Praise for the novels of Lee Tobin McClain

"[A] magnetic second-chance romance.... McClain pits her charming, authentic characters against the realistic problems of everyday life, making for a story that is deeply emotional but never soapy. The welcoming community and beautifully described scenery of Teaberry Island only enhance this cozy romance. Readers won't want to put this down."
—*Publishers Weekly* starred review on *The Forever Farmhouse*

"Lee Tobin McClain dazzles with unforgettable characters, fabulous small-town settings and a big dose of heart. Her complex and satisfying stories never disappoint."
—Susan Mallery, *New York Times* bestselling author

"Fans of Debbie Macomber will appreciate this start to a new series by McClain that blends sweet, small-town romance with such serious issues as domestic abuse.... Readers craving a feel-good romance with a bit of suspense will be satisfied."
—*Booklist* on *Low Country Hero*

"[An] enthralling tale of learning to trust.... This enjoyable contemporary romance will appeal to readers looking for twinges of suspense before happily ever after."
—*Publishers Weekly* on *Low Country Hero*

"*Low Country Hero* has everything I look for in a book—it's emotional, tender, and an all-around wonderful story."
—RaeAnne Thayne, *New York Times* bestselling author

LEE TOBIN McCLAIN

the beach reads bookshop

HQN

Recycling programs
for this product may
not exist in your area.

ISBN-13: 978-1-335-42744-1

The Beach Reads Bookshop

Copyright © 2023 by Lee Tobin McClain

For questions and comments about the quality of this book,
please contact us at CustomerService@Harlequin.com.

HQN
22 Adelaide St. West, 41st Floor
Toronto, Ontario M5H 4E3, Canada
www.Harlequin.com

Printed and bound in Barcelona, Spain by CPI Black Print

To beach readers everywhere

the beach reads bookshop

PROLOGUE

THE LITTLE BOOKSHOP, located on Teaberry Island on the Chesapeake Bay, had once been a fisherman's cottage. In the 1950s, Tom Crockett bought it and made it into a bookshop. Located between the town's tiny business district and the harbor, it soon became a gathering place for the island's residents.

Its weathered porch held chairs and a checkerboard propped on old crab traps, and on warm afternoons as many as ten men would gather there, smoking and discussing the weather on the bay. Fishermen, primarily, but also teachers and shop owners and the town minister. The women of the community tended to congregate inside the shop, drinking coffee from the percolator Tom kept on the stove and catching up on the latest news. More than one moonlit first kiss was shared on the porch, and at least three men were known to have knelt on the weather-beaten planks to propose to their sweethearts.

Inside, volumes of Chesapeake history filled the shelves and nautical maps lined the walls. Regional cookbooks were popular with the island's few-but-loyal summer tourists. *Chesapeake* by James A. Michener was hard to keep in stock, and so was *Beautiful Swimmers*, the Pulitzer Prize–winning study of the blue crab.

As the years passed, people grew busier and Tom's bookshop clientele dropped off. Phone service came late to the island, but it did come, cutting down on the need for in-person sharing of news. People got their hit of history from television, and the old volumes that had once been treasured now gathered dust on the shelves. Tourists walked past the bookshop to trendier places on High Street. Friends told Tom, now nearing eighty, that he needed to modernize, but he resisted the notion.

His sons and granddaughters had bigger things to do than run a retail establishment that, truth to tell, hadn't turned a profit for years. And then Tom died, and the doors of the bookshop closed.

Winter after winter, storms took their toll on the sturdy structure. The weathered boards grew more weathered. Mice and chipmunks skittered across the floors, and a pair of barn swallows took up residence in the eaves. After a large bough from a nearby tree crushed one corner of the roof, rainwater dripped in, soaking some of the abandoned volumes.

One day, Tom's granddaughter Mary Beth, fifty-something and hurting for money after a bad divorce, stuck a For Sale sign in front of the tumbledown building. The local people were too kind to laugh, but privately, they shook their heads. Who would buy such a place? What was the good of a musty old bookshop full of musty old books? And, indeed, the sign stood mostly unnoticed, rattling in rainstorms and bending to the ground when strong winds blew.

No one expected the bookshop's fortunes to change. But Teaberry had always meant refreshment and renewal for tourists, and sometimes the friendly community and natural beauty of the island had brought residents back from the brink of despair. Maybe the same could happen for a broken down little bookshop...

CHAPTER ONE

"HAVE YOU EVER considered slowing down?"

The doctor's words were as out of place as his white coat in Luis Dominguez's busy corporate office. Mergers and acquisitions were what they did here, and at a fast pace. No one slowed down, ever.

"What are you trying to tell me, Doc?" Luis attempted to ignore the text messages that kept pinging into his phone. "I'm only twenty-eight. I can't have something wrong with me."

Dr. Henry fastened the blood pressure cuff on his arm. "My understanding is that you got dizzy at a board meeting. And that you live on coffee and nachos." He tightened the cuff, studied the numbers and frowned. "It's 130/90. That's concerning. Family history of heart or kidney disease?"

"I don't know." Luis didn't want to go into his family medical history, or lack of one, in the middle of a regular work week in mid-April. "I'll try to take it easier. Eat better." Even as he said it, he knew it wasn't true, but he needed to get on with his day.

"I hope you will. Your board members are worried. Apparently, you're indispensable." The man patted Luis's shoulder. "I'll see you next week. We'll need to talk about medication, unless I see significant improvement."

"You'll see it," Luis promised. Ever the overachiever. He was a bit touched that his board of directors was worried enough about his health to set up weekly in-office checkups.

He'd built a life where no one had to worry about him, and he didn't have to worry about anyone else. That was how he wanted it, but every now and then, it was good to know someone cared.

He went to the door and gestured for his assistant, Gunther, to come in. "Everything ready for today's presentation?"

"Slides are all cued up and people are arriving."

Adrenaline surged. "Good."

The doctor clicked his medical bag closed. "How about getting a hobby? Starting a family? Being married is good for your health, you know."

"Not gonna happen." Luis had already made peace with his single status, mostly. He was no good at forming and maintaining relationships. Didn't want the responsibility. Didn't want to *fail* at the responsibility, the way his parents had.

Plenty of women were up for a no-strings fling with a millionaire. The trouble was, that lifestyle got old fast.

"Come on," he said to Gunther, heading for the door. "Let's start the party."

The offices of Dominguez Enterprises buzzed with energy, people leaning over computers, the elevator pinging, voices speaking rapidly into phones. *This* was Luis's hobby. *This* was his family. He was on track to reach his financial goals by age forty, but his lifestyle didn't leave room for coaching Little League or cutting the grass.

"Excuse me, Mr. Dominguez?" A gorgeous blonde woman came out of the reception area and intercepted him. She was holding a toddler dressed in pink, a bow in her dark curls. Cute. Luis liked babies. He reached out and tickled the little one's chin, clicking his tongue, and the child giggled.

"Can I speak to you for a moment, sir?" the woman asked.

He refocused on the blonde. "Not now. Make an appointment with Mrs. Jackson, there at the desk." He gestured toward her then headed into the conference room, smiling at the sight of the suit-clad men and women around the table. Men and women from whom he'd soon make a bundle of money.

Fairly and legally, of course. The small tech firm that was being acquired by the larger one would get a boost of capital and be able to keep all its employees on payroll, and the bigger firm would benefit from the diversification. Ideally they'd all leave as happy as he was.

In fact, two hours later they *did* leave happy. Everyone shaking hands, his own people congratulating him and him thanking them for their hard work.

Who'd have ever thought that a kid from his background would end up making deals with some of the most important businesspeople in Washington, DC?

Then again, maybe his career was at least a little predictable. As a young teenager, he'd borrowed a few bucks from a friend and bought a case of high-caffeine soda, then sold it at a markup on test days. With the profit, he'd bought two more cases and expanded his business from the middle school to the high school. Of course, he'd had to skip class to do that.

"He's not the brightest kid, but he sure does have the Midas touch," the teacher who'd caught him had said to his foster mom.

And Luis had done his best to make the most of whatever talents and abilities he had.

Now, as he walked out of the conference room, the woman who'd approached him before came toward him, this time accompanied by Mrs. Jackson. The woman looked a little disheveled, blowing the blond hair off her face as she shifted the now-sleeping toddler in her arms.

She was still pretty, though. Maybe even prettier with her face flushed and her hair loose.

"I'm sorry, Luis," Mrs. Jackson said. "She wouldn't leave."

"I really need to speak with you." The woman's voice was low, but determined. There was a sexy rasp to it.

He'd have blown her off if it weren't for those stunning slate-colored eyes that seemed to hold all kinds of secrets. But it had been weeks since he'd had a date, and he was feeling celebratory.

"Come on back, I have a few minutes," he said, gesturing toward the hallway that led to his office. He usually avoided women with kids. He definitely avoided women with husbands, so he stepped to the side and checked out her left hand as she passed him. No ring.

She wore a dark skirt and vest and a white shirt, and there was a slight swing to her walk.

He reached the office just behind her and held open the door. "Go ahead, have a seat by the window." He kept his voice low so as not to awaken the child. He nodded an *it's okay* to Mrs. Jackson, who tended to be a mother hen, and followed the woman inside. He knelt down by the minifridge. "Something to drink? I have water, soda. Juice if the kiddo wakes up."

Outside, he could hear people calling goodbyes to each other. He'd given everyone the rest of the day off. They worked late for him plenty of times, so he liked to offer perks when the occasion merited it.

"Water, please." The woman spoke quietly, too, but the child murmured in her arms and opened her eyes. "Juice as well, if you don't mind."

He stood, holding two bottles of water in one hand and a juice in the other. He twisted the top off a water bottle and handed it to her, then did the same for the apple juice.

Sitting on the edge of his desk, he studied the woman. "So what can I do for you?"

She sipped water, cradling the child in one arm, and then looked at Luis with a level stare. "I'd like for you to meet someone."

"Tell me more." So she did have an agenda. Probably some project she wanted him to finance. Bringing her kid was a rookie mistake, but because she looked so serious and earnest, he'd let her down easy.

She nodded down at the baby. "This is Willow," she said.

"Hi, Willow." Luis smiled at the little one, then sipped water.

The woman's skirt slid up above her knees in the low chair.

He lifted his eyes to her face. "What's *your* name?"

"I'm Deena Clark," she said. "But Willow is the important one."

The baby held a small rubber doll out to Luis. He took it from her, hid it behind his back and then held it out again, jiggling it, making her laugh. "Why is Willow the important one?" he asked.

"Because," the woman said, "she's your daughter."

THERE. SHE'D GOTTEN it out. Deena blew her hair out of her eyes and made soothing circles on Willow's back, holding the apple juice for her to sip. She inhaled Willow's baby-powder scent and patted her chubby leg.

She loved the two-year-old fiercely, and she hadn't wanted to give up even the modicum of control that would come with rich Mr. Dominguez knowing he was the child's father. But she was pretty sure Luis wouldn't want much, if anything, to do with the baby. He was too wealthy and entitled.

His wealth would make it easy for him to pay some child support, though. And that would allow Deena to stop working so much, to spend more time at home and to get Willow the services she needed.

Maybe this would go okay. Luis Dominguez wasn't quite what she'd expected. True, he'd made her wait for two hours, but then again, she'd arrived unannounced. She'd heard him saying nice things to his workers, and he'd gotten her and Willow something to drink. So maybe he wasn't as uncaring as Willow's mommy had believed.

He was hot, too. Deena didn't do relationships, but if she did…well. Curly black hair, light brown skin, an athletic body and a dimple in his cheek when he smiled… No wonder Tammalee had gone for him.

He took a sip of water, studying her. "I wouldn't have invited you in if I'd known you were one of *those* women."

"What women?" She bounced the baby doll in front

of Willow, who laughed and grabbed for it then held it to her chest in an adorable imitation of motherhood.

"Women looking to pin paternity on a wealthy man." Luis crossed his arms over his chest.

She raised her eyebrows. "That happens?"

"Pretty often." He took another sip of water and then put the bottle down with a thump. He looked oddly disappointed. "I'm not falling for it, so why don't you take your child and your scam elsewhere."

"This isn't a scam. I'm serious."

"It's a new twist," he said in a fake-thoughtful way, "approaching a man you never slept with. Creative."

That made her cheeks heat. She didn't sleep with anyone, not that he needed to know that. "No," she said, reaching for her phone. "You slept with my roommate." She scrolled through her pictures, found one of Tammalee and held it up for him to see.

He squinted at it. "Oh, yea-a-ah," he said, his brows drawing together. "Sweet girl. But why are you coming here, not her, to claim this is my child?"

Deena glanced at Tammalee's smiling photo, swallowed hard and slid her phone back into her purse. "Tammalee is dead," she said.

His eyes widened. "What? Really?"

She nodded. "An accident."

"I'm sorry to hear that." He stared at the carpet for a minute and then met her eyes. "You realize I'm going to verify all this?"

She blew out a sigh. "Look up Tammalee Johnson, obituary."

He studied her a moment as if wondering if there were even a chance her story was true. She must have looked honest, because he walked around his massive desk, bent over the computer and typed and clicked. He found what he was looking for. "She died two months ago?" He turned the computer so she could see.

The large-size picture of her friend, the one that had accompanied her obituary, made Deena choke up. And that made her angry at herself, and by extension, at this guy. Neither reaction made sense, but then, grief didn't make sense.

The baby stiffened in her arms, probably sensing her tension. Or maybe she'd spotted the picture of her late mother. "Shh, it's okay," Deena whispered, rubbing her back again. But this time, it didn't help; Willow wailed.

The high, keening cry was a sound Deena had heard daily for the past two years, but it still grated on her. "Okay. Okay, honey. Want more juice?"

Willow slapped the bottle away, spilling juice all over Deena, and the guy's fancy carpet.

"Sorry." Although she shouldn't apologize for what his own kid had done.

She rocked Willow in the vigorous way that sometimes calmed her down, trying to gauge whether this tantrum was likely to be a long one. She looked at Luis from under the cover of her lashes. Tammalee had been sure he wouldn't understand Willow, saying he only cared about money. Still, if this meltdown went on, he might require an explanation.

But first things first. She needed to get him to acknowledge paternity before going into Willow's issues.

Willow's cries were softening, to Deena's experienced ear, but they were still grating.

Luis looked uneasy, his forehead wrinkling. "Can't you do something?"

"She's hungry and tired," Deena said by way of explanation.

"You could have found a better time to talk to me about this, when you didn't have to wait."

"You could have given me five minutes before your big important meeting."

But she could see that the baby's crying was impacting Luis, and she didn't want it to make him dislike Willow before even getting to know her. "We can leave," she offered, "but only when you agree to the next step."

"Fine. I'll do a DNA test." He sighed. "There's a doctor I can call."

"I have a test right here." She fumbled in her purse and pulled out the drugstore version. "You just have to rub the swab inside your mouth for fifteen seconds." It had cost a hundred dollars, which was a hardship, but for Willow, it was worth it.

He was already opening it. "How long does it take?"

"Two days from receipt. You mail it in, so…next week?"

"I'll take care of it." He pulled out his phone. "Mrs. Jackson? Hey, before you leave, could you get a courier up to my office ASAP?" He listened. "Yes, I'm still here. I know. Soon." He ended the call and looked at Deena. "I'll have it sent to a better lab and try to get the results faster." He studied Willow, still crying, and shook his head.

She could tell he was hoping he'd get the good news that he *wasn't* Willow's father. Which, she supposed, was a possibility. Tammalee had enjoyed life, and men, and hadn't been particularly choosy about who she'd spent time with—in or out of bed. But she'd insisted that Willow's father was Luis, and Deena believed her.

She swabbed the baby's mouth, making her cry again. Handed Luis the swab, and stood. "She's a terrific kid and deserves the best," she tossed over her shoulder as she left.

Whether the best outcome would be having Luis as a father, or not having him, she didn't know.

CHAPTER TWO

CAROL FISHER SMILED reassuringly at the lanky college student now packing up his textbooks. "You did really well today. You'll handle the class fine as long as you come back to the tutoring center a couple of times a week."

"I will, Ms. Fisher. Thanks." He smiled and waved and walked off.

Carol was gratified to see that his shoulders were straight, his walk brisk. A complete contrast to the way he'd come in, slow and slumped and discouraged.

Amazing what an hour of tutoring on an ordinary Thursday morning could do. She loved her job directing the tutoring center at Baltimore's Watkins College, even during the busy season people tended to complain about. April, toward the end of the semester, was when students needed them most.

She followed her student out into the reception area and there was the part of her job she *didn't* love: her new assistant director, Bambi Gardener.

"Your next appointment is waiting." Bambi forked fingers through her half-buzzed, half-chin-length blond hair and leaned closer to her computer screen.

Did it occur to Bambi to take the appointment herself? They were all supposed to be hands-on here. Carol looked up at the clock. Ten after ten. "I'm sorry to be late," she said to the student waiting for her. "Come on back."

"Excuse me, Carol, can I speak with you?" It was Carol's boss, Evie Marie, standing in the doorway of the center. A sweet woman, but inexperienced. Evie Marie had been at the college only three years, and was twenty years younger than Carol, and yet she was in charge of the entire student-services area.

Still, a boss was a boss. "I have an appointment right now," she told Evie Marie. "Unless... Bambi, would you be able to take it for me?"

Bambi blew out a sigh and turned away from her computer. "Come on," she said to the student, who gave Carol a "save me" look.

Carol led the way back to her office. What did Evie Marie want now? Probably some kind of new initiative that involved collecting and submitting a ridiculous amount of data for every student they tutored. That was education, these days. But Carol hated the time it took away from her real job, the students.

They sat at the little table in Carol's office.

Evie Marie declined Carol's offer of tea. "There's no easy way to say this, Carol," the younger woman said. "We're not going to renew your contract."

Carefully, Carol finished pouring hot water from the old-fashioned hot pot she kept on her desk. She selected a tea bag from her caddy and plopped it into the water. Then she looked at Evie Marie. "Did you just tell me you're letting me go?"

Evie Marie nodded, her thin, folded hands wringing themselves, over and over. "Your contract ends May 1, and we've decided not to renew it."

"May 1, as in...a week and a half from now?" Carol

could barely take it in. She dunked her tea bag repeatedly, as if she could wash away the unbelievable thing that seemed to be happening.

"Yes. I realize it's short notice, but with two weeks' severance pay plus your accumulated sick leave—"

"But *why*?" Carol shook her head and pinched the skin on the back of her hand, hoping to discover this was all a dream. But no; it hurt, and the pinched skin went down slowly. A mark of age she'd read about and then noticed, starting around age fifty. Five years ago.

Evie Marie looked down at her notes. "We've talked about the tech issues," she said. "It's been noted as a problem at your last two performance reviews."

"But I work well with students, that's the important thing. At least…isn't it?" Carol's voice quavered and she pressed her lips together.

"You do work well with the students, and they love you. But we want to take the center online, and you've been resistant. It's been decided that we need some new blood, new ideas."

"I'm resistant because the developmental students need in-person coaching, not just a face on a screen!"

Evie Marie didn't deny that. "I have my directive. We're a tech-savvy school. It's part of our image and our marketing."

"But the at-risk students—"

"Are *not* part of our image and marketing." Evie Marie looked genuinely sad. "I'm sorry, Carol. I know you put your heart into your work, but you've never wanted to embrace the new."

"The new is overrated, especially if it leaves behind the students who struggle! You're the head of student services. Surely you understand that." She was wait-

ing for Evie Marie to admit that letting her go was all
a big mistake, even as the increasing heaviness in her
heart told her this was no joke and she needed to ac-
cept reality.

"You're near retirement age," Evie Marie said in a
soothing voice. "We can bill it that way. And there are
your husband's needs. This way, you can spend more
time with him."

Carol's stomach tightened. Spending more time with
Roger was the last thing that would be a comfort. He'd
be livid. They needed her benefits.

"You're serious about this, aren't you? Have you already started the search for my—my replacement?" Her
tongue tripped over the word.

"We actually aren't doing a search," Evie Marie said.
"Bambi has agreed to take the position."

"What?" Carol's jaw dropped as she stared at her
supervisor. "You know her interpersonal skills are at
the toddler level, and her work ethic—"

"The decision has been made."

The whole place had gone crazy if Bambi was considered a better head of tutoring than she was. "When
do you want me out? Are you going to escort me to
the door?"

"No, no. You don't need to work out the rest of the
month, but we'll of course give you time to gather your
things. By the end of the day, or tomorrow at the latest."
Evie Marie stood. "I know it's a lot to process. HR has
been in the loop on this. They'll be able to talk to you
about COBRA insurance continuation and unemploy-
ment. Why don't you take a few minutes, and I'll let
them know you'll be over, say, after lunch."

Carol nodded, numb.

Evie Marie stood, opened the office door and stopped, waiting for Bambi and the student to walk by. Hadn't Evie Marie noticed that the appointment, scheduled for an hour, had only taken twenty minutes? Didn't she see the miserable expression on the student's face?

Bambi looked in the door at her and her lip pulled back in a strange kind of smile. She knew, obviously. Evie Marie had said it was all decided.

Carol was heartbroken for the students, but also for herself. What was she going to do?

LUIS WAS A FATHER.

He patted the DNA test results in his pocket as he headed toward his meeting with his child's guardian, Deena.

Though it was still April, DC was unseasonably hot and humid, especially in midafternoon. The faint smell of garbage and sweat rose in the commercial neighborhood, crowded on a Saturday. But Luis was too preoccupied to do more than notice. Ever since he'd gotten the results yesterday his mind had been in overdrive, figuring out a plan.

Talking to his family, or what passed for one, back on Teaberry Island had helped him make decisions. Actually made him a little bit excited about what was ahead.

He smiled as he walked into The Book Spot, a local independent bookstore where Deena had wanted to meet. That was one great thing about DC, it was a reading town. Half the people on the metro carried a book, and there were bookstores galore. He hoped to get this situation handled and then pick up the latest Baldacci thriller on the way out.

He welcomed the blasting AC as he strode through

the shop and trotted up the steps toward the café. Deena was at a table in the back, set off a little from the others, reading.

She was *really* pretty. She wore the same white shirt and black skirt that she'd worn before, and he realized it must be some kind of uniform. Plain, but it couldn't make *her* look plain, not with those cheekbones and that curly blond hair escaping from the bun she'd put it in. Her cheeks were faintly pink and she was sipping an iced coffee, engrossed in her book.

She looked up, saw him and tucked a bookmark into her paperback.

It was one of the latest science-oriented, award-winning nonfiction bestsellers; he'd read it himself when it had come out in hardcover. None of his friends or colleagues had read it, and he felt a brief urge to sit down and talk to her about it.

But that wasn't why he was here. "Where's the child?" he asked.

"*Willow* is with the babysitter." She emphasized the name, as if he might have forgotten it.

He took the seat across from her. "Like I told you over the phone, I got the DNA results and they're positive."

"May I see?"

"You don't believe me?"

She tucked a curl behind her ear and gave him a steady, grey-eyed gaze. "Is there a reason I should?"

He guessed not. He'd barely been able to believe it himself. But even if she doubted him, it didn't make sense for her to fight it. It was in her best interest to believe that a wealthy man was the father of her friend's baby; she was likely to get some money out of it.

He shrugged and pulled out the paperwork, slid it across the table to her. She bent over it, and since she was obviously going to read every word, he went and got himself a coffee and her another iced coffee.

As he returned, she pushed back the papers, looked up at him and lifted an eyebrow. "Okay. It all looks legit. Welcome to fatherhood."

Fatherhood. He tested out the word in his head. It didn't match his self-image, not by a mile. He was the hard-driving businessman in his family. His two foster brothers had settled down on Teaberry Island, where they'd all spent their adolescence, and both of *them* were fathers. Both of them had been surprised by it, too. Still, they seemed to relish the role and be made for it. Whereas Luis…wasn't. The little he knew about being a good father had been gleaned from his late foster father, but that had been about being the parent of teens. How to take care of a little girl…a little girl who was his blood… It didn't quite compute.

He had no delusions that he'd be good at this gig, not with his background.

Even so, he wasn't a ditherer. Being in business had taught him to take action. "I've figured out a plan," he said. "Obviously, I'm not set up for taking care of a young child here, so I'm going to take her back to Teaberry Island, on the Chesapeake, where I spent my teenage years. I have family there, people who can help me with babysitting and finding a good childcare provider. I'll have to be here in DC on weekdays, but I'll go visit her every weekend." He smiled at her. "You're off the hook, in other words. I can't tell you how much I appreciate—"

"No," Deena interrupted, cutting him off.

"What?"

"I'm not giving Willow to a complete stranger who only wants to see her on the weekends and who plans to pass her off to other complete strangers to basically raise."

"She's with a babysitter now, and most weekdays as well," Luis pointed out.

Deena looked chagrined. "I know, and I'd love to spend more time caring for her myself. That's why I contacted you. I'd like to see you pay child support. That would allow me to work less and spend more time at home with her." She paused. "You could visit her, of course. We could set up a schedule."

"Obviously I'll compensate you for the time you've spent—"

"That's not what I mean!" Her voice rose and a couple other patrons glanced over. She leaned forward and lowered her voice, but it was still fierce and passionate. "I'm her guardian and I love her."

For whatever reason, Luis felt that as an attack. Like he didn't love his own daughter. Well, he didn't, not yet. He'd barely met her. "Love doesn't stand up in court."

She cringed. "Be reasonable. She can't be so easily moved."

"Why not? Kids adapt." He'd been moved too many times as a kid. It gave him a twinge, thinking he was doing the exact same thing he'd hated about his own childhood. But after this one move, he wouldn't do it again.

"Look, she has issues," Deena said. "She needs consistency."

"What do you mean, 'she has issues'?" The child had looked fine to him when he'd seen her the other day. Beautiful, even. She'd been fussy, sure, but that was normal for a two-year-old. Wasn't it?

There was a pounding in his neck and chest, and his vision blurred. Had he taken his blood pressure medicine today?

"I mean," Deena said, and paused, as if debating with herself. She looked at him, her eyes narrowing, and then she spoke. "I mean, I'm pretty sure she has fetal alcohol syndrome."

CHAPTER THREE

"SLOW DOWN!" DEENA HAD been attempting to match her pace to Luis's angry, fast one since they'd left the bookstore, but keeping up was impossible and she was tired of trying.

He didn't listen. So, as they got out of the commercial district, headed toward her neighborhood, she stopped and crossed her arms.

When he realized she wasn't beside him, he finally stopped and walked back to her. "What's wrong?"

"I can't keep up with you, and you just made a wrong turn. Why are you so angry?" She started walking again, in the right direction, at a much slower pace.

He fell into step beside her. "I don't understand why you didn't seek an official diagnosis."

Deena felt guilty about that, but she also didn't appreciate the way he'd immediately started criticizing her care of the child she loved. "I've been in charge of her for two months, ever since Tammalee..." She swallowed. "Ever since the accident. It's been a little hectic."

"Of course. I'm sorry." He took a deep breath and moved his shoulders like his neck hurt. Obviously trying to calm himself. "What makes you think she has FAS?"

Interesting that he knew the acronym. "She's fussy, harder to console than she should be. Her fine motor skills are behind other babies her age. Plus, I think she has the facial features, or some of them."

"Wow." He nodded and looked across the busy street as if trying to collect himself.

"I've been researching it," she said, to give him time. "I can send you some resources."

He looked back at her and nodded decisively. "Great. Thank you. And I'll take her to a specialist before we head for Teaberry Island."

Men and their lack of listening skills. "Did you not hear what I said before? She's not *going* to Teaberry Island." Of that, she was determined.

He glanced over at her and then looked ahead. The sidewalk was getting more crowded as they approached her street. In the springtime, everyone was out, including a lot of kids and teens. A small group of boys was shoving each other, playfully, and Luis held up an arm and blocked one as he stumbled toward them. "Watch it, pal," he said.

The boy straightened and glared at Luis, and she recognized sixteen-year-old Nicky, a chubby kid who was always trying to prove himself. "Hey, Nicky. Hey, fellas." She smiled at the group and kept walking. They didn't answer, but a couple of them nodded at her.

"My place is two blocks up," she said, gesturing.

"So…if you live over here, why'd you want to meet at the bookstore?" he asked.

She'd wanted to talk with him before inviting him to her place, which was what he'd asked for initially. He wanted to see where his daughter was living. Fair enough, and once she'd seen the paperwork and ascertained that he was at least somewhat sincere about wanting to be involved with Willow, she'd agreed. Maybe seeing her place would forestall a custody lawsuit. "It was on my way home from work, plus I used to work there. Was actually on track to become a manager. I love books."

"Why'd you quit, then?"

She shrugged. "With the baby, I was missing too many shifts."

"This has been a hardship for you."

"It has," she said. "But it's a welcome one, and nothing I can't manage. I still want to take care of Willow."

"Why? I don't get it."

She glanced over at him. In the midafternoon light, his hair shone like polished ebony. He had a strong profile, a sharp nose and square jaw. He was striking, and probably a big hit with women, but he seemed to lack a heart. "I told you," she said. "I love her. Her mother and I were friends and roommates since before the baby was born. I've always helped care for Willow, and I want to keep doing it. I promised Tammalee I would."

"And I want to take her to Teaberry." He frowned, looking around him.

She fumbled for her keys and edged past the silver-haired man sitting on the steps in front of her building. "Hi, Mr. Richards, excuse us."

The man lifted his bottle to her. "Where's that sweet Willow-tree?"

She felt Luis tense beside her. "I'm picking her up soon. If you're still here, we'll stop and say hello."

She opened the door to the building and ushered Luis inside. As soon as the door shut behind them, he exploded. "You know that wino? And he knows everything about my daughter?"

"Come on, I'm on the third floor. The elevator isn't

working." She led the way up the narrow wooden stairs, all too aware of the scuffed woodwork, the torn carpeting on the landings. "Mr. Richards is a sweet old man. I do wish he'd go to AA, I've told him about some of the local meetings, but…" She shrugged. "He has to want to change, and so far, he doesn't."

"If he hasn't changed by eighty…"

"He's only sixty, he just looks eighty." She opened the door to her apartment. "Come on in." Having him walk her home might have been a mistake, since he seemed unimpressed with the neighborhood. But she was proud of what she and Tammalee had done to the apartment.

"Willow's room is here." Deena swallowed hard because it had been Tammalee and Willow's room up until two months ago. She'd occupied herself and assuaged her grief by redecorating the place in little-girl style. A unicorn mobile she'd found at a thrift store, a coat of pale lavender paint she'd coaxed out of the landlord and fresh checked curtains she'd sewn herself. The room looked sweet.

"She still sleeps in a crib?" he asked.

Oh, well, a man wouldn't be impressed by cute decor. "She'll outgrow it soon, sadly, but for now, it helps keep her safe and in bed."

"Speaking of safe," he said, turning to face her head-on, "this isn't a safe neighborhood."

Of course, a couple of police cars drove by at that moment, sirens blaring. That was unfortunate, but it could happen in any city neighborhood. Once they'd passed, she spoke. "It's not the greatest, but people take care of each other. It's basically okay."

"Not for my daughter. I want her out of here."

Her face heated, and she gripped the railing of the crib to keep from smacking the arrogance off his face. "Don't you dare stand there in your designer suit, criticizing the way I've been raising the child you didn't even know you had. Did you ever think of coming home with Tammalee, having an actual relationship before you fathered a child with her, seeing if she lived in a place nice and suitable enough for *her*, let alone the child you were careless enough to conceive?"

"I—"

"You're obviously very privileged, enough that you don't realize this is how a lot of people live."

Something flashed across his face and was gone. "I meant no disrespect."

"Really?" She was breathing hard. She wasn't normally one for outbursts, but he'd provoked her.

"Really. But I'm also not letting my daughter be raised here." His forehead wrinkled as he studied her.

That quiet determination scared her more than open anger would have. "You don't get to walk in here and decide that." She checked the time on her phone. "I need to go pick her up. And no, you're not invited." Because if he thought this apartment was shabby, he'd be horrified by the babysitter's. Mrs. Martin had so much love, and her grandkids were a delight, but with six of them, the house was never neat or quiet. Which, undoubtedly, was what this man would expect.

He snapped his fingers. "I've got it," he said. "You need to come to Teaberry with her, as her nanny."

She'd been walking out toward the front door, wanting to urge him on his way, but at his words, she turned back and stared at him. "Are you kidding me?"

"No. I can see how much you care for Willow, and

it looked like she was pretty attached to you, the other day. You'd get to stay with her, and you wouldn't be leaving much behind. It's the perfect solution."

You wouldn't be leaving much behind. She huffed out a breath, staring at him. "You realize I'm a human being with a life, right? I have a job, and friends, and a support system here. There are lots of people in the neighborhood who love Willow. You can't yank her away from that just because you have a nicer house somewhere else."

"I'm guessing, from your uniform, that you work at a restaurant. I can pay you twice as much as you're probably making there, and you won't have to worry about rent or food."

That made her pause. Did he mean it? What she could do with twice as much money, starting with paying off the credit card balance that had grown so big when she was caring for her mother.

He crossed his arms and had the nerve to smile.

That decided her. "No. Just no. You can't bully me and throw money at me and make me do whatever you say. I have a life." Not only that, but she wanted to be in charge of Willow, and she had the feeling that power would go away if she succumbed to Luis's wishes.

"I'll convince you," he said confidently.

"No, you won't." But as she ushered him out, she had almost no faith in her ability to withstand this wealthy, egotistical man's persuasion.

AT MRS. MARTIN'S PLACE, Deena was so annoyed that she told the woman what had happened. The sixtysomething grandmother of six had been babysitting Willow more often since Tammalee had passed, and she and Deena were becoming closer friends.

They sat on the couch, side by side. Mrs. Martin didn't own a television—said she didn't believe in it—but the floor was covered with toys and picture books. On the wall, a large, colorful crucifix stood prominent, its surrounding tiles depicting what Deena was pretty sure were the stations of the cross.

"You have the opportunity to move to an island and make twice as much money?" Mrs. Martin asked. "If you're not taking the job, tell him to come knock on my door."

Deena snorted. "Your life is here. You know you'd never leave this neighborhood behind."

"True," she said. "But I have a husband, four kids and six grandkids. And three sisters within a few blocks. You have lots of friends, yes, but...you're young and you're not tied down. You should do it."

"I don't even think he'd be a good father," Deena said. "He's all about money. He barely asked about Willow." She twisted the hem of her uniform vest, worrying.

"It's a lot for him to take in, becoming a father. Give him a chance."

"I don't *want* to give him a chance." She knew she was being unreasonable when she heard the way the words came out of her mouth, fast and angry.

Mrs. Martin tilted her head, rocking a baby on her lap. Around them, three of her youngest grandkids stacked blocks with Willow. "What's really bothering you about this man?"

She opened her mouth to answer, but Mrs. Martin held up a hand. "I get that he's acting arrogant, but you've dealt with arrogant men a lot, working at the bookstore and the restaurant by Capitol Hill. What's different about this guy?"

What *was* different? "It's something about the way he looks at me," she said.

"Creepy?" Mrs. Martin's voice went suddenly alert. "I mean, definitely do a background check before you let him have anything to do with Willow. Or with you, for that matter."

"I did research him online. He's not a criminal or anything, and he seems to support good causes, but…"

"You don't feel good about him?"

She wanted to be fair. "It's not creepy, exactly. I don't feel like he's sneaky or out to hurt anyone. He's more… watchful. Like a tiger on a hunt."

Mrs. Martin laughed. "Oh, I see. And is he handsome, this Luis Dominguez? A Latin lover type?"

Deena rolled her eyes. "How would I know what a Latin lover is like?"

"Maybe it's time you found out," Mrs. Martin said. "I know you had a bad experience when you were younger, but is that a reason to stay away from all men?"

Deena wished she'd never told Mrs. Martin about that, and she certainly didn't want to go there now. "All I know is that he scares me, and he wants to take away Willow, and I'm not letting him get away with it."

CAROL'S MOOD IMPROVED as she pulled up to the house she shared with her husband and started unloading boxes onto the driveway.

It was Sunday morning, about 11:00, and she could hear church bells from the cathedral down the street. She'd chosen Sunday as the day to move her things out of her office, partly so that no one would be there to see her humiliating departure, and partly to put off the move until the last minute. She'd been told to be out by the end of the week, but there was always the chance that Evie Marie and HR would change their minds.

That hadn't happened; on the contrary, someone had come in and boxed up all her things and left them in the lobby of the tutoring center, topped by an index card with her name on it. Irritating, the thought of someone else handling her stuff. That weasel Bambi had already taken over the director's office; Carol had peeked.

But she wasn't going to think about that on this beautiful April morning. As she rested from lifting boxes out of her Honda, she surveyed the house she and Roger had lived in for the past fifteen years. It was a small frame structure, plenty big for the two of them, but looking a little neglected these days. She was going to pull weeds and plant spring flowers, make the place look nice. Since she'd gotten home earlier than expected, she might even do some yard work today.

Maybe she'd even put a couple of lawn chairs out here. She and Roger could sit outside in the evenings and drink iced tea and chat about their days.

Not that either of them would have much to chat about, now that neither of them was working. Roger had been on disability for five years, ever since his crane had tipped over at the plant where he worked and thrown his back out. He spent a lot of time watching cable news these days.

She shuddered to think of listening to him spout his opinions on world events for hours on end. Well, maybe they'd stream a new series together, really get into it. Or they'd cook together and invite people over.

Losing her job had been a wake-up call, emphasizing the importance of the other aspects of her life. You shouldn't put all your eggs into one basket, say for instance a job; that wasn't reliable. But marriage was for life, and she was going to work on theirs.

She hoisted the heaviest box with some difficulty and opened her mouth to call for Roger to help. Then she closed it again. He might try, but he really wasn't supposed to lift anything heavy. She staggered to the door, put the box down on the concrete stoop and opened it.

And there was Roger, carrying something quite a bit heavier than her box; he was carrying his giggling caregiver, Misty, toward the hall that led to the bedroom.

"What on earth!" Carol burst out, staring.

He didn't hear her—his hearing was bad—but Misty did, and she struggled out of his arms, escaping his playful efforts to grab and lift her back up. She straightened her old-fashioned nurse uniform, whacked Roger on the shoulder and pointed toward Carol.

Roger turned around and saw her. His face flushed a dark, dangerous red. Good heavens, was he going to have a heart attack?

Carol said the first thing that came into her mind. "You're going to hurt yourself! She's way too heavy for you!"

"I beg your pardon." Misty's expression changed from guilt to anger. "I'm smaller than you are."

Around the roaring in her ears, Carol walked right up to Roger, propping her hands on her hips, ignoring Misty. "Your health isn't good enough to do what you were about to do." The Lord knew, she and Roger hadn't made love for months.

"I, uh, I thought you wouldn't be home until this afternoon."

"I see that." She kept her spine straight, trying to disbelieve what was right before her eyes. Roger couldn't be having an affair with Misty. Could he?

Even as she had the thought that it was impossible, various puzzle pieces fitted themselves together in her mind. Roger had insisted on hiring Misty rather than the caregivers with more credentials. Misty always wore that short, tight nurse uniform that looked more like a Halloween costume than something a professional caregiver would wear.

They were all three caught in a tableau of staring at each other: Carol in the living room, Roger in the hallway and Misty partly behind him. Finally, Carol lifted her hands, palms up. "Are you going to explain what's going on?"

Roger cleared his throat, the color in his face still high. "I've changed, Carol," he said, "but you can't see it."

That wasn't the kind of explanation she was looking for. Trust Roger to turn things around so it was her fault. "I wish I could *unsee* you hoisting that tramp like a sack of potatoes."

Misty sidled past Roger and Carol and grabbed her purse from a living room chair. Hand on the front door, she looked back. "I'll leave the two of you to work this out."

"You'd *better* leave," Carol said in a voice that was almost a shout. "Don't come back!"

"I'll call you," Roger said almost as loudly.

Misty didn't answer. She hurried out the door, tripped over the box on the porch and went sprawling.

Her short nurse uniform was no protection against the hard cement; she was going to have a bad scrape. Involuntarily, Carol took a step toward the door. What if Misty had really hurt herself?

But the woman picked herself up quickly and scrambled toward her car, which Carol only now realized was parked across the street and a house down. She rolled her eyes. *Very sneaky, Misty.*

After Misty was in her car, Carol spun and glared at Roger. "You'll *call* her? And you said that right in front of me?"

Roger walked into the living room and sat down heavily on the couch, wincing. Evidently that macho ploy of carrying, or attempting to carry, Misty back to the bedroom had cost him. Good. Men were such idiots. If the disability office could have seen him, they'd have stopped his checks in a heartbeat.

"Sit down, Carol." He picked up the TV remote and turned it around and around in his hands, as if eager to turn on the Sunday morning news shows.

Should have thought of that before Misty came over, buddy. "Don't tell me to sit down when you're cheating on me." But she did sit down. Her legs felt shaky.

He leaned forward and set down the remote. "I want a divorce."

She blinked. "You?" The truth was, she'd occasionally thought of leaving Roger. Their marriage had lost its spark years ago. But she'd stayed because she felt obligated to him in his infirmity. And because she'd always expected to stay married for life. "You can't take care of yourself."

"I'm stronger than you think." The weary sound of his voice and the slump of his shoulders defied his words. She was about to point that out when he added, "I'm not happy with you."

Whoa. Carol closed her mouth, her body deflating like a leaky tire.

How could Roger get up the gumption and the strength to ask her for a divorce? How could he think he could get along without her? "How can you manage?"

"I want to keep the house. It's all set up for me."

It was true; when he'd first come home from rehab, using a wheelchair, they'd gotten help widening the doorways and installing ramps and grab bars. He still used the latter two; she'd thought he needed them. He *did* need them, some days more than others.

The question that kept spooling through her mind was, how could a man who often walked with a cane, who sometimes needed help getting up off the toilet, have an affair?

"You don't mean it," she said. "Have you been taking extra pain pills?"

His face twisted into an expression a lot like pity and it hit her like a blow, and then he pounded her again with his words. "I'm stone-cold sober, Carol, and I don't want to be married to you anymore."

Words failed her then. She looked at his face, the face she'd seen expressing pleasure and pain, happiness when his team won, grief when his father had died. After thirty years of marriage, it was more familiar to her than her own.

And it was set now, unyielding. He meant it; he wanted a divorce.

"My car is full of boxes from the office," she said in a low voice. "What am I supposed to do?"

He looked relieved to get out of the emotional weeds

and onto something practical. That was so Roger. "I've thought about that. You could go live in the family place on Teaberry Island. Your sister isn't coming until school's out, is she?"

That was true, and she liked the place. But she was stuck on what he'd said: *I've thought about that.* For how long?

She sucked in a shaky breath. "How am I supposed to earn a living on a tiny island like that?"

"Didn't some of your relatives own a shop there?"

"Yeah, but it's long gone." She couldn't believe they were having a civilized conversation about the details when he'd just betrayed her in the worst way possible. The image of him carrying Misty, the woman's skirt riding up her legs, was burned into her brain. The worst of it wasn't Misty's legs, though; it was the smile on Roger's face.

She hadn't seen that smile in years.

It was that smile that made her know he was serious about leaving her. Or rather, kicking her out.

She could fight him; she knew that. Friends at work had gone through divorces and talked about maintaining occupancy in mutually owned homes.

Come to think of it, was her name on the deed of the house?

Tears pushed at the backs of her eyes and she felt like something heavy was shoving her entire body down into the sofa she sat on. How would she muster the energy to deal with her life?

Although the truth was, there wasn't much of a life left to deal with.

"Aw, Carol, don't take it so hard," he said. "Wouldn't

you be happier with a whole man, someone who has more of the same interests?"

"Shut. Up." She glared at him. "Since you're so strong and fit all of a sudden, you can load that box Misty tripped over back into my car. I'm going to call around until I find a moving company that can get me packed and moved in the next day or two. Meanwhile, I'm staying at a hotel. And—" she fixed him with a teacherly glare "—don't you even *think* of emptying out our checking account. I'll take my half of what we have and start new accounts in my name tomorrow."

Roger looked disconcerted. "I haven't really thought about money yet—"

"That's because you're not thinking at all. But you're right. I *will* be happier with someone else. Someone who doesn't pick his teeth at the dinner table or blow his nose on my cloth napkins." Her voice rose at the end. She was getting hysterical, so she pressed her lips together and gestured toward the box.

She supposed the next step was to call her sister and make sure she was okay with Carol living in the house. Come to think of it, Mary Beth might be there now, since it was Pete's spring break.

She'd make a list of what she needed to do. Carol was efficient, despite wretched Evie Marie's denigration of her technology skills. She could survive.

But the trouble was, she didn't know what she'd survive as, who she'd become. If she wasn't Roger's long-suffering wife, and she wasn't the warm, compassionate head of the tutoring center…who *was* she?

CHAPTER FOUR

ON MONDAY NIGHT, Luis trotted up the steps of the Dockside Diner, a Teaberry institution. He hadn't spent much time on the island since graduating high school, but he was surprised to hear a couple of friendly greetings and to see a few familiar faces. The diner might have a fresh coat of paint and look a little more upscale, but it had the same feel as it had when he'd arrived on the island as a teenager. And the people here had long memories, apparently. That, or they just didn't meet a lot of new people, so they remembered those they'd known years ago.

Across the outdoor deck, his two foster brothers waved him over. That was nice, too. The only time he really felt like part of a group, like he had a family, was here with his brothers and foster parents. Foster mom, now, since Wayne had passed away.

"Thanks for coming out on a weeknight." He gave both Ryan and Cody a half hug, half back-pounding, ordered a beer and then looked around appreciatively. The sun was low in the sky, turning the scudding clouds pink and orange and gold. The Chesapeake, flat as a mirror today, reflected all of it back, doubling the beauty.

"Is this what it takes to get you to come visit—news that you're a father?" Cody gave him a light punch in the arm. Luis had told his brothers and foster mother the skeleton outline of what was going on with Willow, but the word *father* still jolted him.

Luis's beer was delivered, along with a hug from the waitress, one of their high school classmates. She was pretty, but Luis was too preoccupied to do more than notice.

"Here's to fatherhood," Ryan said after she'd left, lifting his glass.

Luis clinked both of their glasses and took a long draw on his beer. He wasn't much of a drinker, but the past week merited at least a minimal amount of alcohol. After a pause, he said, "I need help figuring all this out."

Cody pretended to collapse in his chair. "I must be hallucinating. My little brother just admitted he needs help."

Ryan lifted his hands in fake confusion. "How can you need help when you already know everything?"

The teasing was well deserved. Luis had never liked advice, never appreciated being told what to do. Probably a function of his role as the youngest of the three brothers. But assuming custody of a child he hadn't known he had was so far outside his experience that even he had to admit he needed counsel. That was a big part of the reason he'd asked his brothers to meet him here.

Both of them had recently become fathers themselves, or in Cody's case a father figure to his much younger siblings. It had been unexpected, but both were making a success of it.

They were doing it right here on Teaberry Island. That was part of the reason Luis had decided Teaberry Island should become Willow's home, too, but he had no clue of how to make that work. "I'm serious," he said. "This is complicated."

Cody raised a hand to the waitress, holding up three fingers. Then he turned back to Luis. "Complicated how?"

"Do you have a picture of the child we're discussing?" Ryan asked.

Luis pulled up a picture of Willow on his phone and showed them. After they'd both agreed that she was exceptionally cute, he explained, "I want to make sure she has a good life, a better life than she has right now, but Deena, the woman who's been taking care of her, is against making a change."

"What's she like?" Ryan asked.

"Who, Willow or Deena?"

"Both," Ryan said.

Luis blew out a sigh. "Willow is... I don't know, I don't really know her at all yet, but she's cute. Playful. Kind of fussy. Deena thinks—" He broke off, uncomfortable. Cody's young siblings had had their struggles but seemed basically fine. Ryan's son was a certified genius. What would they think of Willow's apparent issues?

"She thinks what?" Cody asked.

There was no way around telling them, not if he wanted their help. And he had to get used to saying it. "Deena thinks that she might have FAS."

"Wow." Neither brother needed the acronym explained. They'd had rough upbringings, just as Luis had. They'd known kids in the system with all manner of problems, most likely including fetal alcohol syndrome, or fetal alcohol spectrum disorder as it was more often called these days.

"So," Cody said, "her mom drank. Did you know that?"

Luis glanced at both of them and then shook his head. "I'm not proud of this, but the relationship wasn't even worthy of the name. I met Tammalee at a club, she was pretty, I was lonely. We had a couple of fun nights together, and then I got busy with other things and never saw her again." He paused and looked out over the water to make sure he didn't get emotional. "Like I mentioned when I told you about all of it, she recently passed away in an accident." He swallowed hard. "So I don't know much about her habits."

"It doesn't take much alcohol to affect a developing fetus." Ryan's voice shifted subtly into professor mode, accurate enough since he was a scientist and sometimes a professor. "Even one episode of binge drinking can hit a child hard, depending on the timing."

"You're sure you're Willow's father?" Cody asked abruptly.

Luis nodded. "Yep. DNA."

"Ah."

They all three sipped the drinks the waitress had brought and watched the sun sink into the water. People were leaving; it was a weeknight, and most people on Teaberry worked in the fishing industry and kept early hours. Luis inhaled the mixed fragrance of fried food and salt water, lifted his face to the cooling breeze and tried to still his mind. His doctor had suggested meditation, which Luis was way too antsy to do, but he had been practicing deep breathing in stressful situations.

Thinking about Willow and how to properly assume control of her life was definitely stressful.

"I want to bring her up here," he said. "This island is going to be the best place for raising a kid, especially if you two will lend a hand sometimes. Betty already said she can babysit, but I'll need more than that." He took a breath. "If it's true Willow has FAS, she'll need more, a lot more. Can I get her services here?"

Both brothers nodded. "It's not like living in a city, but we've managed to get gifted services for Alfie," Ryan said.

"Danny and Ava have weekly counseling," Cody added. "I generally take them over to Pleasant Shores, but we've had social worker visits here, as well."

"That's one obstacle overcome, then," Luis said. "But there's another one, a big one. Deena."

"The caregiver," Cody said, his eyes narrowing. "Tell us about her."

"Sure." Luis conjured up a vision of Deena in his mind and was struck dumb. Where to start? "She's a waitress, a good friend of Willow's mom. They lived together, so Deena helped with Willow's care from birth, and when Tammalee was in the accident, Deena took over."

"Anything official?" Cody asked. "I can put you in touch with social workers who can start an investigation if you think she's an unfit guardian." That was what had happened with Cody's siblings; after their mother had basically dumped them on Cody's doorstep, he'd done some digging and then gotten himself declared their legal guardian. His mother had visitation rights, but nothing more.

"Deena's not unfit," Luis said. "She's taking good care of Willow. But she lives in a bad neighborhood, and she has to work a lot. And she's not a blood relative, though Tammalee did sign a paper saying if anything happened to her, Deena was to assume Willow's care."

"So how'd you get involved? Why did you even find out about Willow, if you hadn't been told up to this point?"

Luis spread his hands. "Money. Tammalee had contact information for me and told Deena to get in touch and get me to pay child support. That's really why they came to see me. Of course I'll support Willow, that's not a problem. But I want control, too."

His brothers glanced at each other. "What a surprise," Ryan remarked.

Cody snorted, and then his face went serious. "You also need to start connecting with Willow. You're the only father she has, the only parent. She needs you."

That made Luis all kinds of uncomfortable. "So anyway, since Willow's attached to Deena, I want to hire her as a nanny."

Ryan raised an eyebrow. "That can go places you don't expect. Our friend Hank thought he was hiring a companion for his daughter, and he ended up with a wife."

"That's not happening to me," Luis said. Although the idea of Deena as a wife was more appealing than he would've thought, given that he was a confirmed bachelor. "The problem is, she's not interested in moving here. Says she has a life and doesn't want to leave it."

"So you take Willow," Cody said. "This Deena isn't a blood relative. Her claim for custody wouldn't hold up in court."

"Right, but antagonizing her and separating her from Willow isn't going to make things right. They're attached, and Willow's already had a big loss. She doesn't need another. That's why I want Deena to come here."

"If Deena is committed to living in DC," Ryan said, "why don't you just have her as a nanny there?"

Luis blew out a sigh. It was hard to explain all the reasons that didn't appeal.

To his surprise, Cody said it better than he could have. "The island is a great place for kids, especially kids with issues," he said. "Willow will have a good childhood here. And this is where her family is."

Luis fist-bumped Cody, his throat tightening. He, Ryan and Cody weren't blood brothers. They'd all three come to the island separately as troubled teens. They'd first met in Wayne and Betty Raines's foster home, and they'd had their difficulties, but with love and the healing power of the bay and the island, they'd become family.

He wanted that for Willow, and he didn't want to wait until she was a teenager to do it.

Ryan was nodding. "Okay, makes sense. So think about this logically. What does Deena like? What would bring her here?"

Luis frowned. "I don't know her well. She likes... books."

"You mean reading?" Cody asked. They were all pretty serious readers; Betty had forced them into it as teens and it had stuck.

Luis shook his head. "That, but she had me meet her at a bookstore. She used to work there, was working her way up hoping to become a manager, until taking care of Willow lost her the job."

Ryan looked at Cody. "There's that broken-down bookshop," he said, gesturing off to the north.

"That one at the edge of downtown?" Cody frowned. "It's been closed forever. There's been a For Sale sign up ever since I got back to Teaberry. Looks like it's been there a long time."

"Wayne said that bookstore was a great place," Ryan said. "Had some kind of special meaning to him and Mom."

Luis remembered the building, vaguely. "That little red place? Is it still solid?"

"Windows are boarded up," Ryan said, "and there's some roof damage, but it's stood through a bunch of storms and winters, even a flood."

"Then it would be a project to set up," he said.

"A big one." Ryan looked thoughtful. "Do you think she's the type of person who likes projects?"

"She took on Willow." Ideas were sparking in Luis's mind. "I could buy it for a song and give it to her. That would interest her and keep her here, more so than being just a nanny."

Cody looked skeptical. "Money doesn't solve everything. She might not go for being handed a bookstore. She doesn't want to come, right?"

"Right. The alternative is fighting her in court, but... I just know she'll like this better." He stood, energized, and threw a fifty on the table. "Betty will know who owns it. Let's go talk to her."

Ryan and Cody rolled their eyes at each other. "Biggest tip Jennie has had in a year," Cody said, waving to their waitress and pointing at the table. They followed Luis down the steps.

Half an hour later they were around Betty's kitchen table, where they'd spent so much time as teenagers. Luis had explained the situation and what he wanted.

Just as in earlier years, Betty served them lemon cake and then put her hands on her hips. "You have high blood pressure and Lord knows what else, Luis. You're about to take on fatherhood. Are you sure you want to take on a new side business, as well?"

"You need exercise, dude," Cody said. "Not more work."

"Hey. I swim." Although he hadn't been to the pool for weeks. "Anyway, working on a little seasonal bookstore? This will be relaxing," Luis said with confidence. "I know business, and Deena knows books. It'll be good for the island."

She shook her head slowly. "That may be," she said, "but having a baby won't be relaxing. It's going to be the main thing for you, for a while. You can't live in DC and commute here and run a bookshop and become a father. You'll wreck your health."

"But with Deena to take care of Willow, it'll work." Now that he had a plan, Luis felt back in control. He wanted Willow here, in the safe, supportive environment of Teaberry Island. And he wanted other people taking care of Willow, since Luis himself was bound to be bad at it. "You said you know the Realtor who's handling the bookstore property?"

"I do. But you should look at the building, inside and out, and give this some thought."

Luis shook his head. "No, this will work. I'll buy it, sight unseen."

ON WEDNESDAY AFTERNOON, Deena leaned against the ferryboat railing, Willow sleeping in her arms, lulled by the gentle rocking of the Chesapeake waves.

"There it is!" one of the other passengers called, and five or six of them gathered at the railing to watch as an island, complete with quaint harbor and old-fashioned-looking fishing boats, came into view.

The place actually looked like several marshy islands, with docks poking out into the bay. White frame houses with red or gray roofs stood above the flat landscape. Off in the distance, green and brown wetlands were visible. Deena had learned that the island's main industry was fishing, which made sense when she saw how water-bound the place was.

"Pretty, isn't it?" Luis said beside her.

"I don't want to give you the satisfaction, but yes, it is." Deena had come to see the island mostly to humor her friend Mrs. Martin and to placate Luis, who'd visited Willow Sunday, called Deena to check on her Monday, and visited again Tuesday, that time meeting them at Mrs. Martin's place so he could understand more about Willow's living situation. The visits were brief, as was the phone call, but each time he'd painted for her the benefits of raising Willow on Teaberry Island.

She felt like her life had been infiltrated.

Mrs. Martin had told her she should go to the island just for the fun outing and a boat trip with a sexy man. Deena was trying to look at it that way. Luis was attractive, no doubt about it. That was part of what made Deena cautious around him. Men that good-looking, in her experience, couldn't be trusted.

Well, men in general couldn't be trusted. She'd learned that young, from her mother's stories about how Deena's father had left her as soon as she'd gotten pregnant. The lesson had been reinforced when her stepfather, Andrew, had abandoned her and her mother in their hour of need. As for personal experience…she didn't even want to think about her own disastrous attempt to date in high school.

But men as good-looking as Luis were even less trustworthy than most.

It had taken two hours to drive from DC to the ferryboat station in Pleasant Shores, Maryland, but part of that was traffic. Although, with the way Luis had driven, weaving smoothly in and out of lanes in his powerful, purring black sports car, traffic hadn't seemed to cause much of a problem.

As the boat docked, some on the ferryboat hurried off, dressed in work uniforms. Most likely, there weren't a lot of jobs on the island. The uniformed folks must be returning from early shifts working on the mainland.

A crowd of shorts-clad vacationers waited on the dock for the return trip. Tourist season hadn't started, but there looked to be several families squeezing in an early vacation.

After the push was over, she and Luis headed down the gangplank and onto the dock, Deena holding Willow while Luis unfolded the stroller she'd brought. "This doesn't seem very sturdy," he said.

"It's lightweight and cheap, and it works." She plunked Willow into it and the child stretched and snuggled in, her eyes closing. They'd gotten up early this morning to be ready for their little trip. Willow was tired. Fortunately, she was getting back to being a good sleeper after the trauma of losing her mom, and Deena counted her blessings for that.

They walked down a semi-gravel road toward a cluster of buildings that looked like a small downtown. Here and there, side streets branched off to houses ranging from small shacks to well-kept cottages with picket fences. A couple of bigger places suggested there were a few wealthy folks living here, too. Deena saw a car in front of one place, a golf cart in front of another. An SUV passed them, heading downtown. Mostly, though, it looked like distances were short enough for walking.

Compared to the congestion of DC, it *would* be nice not to need public transportation or a car.

Shimmering to their right and behind them was the bay, the island's dominant feature and probably visible from most homes and businesses. Its water was a deep blue-green, although Luis had told her on the way over that its color varied, depending on the time of day and whether it was sunny or overcast. Today, the sky was cloudless. A few fishing boats were tied up to short piers, one occupied by two men whose indistinguishable words drifted toward them on the salty breeze.

"Let's walk through the town so you can get a feel for it," Luis said. He was carrying the diaper bag and pushing the stroller, leaving Deena unencumbered. Even at work, when she didn't have Willow with her, she was mostly carrying trays of food or dirty dishes. Having nothing in her hands, swinging along in the sunshine, made her feel like a girl again.

She glanced over at Luis to find him watching her. "What?" she asked.

He smiled. "Sorry. I'm just hoping you like the place. And…to be honest, you're very pretty."

Heat rose up in her and she looked away. She couldn't help but feel a little thrill that a man as handsome and important as Luis thought her pretty. On the other hand, men like that usually had a plan when they smiled and paid compliments. No way would Deena play that game. She looked away, focusing on the way the wind rustled the grasses, the sound of a woodpecker tap-tap-tapping on a tall, branchless dead tree.

As they approached the town, the houses got closer together, most gray-shingled with white trim and window boxes filled with bright flowers. Luis stopped by one that had a low picket fence and children playing in the backyard. He beckoned her over. "This is the day care home my brother recommends," he said.

A little girl, maybe four years old, ran to the fence. "Uncle Luis!" she crowed, lifting her arms.

"Can't pick you up, sweet Ava," he said, squatting down to be at her level. "Miss Arletta wouldn't like it. Peek through the fence at me."

The child giggled and did what he said, and a couple of other kids came running over, followed by a tall woman with salt-and-pepper hair and a You Can't Scare Me: I Teach Toddlers T-shirt.

The woman greeted Luis warmly, the kids swarming around her legs with easy affection, and the backyard was a dream, full of kids' play equipment. There were only five kids, so clearly there was individual attention.

But what about safety? Deena couldn't forget that Luis could have picked up the little girl and taken off. Back in DC, Mrs. Martin kept a close eye on all her kids when she went to the park, sometimes enlisting a niece or nephew to help her.

"This is Deena, and that's Willow, just waking up," Luis said. "This is Miss Arletta." The two women shook hands. "There's a chance Willow might come to stay on the island, at least part-time," Luis continued. "Do you happen to have a space for her in your group?"

Miss Arletta tilted her head to one side, looking at Willow. As the child opened her eyes and reached for Deena, the older woman continued to study her.

"I might have space," she said. "Does she have any issues?"

Deena glanced at Luis, then back at the woman. "Why do you ask?"

"I'm not a medical professional, but I do deal closely with children on a daily basis."

Deena held her breath. Had the woman noticed signs of FAS in Willow, signs that had taken her a while to notice, that Mrs. Martin and even Willow's own mother had never noticed?

"It's just good to know whether she has any particular needs beyond what any kid would have. That way, I can assess whether she can get the right attention and services to thrive here."

"Would you turn her away if she had issues?" Luis asked.

"Not unless we didn't have the equipment or manpower to handle them. I have two helpers who work with me part-time."

Willow pumped her arms up and down, looking at the colorful play structure in the backyard.

"See the slide, honey?" Deena asked, bouncing her. She felt defensive, like Willow was on trial.

Willow smiled but didn't speak.

"How old is she?" Miss Arletta asked.

"She just turned two, but she was premature."

"So she's running a little behind," the older woman said, nodding.

A couple of the boys at her feet started pummeling each other, and Arletta separated them. "Tommy, Justin, you may not play together for ten minutes."

Both boys began to cry.

"Go on and dig in the sandbox, Tommy," she ordered. "Justin, you may climb or collect sticks for our craft."

The two little ones slumped off, and Arletta smiled. "That's about the top level of punishment we use here. The kids are pretty well-behaved and they like each other. Being separated is the worst thing they can think of, even if it's just for a short time."

Deena realized then that she ought to be evaluating Miss Arletta and her childcare approach, too. What she saw, she liked. The woman seemed knowledgeable about child development, kind but adept at maintaining order. The big backyard would be both more calming and more stimulating than Mrs. Martin's small apartment.

"We're working on figuring out a few issues with Willow," Deena said, taking charge. "If you think you might have a place for her, and she ends up spending time here, may we get in touch?"

"Of course. Phone number's on the sign in front. And now I need to get everyone organized for snack time. Good to see you, Luis. Nice to meet you, Deena." She leaned over the fence and patted Willow's leg, gently. "Bye, honey," she said, and then hurried off.

Deena and Luis walked on, Willow riding in the stroller and taking in the scene as they came into the tiny downtown, passing a hardware store and a hair salon. The shopping district was maybe four blocks long, although blocks didn't seem to be the governing principle; instead, streets and a small park followed the curves of a couple of streams that ran alongside the main street. Luis greeted several people, including a pastor who invited her and Willow to come to church. When they reached a small market, Luis paused. "If you don't mind coming inside," he said, "we can meet my foster mother and get the best ice cream on the island."

"Big mistake," came a voice behind them. "You don't want to get your ice cream at Betty's market when you can have your pick of flavors at my cart."

Luis grinned, revealing that dimple again. "You're Goody, right? I've heard something about this rivalry, but you know I've got to be loyal to my foster mom and teaberry ice cream."

"Your loss," the woman said, spinning and marching back toward a pink-and-blue truck with a big ice cream cone decorating the top and a window where several tourists were lined up, waiting.

"Luis, *mi amigo*!" An older man hurried across the street to greet Luis. "Woo-hoo, things have improved in your life!" He looked Deena up and down, his once-over so comical that it didn't annoy her. Much. "Is this your bambino?" he asked Luis, pointing at Willow.

Luis unclipped Willow from her stroller and swept her into his arms, conveniently keeping the little old man from touching her, for which Deena was grateful. "This is Willow," he said, "and this is Deena. Deena, Hector Lozano, who has a monopoly on the bike and golf cart rental business during tourist season." He gestured toward an open stand where several bikes and golf carts were lined up.

"Speaking of that, I have customers. First rental is free," he added to Deena, winking.

Luis handed Willow back to Deena and then led the way up the steps of the market, laughing. "Hector likes to joke around, but he's a good guy," he said. "When I was a teenager, he took a special interest in me because of my Mexican heritage. Cooked me Mexican food and spoke Spanish to me. Not that I'm fluent, I didn't live with my birth family long enough to be, but the sound was a comfort."

Deena felt a little breathless with all that information, which Luis had conveyed as if talking about someone else. Hmm. There was a lot going on underneath that millionaire surface, but he wasn't going to reveal it easily.

For the first time, she felt curious about him beyond his being professionally legitimate and a potentially decent caregiver for Willow. What kind of background did he have? What kind of man was he, really?

Inside, the market was dark and cool, with scents of coffee and baked goods and a faint smell of appliances and oil. "It's a food market but it sells basically everything," Luis explained, pointing toward cookware in one section and clothing in another. "And here's the queen of it all, my mama, Betty. Mama, this is Deena."

He reached out and gave a pretty older woman a big hug. She patted his cheek as if he were a kid and then turned to Deena. "I'm pleased to meet you," she said, "and I'm delighted to meet this little lady." She held her arms out for Willow.

Willow buried her face in Deena's chest. Too bad. She'd hoped Willow would be friendly and charming toward this important person in Luis's life.

But then again, Willow was just a baby. She wasn't concerned about first impressions, nor should she be.

"I'm sorry. Too many new people, huh, sweetie?" Deena joggled Willow and kissed her head until she smiled and peeked out at Betty.

Betty didn't look put off by Willow's shyness. Instead, she looked thoughtfully from Willow to Luis. "I do believe she has your eyes," she said. "Can she have a *c-o-o-k-i-e*?" she asked Deena.

"A little one," Deena said.

Betty went behind the bakery counter and brought out a small cookie shaped like a star. Instead of handing it to Willow, she offered it to Deena. "She might not take food from my—"

Willow grabbed the cookie and stuffed it into her mouth.

"Oh, I guess she will," Betty said, laughing. "Now, for you grown-ups, can I get you some teaberry ice cream?"

"That's what we came in for," Luis said. "Better give me mine in a cup. I'm not used to juggling a stroller and a diaper bag. A cone might end up on the ground."

Deena put Willow into the stroller. Then, hands free, she opted for a cone. When she licked the pink ice cream, expecting a fruity taste, she was startled at the light, sweet mint flavor. "This is so good!" she exclaimed, earning a wide smile from Betty.

As they walked through the rest of the largely car-free downtown, passing a park, a tiny post office and a library, Deena processed what she'd seen.

There was definitely a community here, one that seemed like a caring one. If Willow became a part of it, Deena could see the benefits.

"If my guess is right," she said to Luis, thinking aloud, "Willow will need a lot of support as she grows. Impulse control, remembering, various cognitive and behavioral symptoms could come up. Are you up for all that, and is this the place for it?"

"From what I hear, yes. Some social workers and counselors and the like visit the island, and more are available just a short ferry ride away, in Pleasant Shores."

She noticed he'd talked about the place, and not his own capacity to deal with Willow's issues.

"Teaberry's kind of magical," he went on. "My brothers and I were basically reborn here when no one else thought we would amount to anything. Once we got here, we thrived." He frowned. "I think Willow could do well here, especially if you'd come help with her care, so she has a bridge to what's familiar."

"I see the benefits," she said, "but like we've discussed—"

"In fact," he interrupted, "here's the cherry on top of the offer." He pointed at a weathered red clapboard building with a faded sign that said Books. Old-looking, leather-bound volumes were stacked in the front windows, and there was a small, dilapidated shed in the back.

"I just bought this bookshop," he said, "and you can run it."

She stared at the adorable little shop, her heart leaping.

"No, she can't," said a voice behind them.

CHAPTER FIVE

EVERYTHING CAROL WANTED was slipping away. "What do you mean, it's under contract?"

She was standing in front of the old bookshop, which was way more run-down than she'd expected. Seeing it was discouraging, and as she'd approached, she wondered if she actually wanted anything to do with it.

As soon as she learned someone had bought it, though, it was all she craved.

"Your sister and I met yesterday and signed the paperwork," the man said. "I'm Luis Dominguez, and I can show you a scan of the contract if you'll just let me see some ID, so I know for sure you're who you say you are."

The nerve!

The blonde woman nudged him. "Luis. You made an impulsive decision to buy the place. Maybe this is your God-given way out."

"I don't want a way out. I bought the bookshop, and I'm already renovating it, and you're going to run it. If you're amenable."

"I mean…" The woman frowned. "I loved working at the bookstore in DC, and I did hope to become a manager someday. But I never imagined… I'm not sure I can do something like this, here."

"There, see?" Carol lifted a hand, palm up. The

woman's reluctance could work in her favor, even though personally, Carol thought she must be a fool for turning down such an offer. "She doesn't want to run it. I do. But I don't just want to run it, I want to own it."

"That's not going to happen," he said. "The deal is done."

Carol spent half an hour arguing with the man, but he continued to insist he owned the bookshop. Had the paperwork to prove it, too.

So she returned to the family home where her sister and nephew were staying during spring break and where Carol planned to live for the foreseeable future. Unless this upstart stranger spoiled everything by removing the only means of earning a living Carol could currently think of.

She was in the bedroom she'd always used, unpacking her bags, when she heard her sister and nephew come home. She gave them a few minutes to settle in and for Pete to go off in his own direction, and then came down to the kitchen to confront her sister.

"You sold the bookshop!" she said to Mary Beth. Then she regretted her tone. Mary Beth was easygoing, for a lawyer, but she'd had a rough divorce and financial troubles and was raising a teenager basically alone. She didn't need her sister being harsh with her.

"What?" Mary Beth had the refrigerator open and was looking inside. She grabbed a hunk of cheese and a gallon of milk and nudged the fridge door closed, then turned to Carol.

"The bookshop. Why'd you sell it without asking me?"

Mary Beth put the items down on the counter. "I was so glad to get it off my hands that I didn't even consider asking you, to tell you the truth. It's been for sale for two years. I was shocked someone wanted it."

"*I* wanted it," Carol said.

"You *did*?" Mary Beth glanced at her sidelong, then knelt and pulled a grater out of the cupboard. She unwrapped the cheese and started grating it.

"Yes, I did!"

"Since when?"

Since I lost my job and my marriage. She'd told Mary Beth the basics of what had happened. She didn't necessarily want to dig into the details now.

Pete came in and grabbed a handful of grated cheese.

"Stop! That's dinner!" Mary Beth smacked at him half-heartedly.

"It's good," Pete said. "What are you two arguing about?"

"I came here to reopen our old family bookshop," Carol said, "and your mother sold it out from under me."

"You mean that shack on the harbor end of downtown?"

"It's not a shack! In its day, it was a very important place for those interested in the history of the island."

"Um," Pete said, grabbing more cheese, "is anyone actually interested in the history of the island?"

"No," Mary Beth said.

"Of course they are!" Carol said at the same time. "Plus, I need some way to make a living over here, and I was counting on reopening the bookshop."

"I'm sorry." Mary Beth put a chunk of butter into a saucepan and reached for the flour. "You'd probably do better to find a job, though, rather than starting something up. That bookshop never made much of a profit."

"You're not taking this seriously!"

Mary Beth gave her a side-eye glare as she sprinkled flour into the sizzling butter. "Carol. You've been in Baltimore for years. You never said you were interested in the shop when you visited here. Never even looked at it, as far as I know. How was I supposed to guess that you'd suddenly show up wanting to live here and open the shop?"

"I still wish you'd asked." Carol hated change. Hated having her own plans abruptly fall through.

"You'll get half of the proceeds from the sale, if that's what you're worried about. Guy paid the asking price, sight unseen."

The thought of the extra money eased Carol's mind a little. She'd known Tom had left the shop to the two of them, but she hadn't really considered the monetary value. Hadn't thought it was worth anything in its current condition. "I'm not worried about that. I knew you'd give me my share. And you should take more because you've dealt with it these past few years." She looked around, noticing the scratched floors and grimy cupboard doors. "You've dealt with this place, too. I'll do some work on it. It's my turn."

"Be my guest," Mary Beth said, stirring the roux she'd made. "We've done a little this week, and Pete promised to help me do more this summer. We're back for the summer on June 12, but until then, you've got free rein."

Carol definitely liked free rein. She went to the fridge and looked inside. "Do you want me to make a salad?" she asked doubtfully, holding up a browning half head of iceberg lettuce.

"No. I meant to pick up some stuff at the market, but time got away from me. Just open a can of green beans so we can say we made an effort." She gave Carol a tired smile.

"I should've shopped and fixed dinner." Carol didn't want to be a burden. "I'll help you more tomorrow and we can do a nice picnic together over the weekend."

"Sure, if my little angel wants to spend time with family." Mary Beth softened her sarcastic words with a pat on Pete's back. "Go clean up. We'll eat in half an hour."

After he'd left, Carol opened a bottle of wine she'd brought and poured glasses for both her and Mary Beth. "That man who bought the shop, he had the audacity to offer me a job working there."

"Really?"

She nodded. "Once it's operational, which will take a while."

"That's great, right?" Mary Beth sipped wine, eyeing Carol over the rim of the glass.

"Not really. I planned to run the bookshop myself, the way I want to run it. The way our family always did."

"Or didn't. Grandpa opened it whenever he pleased and stocked whatever he was interested in. Not the best way to run a business."

"This Dominguez guy was talking pie-in-the-sky changes."

"Not your favorite thing," Mary Beth said. "And I'm sorry about selling the shop, but the truth is, I need the money. Trying to be here for Pete and also practice law remotely…well, it's tough."

"Hugh isn't making the child support payments?"

"No, but that's nothing new." Mary Beth shook her

head and waved a hand, indicating that she didn't want to talk about it. "So tell me about you. What's going on?"

Carol rolled her head between her shoulders, trying to ease the ache there. "You're right about how I don't like change. I've been criticized for that a lot recently."

"Such as?"

"My boss at work wanted me to take the tutoring center online. I balked—for good reason—and that's the main reason I lost my job. And…" She trailed off, feeling embarrassed.

"What else?"

She sighed. "Roger said he'd changed but I refused to see it." She'd told Mary Beth the bare outline of losing her job and her husband when they'd spoken on the phone, but she hadn't felt like sharing the details. Still didn't, but if she couldn't admit the truth to her sister, who could she tell?

Mary Beth squeezed her shoulder and sank into a chair across from her at the table. "You've really gone through it, haven't you? I'm sorry I haven't been very supportive. I had no idea things were deteriorating for you at work or at home."

"Neither did I, honestly." Which was eye-opening. There must have been plenty going on right in front of her, and she hadn't even noticed. "I appreciate you letting me take over the house. I'll work on it while I figure out what to do with my life."

"Take the job at the bookshop. Get out and meet people." Mary Beth drank a deep gulp of wine. "It's a friendly island. I'd live here full-time, except I don't want to mess up Pete's high school years with a big change." She frowned. "And speaking of changes, what are you doing as far as Roger goes? Are you two going through with a divorce?"

Carol shrugged. "I guess so." She'd thought maybe the incident with Misty was a brief aberration in Roger's fidelity to her, but he'd continued to assert that he wanted a divorce the couple of times they'd spoken since she'd moved out. "I'm going to need your legal advice. I'm thinking about taking Roger to the cleaners, along with his little nurse buddy."

Mary Beth grinned. "I'm on board to help with that. What about your workplace? Doesn't seem like they had legitimate reason to fire you. You should take *them* to the cleaners, too."

"Well… I *guess* an age discrimination case isn't a bad idea." But it didn't give her much satisfaction. Neither did turning the screws on Roger, to be honest. "For now, I want to settle in and rebuild a little."

It was foreign to her, but she sensed that she needed to look forward. And sitting here with her sister, looking out the window at the bay, she felt an unfamiliar twinge of excitement.

It told her that looking forward just might be the right thing to do.

On Sunday, just four days after he and Deena had visited the island, Luis set down a load of boxes in a pair of attached bedrooms in Betty's farmhouse. Deena was across the room, opening another moving box and pulling things out. Willow bounced in a plastic chair-walker combo, batting at the colorful toys and bells that adorned it, seemingly content.

Luis was as pleased as when he completed a major business deal. Getting Deena here to look at the island, to see its charms and imagine living here with Willow, had been the right first step. Buying her the old bookshop had sealed the deal, and she'd agreed to come.

He'd pulled a few strings and spent some money to make the move happen fast, before she changed her mind. Movers had packed up her things while she'd dealt with quitting her job and notifying her landlord and changing her address. They'd signed an employment contract.

And here they were, moving her and Willow in.

Living in the big farmhouse with Luis's foster mother wasn't ideal, but it was temporary. Thanks to Betty, the place was comfortable and homey. He could tell Deena liked it from the way she ran her hand over the iron bed frame and kept glancing out the tall, narrow windows that faced the bay. Attached to this large bedroom was a smaller one, perfect for Willow. Rocking chairs and antique-looking dressers, one in each room, made it all ready to move in.

Luis was staying at the other end of the hall, in the bedroom his brother Ryan had used when he'd first returned to Teaberry Island. It was actually the bedroom Luis had lived in as a teenager, and it felt like home.

What *wasn't* sweet and comfortable and homey was being in a bedroom with Deena. That was a different kind of feeling entirely. What was wrong with him that his mind kept picturing what they could do together on that narrow, iron-framed bed?

Not that she was dressed provocatively, not at all. She wore a plaid shirt with the sleeves rolled up, frayed jean shorts and sneakers.

Different from the way women dressed to impress in DC. She'd fit right in on the island. And that was what he needed to focus on, not those long, perfectly shaped legs.

What he really needed to do was get back to work. He needed to complete this move-in and then get on his computer to prepare for tomorrow's meetings. Sundays weren't a day of rest, not in Luis's business.

The man he'd hired to help with the move-in, an island fixture named Weed, came huffing into the room, carrying two boxes. Weed was a Vietnam veteran who'd had an obvious drinking problem when Luis was a teenager on the island. Now he was sober, a friend of Luis's brother Cody, but he still lived a somewhat itinerant lifestyle and made his living doing odd jobs.

"Last ones," Weed said, setting the boxes gently on the floor.

"Thanks, man." Luis looked in his wallet, didn't find a fifty, and handed Weed a hundred-dollar bill. Guy looked like he could use it.

Weed's bushy gray eyebrows lifted. "You sure?"

"Yep. Appreciate the help."

Deena came over and shook Weed's hand, smiling. "We couldn't have done it without you. Thanks for being so careful."

"My pleasure," he said, his cheeks reddening.

And no wonder. Deena was warm and friendly, a beautiful woman. To shake her hand had probably made Weed's day.

Focus on business, he reminded himself as the older man headed down the stairs.

Willow had seemed content in the bouncy chair, but now she rubbed the backs of her hands over her eyes. Her face screwed up, which Luis had already realized meant a big fuss was coming.

Deena must have noticed it, too, because she swooped Willow out of the chair and planted a big, noisy kiss on her belly, making her chortle. Then she turned to Luis with Willow propped on her hip. "Would you mind holding her while I make up our beds? I'm so glad Betty had a crib available."

"Benefit of all her years doing foster care," Luis said. Last fall, Ryan had helped Betty clean out the farmhouse, rescuing it from a near-hoarding situation, but Betty had insisted on keeping certain items of furniture, including a crib and a couple of booster seats. Now that was proving to be a wise decision.

He took Willow from Deena and sat down in the rocking chair, holding the child on his lap, chattering nonsense to her. She laughed easily and reached up to explore his face with her chubby, slightly sticky hands.

Luis still wasn't quite used to the notion that this was his child. He found himself studying her face for similarities to his own. Maybe their noses? Betty claimed to see a resemblance around the eyes, but Luis wasn't sure. He rocked her, gently, and she stuck her thumb in her mouth and leaned her head against his chest.

Luis melted, his eyes tearing up.

He looked at Deena to see if she'd noticed, but she was making the bed. Bending over to do it, and…wow. The woman had beautiful curves.

He forced himself to turn away.

Willow sighed. Her eyes had fluttered shut, her long lashes dark against her cheeks.

Women had always told him his eyelashes were too long and pretty for a man. Apparently Willow had inherited those. He studied her face, his heart warm, while Deena went into the adjoining room and shuffled around in there, probably making up the crib.

When she came back into the room, he climbed his way out of his emotions and stood, careful not to jostle Willow. He handed her back to Deena and brushed his hands together. He needed to get back to business. He straightened and said the first non-gushy thing that came into his head. "Could you get me a spreadsheet of any extra hours you've put in by tomorrow morning?"

She tilted her head to one side, looking puzzled. "What's wrong?"

"Oh! Well, it's just… I'm not used to thinking of hours, I just take care of her. She's my…" She trailed off, biting her lip.

Her very full, very pretty lower lip.

"That was good of you, but please keep track from now on," he said, trying to get his brain into boss mode. "I'm going to need you to work some extra hours, but I want to be fair."

They were standing close together. This beautiful woman, this child of his, they were calling to him. Begging him to relax, sink in, embrace the moment.

It was a longing feeling he wasn't accustomed to, and he shoved it away. He checked the time. "If you're settled," he said, "I have a couple of hours of work."

"Oh!" She looked disconcerted. "Um, okay."

"What's wrong? Is there something else you need?"

She shook her head rapidly, as if to clear it. "No, I guess not. I'm just…normally, I take a little more time to make a major life change. Four days ago, Willow and I were living in our familiar neighborhood in DC."

She sounded…lost.

Her vulnerability tugged at his heart, but he shoved

away the feeling. "Second thoughts? We have a contract."

She stiffened. "I understand. I'm not going to abandon Willow. Go ahead, go do your work."

He nodded, turned and strode away. He'd been too abrupt and brusque, most likely, but he couldn't stick around and fix it. He had to get out of there. Because... His steps slowed for a moment.

Because in truth, he didn't want to go. He wanted to stay and melt into the sweet warmth of this pretty woman and his amazing, newly discovered daughter. But getting attached was way, way too dangerous when he knew he couldn't follow through.

THE MORNING AFTER moving into the farmhouse on Teaberry Island, Deena brought her coffee out onto the front porch. It was May 1, May Day, and the sky was a deep blue. The bay wasn't visible from here—it was behind the farmhouse—but she could hear the gulls fighting and the sound of a boat motor, and the air had a soft, slightly salty tinge to it. The place was gorgeous, and relaxing in a way that a city could never be. She'd worried that she had made a too-hasty decision, based on the island's surface appeal and the promise of caring for Willow and running a bookstore. But the charm of the place ran deep. She was pretty sure she could learn to love it here.

"Thank you again for letting us stay with you," she said to Luis's foster mom, who sat on the porch swing, moving it with the occasional shove of a bare foot.

"Glad to have you." Betty glanced toward the house, where Luis was feeding Willow breakfast. "It's been rare enough that Luis would come and stay here, even for a few days. I'm delighted you all have pitched your tent with me for a while."

Deena sank down onto the top step and leaned against the pillar, gazing off in the direction of the bookshop that was to be hers to run. "You have a business on the island," she said. "Do you think a bookshop will make it here?"

Betty was quiet for a minute, her forehead wrinkling. "You can tell me."

"I'm skeptical," Betty said. "That place is a mess, and it never was real viable. You'll need to find a niche and do some market research, and even then…" She shrugged. "A lot of folks on the island like to read, but we're a small population. And people use the library. Speaking of which…" She stood and put two fingers in her mouth and whistled. The sharp sound halted a woman who was riding by on a bike.

Betty waved and beckoned. "Come on up here. We're talking books."

The woman coasted along the grassy stepping stone path and leaned her bike against a small apple tree. She strode briskly to the porch. "Talking books, are you? That's no surprise. I'm Linda," she added, holding out a hand to Deena. "I run the library. And you must be a visitor?"

"Actually, I'm going to be living here," Deena said. "At least for a while." She wasn't sure how, or how much, Luis intended to tell people about Willow. Until she knew, she'd focus on business. "I'm planning to renovate and reopen the little bookshop at the edge of town." She gestured in its direction.

"Really?" Linda sounded surprised, and not pleasantly so. "Now, why would you want to do that?"

Deena's stomach tightened. Sensing animosity from the woman, she wasn't sure how much she wanted to say.

"Luis, my foster son, decided to give it a go and hired Deena to help him," Betty said. "He's normally a genius at business, but... I'm not sure about this particular decision. You think a bookstore's going to make it here?"

Linda puffed out air. "Honestly? I doubt it." She crossed her arms over her chest and frowned. Her stance suggested that she didn't *want* the bookstore to succeed. "Pretty sure you hitched your cart to the wrong horse, honey."

"It's not competition for the library," Betty said mildly.

"How do you figure that? I've spent years building up the literary community on this island. It's been an uphill battle, and I don't want some new business poaching on my hard work."

Deena blinked.

"Good heavens, Linda," Betty said, "I don't think Deena and Luis have come here with the intent of taking away library customers."

"I'd rather cooperate with you," Deena said, "and I think Luis would, too. It would be nice to plan some joint events, if you're open to that." *Nice if you turn your attitude around. Otherwise, not so much.*

Linda shrugged. "We'll see how your business comes along. I'm not optimistic."

"Linda!" Betty gestured toward Deena. "This young woman is a friend of my Luis, and she's basically uprooted her life to come here and make something of the place. We need to be supportive."

Linda spread her hands and tilted her head from side to side, meeting Deena's eyes. "I don't know what Luis was thinking, but apparently he's not the only one. That Carol woman has already been to see me. She's up in arms about her family selling it out from under her when she wants to reopen it."

"We've met." Deena pressed her lips together to keep herself from saying more. The woman had been extremely angry and rather rude. Deena was accustomed to dealing with people of all sorts, but it felt a little more personal here on the island, compared to customers in a busy city restaurant or bookstore.

"I don't think I know her," Betty said.

Linda glanced at Deena and then addressed Betty. "Carol is living here now. She's Mary Beth's sister, the one who spends summers out on Sandy Point. Single woman with a teenage boy?"

"She's staying in their summer house year-round? Wonder why?"

"Long, gossipy story. You'll have to ask her."

Deena found it a little worrisome that the two women seemed to know everyone on the island, everyone's history, and to have an opinion about each one. Then again, her neighborhood in the city had been a gossipy place. Human nature, she guessed.

She didn't have much time to ponder that before Luis came out. He was dressed in business casual clothes. A different shirt than he'd worn before, and in fact, he was still buttoning it up.

A woman would have to be a corpse—or Luis's mother—not to appreciate that glimpse of man-chest. Deena was pretty sure Linda the librarian noticed, and she was Betty's age.

"Hey, Linda," he said, flashing a smile. "Mama, I'm

sorry we're imposing on you like this. I'm going to find us another place soon."

"Wait, what?" Deena was just getting her bearings, and so was Willow. They'd only been here twenty-four hours.

"No need to find another place. I have all kinds of room, since Ryan and Mellie helped me clean the place out." Betty patted the porch swing beside her. "Come sit. You need to relax."

Deena figured she'd better speak up so as not to get steamrolled by Luis's intensity. "I'd like to stay here. I mean, as long as Betty's willing. She's babysitting Willow some, which is wonderful. And it's close to town and the bookshop. I don't want to live in some isolated place with you."

"Family discussion. I'm outta here. Have to open the library." Linda waved and headed for her bike. No "nice to meet you" was forthcoming, which, given her attitude, didn't surprise Deena.

"Very sensible." Betty smiled at Deena. "This is an old-fashioned island. It wouldn't look good for the two of you to stay alone together."

Luis shook his head, laughing a little. "It's the twenty-first century. Surely nobody will judge." He turned to Deena. "I promise, your virtue is safe with me."

In Deena's experience, men's promises lasted about as long as a Chesapeake wave. "I'd rather stay here." When Luis opened his mouth, most likely to argue, she quickly changed the subject. "Betty and Linda aren't optimistic that the bookshop will work."

Luis shrugged. "It's worth a try."

Why wasn't he concerned?

And then it dawned on her. "Wait a minute. Did you just buy it to get me here, to placate me?"

"No!" he said. Then that dimple flashed again. "Well, maybe. Sort of."

The excitement Deena had held inside her ever since Luis had mentioned the bookshop leaked away, leaving Deena deflated. Luis was just a manipulative man, like all the other manipulative men she'd known.

"I have to leave," Luis announced. "I'm going to run upstairs and grab my suitcase. Have to catch the ferry in a few."

She tilted her head, looking at him. "What do you mean, leave?"

"I need to get back to DC. It's Monday morning."

"But what about Willow?"

"She's watching a kids' TV show in there." He gestured toward the house. "Ate breakfast like a champ." He looked proud of himself.

Deena felt panicky. She wasn't ready to be left alone and in charge of Willow in a strange place. "You're leaving the moment you got us moved in?"

"I told you I'd have to work a lot."

"Yeah, but…that can't be the default. You can't feed her breakfast and take off without even giving me a heads-up." They'd talked a little about her duties when they'd drawn up a contract, but they hadn't pinned down the exact days. Now she realized that had been a mistake. Ugh.

"Look, of course I want you to have a say in how all of this plays out," he said. "But you can't dictate my schedule. I have a lot going on."

Deena's heart started pounding faster as heat rushed to her cheeks. She opened her mouth to speak.

Betty beat her to it. "You're a father, Luis. Your child and her needs should dictate your schedule."

Relief washed over Deena. Betty was on her side. On Willow's side, really, but it was the same thing. Shifting her mindset from being the parent figure who raised Willow to guiding Luis in how to parent... It wasn't easy. But it was what she had to do. "Right now, she needs you here," Deena said. "She's just had a major move, and she's unsettled. Now would be a good time for her to learn to depend on you. She needs to get to know you."

"Plus," Betty said, "remember how May Day is a holiday on the island. All the shops are getting ready for tourist season. And your brother—" she gestured toward the house next door "—he and Mellie are planning a cookout tonight. It would be nice if you, Deena and Willow could come. Help Deena get to know some people before you leave her here."

Exactly. Deena shot Betty a grateful smile. That was what Deena had left unsaid, hadn't even articulated to herself: she'd glommed on to Luis because she felt isolated in a new place. She didn't want him to go, not yet.

Don't get too dependent. You can't rely on him.

Luis glanced toward the docks, where a ferryboat was arriving. "I have meetings this afternoon in the District," he said.

Well, fine. He could just go. Deena opened her mouth to tell him so, but Betty spoke first. "Are your meetings more important than your daughter?"

A trapped expression crossed Luis's face. "Of course not."

"Then...you have to make sure your actions align with your values." Betty put an arm around Luis, a smile tugging at the corner of her mouth. "I'm sorry, honey. I know you're a grown man, but I can't turn off the motherly advice just because you're taller and richer and smarter than I am."

He let out a little snort. "Not smarter." He looked again toward the ferry and then back at the house. "All right. You're both right. I'll stay the rest of the day and head back in the morning."

Relief washed over Deena, followed immediately by a wave of anxiety.

Deena hadn't wanted to be left on her own on the island, but she wasn't sure she was prepared for an entire day spent with Luis.

Obviously she should have done more thinking about what it would be like to move to the island and co-parent, basically, with Luis. What had she gotten herself into?

CHAPTER SIX

BY LATE AFTERNOON, Luis was freaking out. Freak. Ing. Out.

Willow had been screaming for an hour, solid. After trying to comfort her in Betty's house, he brought her outside and paced with her. His brother Ryan, who lived next door, had beckoned him over; he and Mellie were preparing for a May Day cookout to which all of them—he, Willow, Betty and Deena—were invited.

Luis hurried over into Ryan's yard, feeling like his brother had thrown him a life preserver. Willow continued screaming, but at least Luis wouldn't be alone in dealing with it.

Mellie tried to comfort her, checked for fever, encouraged Luis to change her diaper again.

None of it helped. Where was Deena?

But he knew where. Betty had taken her downtown, where all the shops were throwing open their doors, showing off their new wares for the upcoming tourist season, serving cookies and lemonade. And Deena had looked extremely happy to go, leaving Luis in charge of the baby.

Betty had wanted to take Deena to see the town when most of the shops were open. She'd taken to Deena, and she'd *really* taken to Willow, and she'd told Luis she wanted to introduce Deena to people and give her every reason to stay on the island.

"Can't you shut that child up?" The voice, and the accompanying whack on the shoulder, told him his other brother had arrived. Although Luis knew the remark was a joke, he didn't find it funny. "*You* try," he said, holding Willow out toward Cody.

Cody backed up hastily, hands rising like stop signs. "No, not me. No way. I don't do babies."

"Not *yet*. Someday you may, so watch and learn." Cody's wife, Taylor, nudged past him and held out her arms for Willow. "Let me try. Mellie said Willow's having a bad day."

"That's an understatement." Luis relished getting a few feet distance from his screaming daughter. Bemused, he watched as Taylor patted her back and bounced her and made soothing noises. Women had a way with babies.

Or maybe not. Willow was still going strong. Maybe women just had more patience. He and Cody watched as Taylor carried the baby onto the porch, sat down in a rocking chair and started rocking back and forth, harder than Luis would have thought was a good idea. Cody and Taylor's kids, and Ryan's son, Alfie, watched for a few minutes and then ran off to play with one of the island dogs that had wandered into the yard.

"Rough day, huh?" Ryan came over, holding beers for both of them.

Luis grabbed his and drank deeply. "I want to raise her right but I can't even quiet her down." He looked from Ryan to Cody and back again. "The truth is, I feel like turning tail and running back to DC. At work, at least I understand the rules. I can fix what goes wrong."

Cody laughed. "I felt that way some, when my little brother and sister landed on my doorstep."

"Hard becoming an instant father," Ryan said. "But…" He shrugged. "No choice, right?"

"Right." No choice. He was stuck. The beer suddenly tasted sour in Luis's mouth. He loved Willow already, and he wanted to raise her, but he felt totally incompetent. Totally incompetent at a job he had no choice but to do. "It's not Willow's fault. She's had a lot of changes, and on top of that, the FASD." He was pretty sure that Deena's FAS theory was going to prove true. He'd stayed up until the wee hours researching the condition and comparing it to Willow's features and behavior. Betty, who knew more about babies, agreed with him.

Both brothers nodded, watching the porch, not speaking. Taylor appeared to be getting Willow calmed down. Her wails were getting further apart.

Deena and Betty pulled up next door in Betty's car and relief washed over Luis. He wouldn't be in charge of a child he couldn't handle anymore.

But rather than immediately taking over Willow's care, they went into the house. And Luis realized he had to stop making assumptions that women loved hanging out with babies all the time, that they had a way with them, that men could sit back and let the women handle any kid-related problems. Apparently, it didn't work that way.

"So, uh, Deena's going to be her nanny?" Cody asked.

"Yeah. We still need to work out the day-to-day arrangements, but we have a contract." And the sooner Deena and Willow got into a routine, the better. He knew Deena had been right this morning, insisting that he stay for an extra day before heading back to the city, but he felt slightly panicky about the constant pings on his phone, the long list of emails piling up. He was accustomed to being able to work whenever he needed to. Thrived on it, in fact.

"And you're going to help her open the bookshop?" Ryan asked.

Luis blew out a breath. "Yeah. I guess. We're going to take a look at it next time I'm here."

Cody wandered off to do something with his kids, and Ryan slung an arm around Luis and urged him toward the house. "Come on. You can help me grill and tell me how you're going to manage all you have on your plate."

If it would buy him more time away from the baby he couldn't handle, Luis was up for it. "Thanks, man."

In the cozy, homey kitchen, Ryan handed him a big tray of raw crab cakes. "Take those to the grill. I'm right behind you with hot dogs and buns."

Luis carried the tray down the steps and across the yard. To the right, he glimpsed Deena holding Willow on her lap on a rocking chair and talking to Taylor, who sat beside her. Betty was admiring something Ryan's son, Alfie, had brought up from the creek. The sun shone down and a cool breeze came across the bay, bringing the half-ocean, half-freshwater smell unique to the Chesapeake.

He was lucky, he knew that. Lucky to have this family. Lucky to have a home base here.

Lucky to get to know his daughter, even though the circumstances were terrible and he was no good at baby care.

The lawn shimmered and blurred and seemed to be coming closer. Trying to keep the tray steady, he sank to his knees without meaning to, and then sat down abruptly in the grass. The next thing he knew, he was falling backward and looking up at the sky, and the dogs were scarfing down the raw crab cakes, and people were yelling and rushing toward him.

He drifted for a few minutes. A car squealed up and some woman he didn't know came rushing over with a medical bag. She started taking his vital signs. "Has this ever happened before?" she asked.

"Ye-es." He had a little trouble getting the words out; his tongue felt thick. "It's blood pressure. Guess the new meds…need…to be adjusted."

Cody was going through his wallet. "Is this your doctor?" he asked, waving a card in front of Luis's face. "Dr. Henry Greeley?"

Luis nodded and leaned back, feeling more exhausted than he'd ever felt in his life.

But he couldn't be exhausted. He had a job to do, a child to raise. A bookshop to open, for pity's sake.

He sat up by sheer force of will, rubbed his eyes and got to his feet with the help of Ryan on one side and Cody on the other. "Things…to do," he said.

"Not tonight." His brothers walked him over to a chair and sat him down, and try though he might, his muscles wouldn't let him resist.

The breeze still felt good. The sun was sinking down, though. How long had he been out, anyway?

Betty came bustling over, spoke briefly to the nurse and then knelt in front of him. "We're taking you over to the mainland tomorrow to get you checked out," she said. "And then you're going to come back here and let me take care of you until we know what's going on."

"No time for that," Luis rasped out.

"Yes, there is. You're going to make time." She

looked over at Deena and held out her hand, and Deena helped her to her feet. Then Deena put the baby into Luis's lap and sat down beside them, one hand on each of them.

"You have to take care of yourself," she said, her voice firm. "Not just for yourself, and not for Betty. For your child."

ON THE THURSDAY morning three days after the dramatic cookout incident, Deena sat in Betty's kitchen, feeding Willow oatmeal and talking with Betty, who was putting together a casserole for later.

The farmhouse kitchen had high windows and a big old-fashioned ceramic sink. Dishes were stored in glass-fronted cabinets and a large white corner cupboard. Herbs grew on the windowsills, and onions and mushrooms sputtered on the stove, their delicious buttery smell permeating the air. The large, sturdy table's surface revealed scrubbed-over scratches and stains, and it was easy to imagine Ryan, Cody and Luis sharing raucous meals here with Betty and her late husband.

Deena and Betty had fallen into an easy rhythm in the past few days, communicating their plans, figuring out Willow's needs and dividing up her care. Deena kept the kitchen and bathrooms clean and did some vacuuming and dusting while Betty was at work at the market. Betty was a talented cook and often brought home fresh food from the market for supper.

Luis was unexpectedly staying here, but his presence was muted. He'd gone to the mainland for tests the day after the cookout, accompanied by his brothers, and the day of medical procedures had clearly wiped him out. It didn't help that his phone was constantly buzzing. Nor that there was little data available about his family of origin and any genetic health concerns.

The biggest problem, from what Deena could see, was that he pushed himself relentlessly. At the moment, he was talking with his board of directors on a video call in the other room.

"I hope the Wi-Fi signal holds up," Deena said, glancing toward the closed door of the dining room, where the call was taking place. She had already figured out that it was touch and go.

"I hope *he* holds up." Betty looked worried. "He's always driven himself so hard, and it's always been all about money, ever since he was a teenager. He needs to learn there's more to life."

Deena lifted Willow out of the high chair Betty had borrowed for her and sat her in her lap, her back to Deena's stomach. She patted Willow's little hands together. "You'll teach Daddy there's more to life, won't you?"

"Dah!" Willow said, and laughed.

Betty's eyebrows lifted. "Did she just say Daddy?"

"I think maybe," Deena said. Hope and happiness bubbled inside her. She *knew* Willow was smart and could catch on to things. A few people in the old neighborhood had seemed to doubt it, and Deena relished anything Willow did that proved them wrong.

The door from the dining room opened and Luis came out, groaning. "My board wants me to stay here on the island," he said. "They're worried about me. I wish they hadn't found out—"

"Dah!" Willow interrupted, lifting her arms toward him.

Luis's face broke into a smile so gorgeous that Deena

had to look away. No man had a right to be that handsome. He took Willow into his arms and swung her high, and she laughed uncontrollably.

Then she vomited up her breakfast.

Both Betty and Deena burst out laughing at Luis's horrified face. He'd put on a dress shirt for the video call. He'd definitely have to change it.

For now, he wiped himself and Willow with a paper towel and handed her to Deena.

"So how would you do your job, staying here?" Betty asked, layering vegetables with corn tortillas in a casserole dish. "Could you do your work on video conferences? Or can you get some time off?"

Luis grimaced. "Both. They seem to think I can work half-time for now, and that my assistant and a couple of others can handle more of my responsibilities. I'd need to go into town for a couple of days a month, occasionally more, but I could do a lot of it long-distance."

"That would be wonderful." Betty walked over and wrapped her arms around Luis. "I'd love to have you and your family here for as long as you can stay."

The word *family* took Deena aback. They *were* kind of like a little family, Dad and Mom and baby. Except she needed to keep reminding herself that she wasn't Mom, she was a paid caregiver. And she didn't have a relationship with Luis.

An unexpected surge of bitterness rose up in her. She'd gone to Luis because she'd wanted his financial help so she could be with Willow more. And, okay, she'd gotten that.

But it wasn't what she'd pictured. She'd expected to raise Willow herself as Tammalee had asked her to do.

Instead, she was the paid help.

"I just don't know if I can do it, Mama." Luis poured himself a cup of coffee from the old-fashioned electric percolator Betty used. "This is a complete change for me. I'm used to city life and business life." He looked over at Deena and Willow and sighed, as if they were millstones around his neck.

When in fact, Deena was helping him, and Willow was his *child.* Anger on Willow's behalf, and maybe on her own as well, boiled up inside her. "I'm sure it's rough for you to change your routine," she said, hearing the sarcasm in her own voice, "but there's been a change to Willow's routine, too."

"And to yours," Betty said. "You're not exactly used to island life."

No, she wasn't, and it was an adjustment, but not as much as she'd expected. The slower pace, the friendly people and the natural beauty soothed her soul in ways she hadn't known she needed.

Which didn't mean Luis could dodge all responsibility. "We need to meet with the Early Intervention people next Monday to get her evaluated. You need to be here for that as well as for whatever treatments they recommend."

"Can't you do it?" Behind his words was the unspoken reality: he was paying her to take care of his daughter.

For whatever reason, that hurt. Actually, she knew the reason. She felt more like a friend or relative to Willow, someone collaborating with Luis for Willow's care. She loved the sweet child like a mother. His "can't you do it" pressed her firmly back into her place.

"I *could.*" She glared at him. "If you want to be the kind of dad who foists his daughter's needs off on the babysitter."

Willow looked up at Deena, eyes wide, forehead wrinkling.

"Whoa whoa whoa." Betty came over and swooped Willow out of Deena's arms, blowing a raspberry on her chubby belly and making her chortle. "You two need to get out of the house to figure this all out. Or better yet, to forget about it and do something else, something less likely to send your blood pressure through the roof again." The tests on Luis had been inconclusive, but he'd been warned to avoid stress lest he have a stroke. Which, apparently, was something that could happen even to a man in his twenties.

"Fine," he said. "Let me change my shirt and then we'll go look at the bookshop. I'll need to have *something* to do if I'm stuck on the island." He stomped off toward the stairs.

Betty and Deena looked at each other, and Deena was delighted to see that Betty was stifling laughter, just as Deena was.

"He's acting like he did when he was a teenager," Betty said.

"Cranky," Deena agreed.

"Don't take it personally," Betty said to Deena once he was out of earshot. "Luis has a good heart despite all that he's been through. And he's been through a lot. It's left him pretty one-sided, but I suspect that you and this sweet baby are going to be the ones to help him grow into a well-rounded person."

"Maybe." Deena gathered her things. Helping an emotionally stunted man to grow up was a whole other task, in addition to being a caregiver to Willow and starting a business.

She was game for the latter two tasks, but whether

she could provide that kind of support Luis needed to grow—whether she even wanted to or should—she just didn't know.

LUIS AND DEENA were almost to the bookshop when he realized that she was carrying a blanket and a basket. He'd been distracted by the meeting with his board members and the new realities of parenthood, and as a result, he'd forgotten his manners. Not that his sulky display of anger earlier had been exactly polite. "Give me that stuff. You shouldn't be carrying it. What even is it?"

She kept ahold of both. "*You* shouldn't be carrying things. You're an invalid, after all." She said it with a twinkle in her eye, teasing him.

The fact that she was willing to be playful after he'd acted so immature made him like her even more. She'd changed into a casual white dress, her hair loose, and the force of his attraction to her almost bowled him over. "I'll show you an invalid," he said, pretending to tackle her and in the process, neatly taking away both blanket and basket.

She was laughing, her head thrown back, and he realized he hadn't seen her look carefree before. She always had Willow with her and was always worrying about something. Now the long column of her throat, her hair cascading down her back, her undeniably stellar figure... Wow.

She must have noticed him looking, because she stopped laughing and turned away. A tiny smile remained on her face, though.

"So what is this?" he asked, holding up the basket as they reached the little shabby building that was the bookshop. He set down the basket and peeked inside. "A picnic?"

"Betty threw it together. She wants me to keep you out here awhile, lower your blood pressure."

Getting close to Deena was much more likely to *raise* his blood pressure. "Let's look through the shop and then eat," he said. "I have the key right here."

The red clapboard building was almost like a house. In fact, that might be what it had been at one time. Two big display windows stacked with books in the front, a faded sign above the door and a shuttered upstairs. A tangle of weeds filled the narrow garden space in front.

He opened the door and peeked inside, then stepped back so she could enter first. She immediately started coughing. "Dusty," she said when she'd caught her breath. "So, um, you bought this, sight unseen?"

"I did." Because he hadn't really cared if it was functional or not. It had already served its function, in fact; it had gotten Deena to the island.

Now, though, seeing her stepping around gingerly looking at everything, watching the excitement grow in her eyes, he wondered if, in fact, they might be able to make a go of it. He was willing to try if it would keep her happy. And keep that sexy enthusiasm alive in her.

Deena ran her hand along a row of old volumes. "They left so many behind." She bit her lip, looking for all the world as if she were worried about the books' feelings.

Luis nearly tripped over a box, so focused was he on Deena. He tried to disguise his interest in her by opening the box's flaps. "Old papers, too. Wonder if this is family stuff that woman, Carol, would want?"

"We should hold on to it." Deena narrowed her eyes,

surveying the crooked shelves, the rickety-looking front counter, the dusty nails and other detritus covering the floor. "We'll shove all the stuff over there, to save and go through later," she said, pointing to a back corner. "Then we can see what kind of space we have here."

"Big picture first," Luis said. "Let's go have lunch and talk over what we've seen." The truth was that he felt more like relaxing with a beautiful woman than working on a new business. That, for him, was a rare thing.

"But…" She looked around longingly. He recognized the look: she wanted to get to work. He'd had that feeling himself, many times—itching to get going on a new project, feeling the pure joy of creativity tuned in a business direction, to do something that would make the world better. Not in some theoretical way, but rather, helping people find jobs, earn good salaries, pay their bills. The nitty-gritty of life.

He supposed books could fit into that category of making the world better. He could get excited about the project right along with Deena. He'd rarely felt that kind of kinship with a woman. With anyone.

But not now. Now he wanted to get to know her. For professional reasons and maybe more.

The truth was, seeing her flushed cheeks and sparkling eyes as she got excited about the bookshop project drew him like a magnet. Made him want to be close to her.

So they went outside and spread the blanket in the grass beside the shop. The afternoon had gotten warmer and the breeze had stilled. You could see the bay and the harbor, a few boats. Ospreys and gulls swooped, calling, but beyond that, the day was quiet. The island's usual salty, oyster-shell smell mingled with the fragrance of fertile soil and new vegetation.

Deena was pulling things out of the picnic basket in a haphazard fashion: thick sandwiches on homemade bread, a variety he recognized from the Bluebird Bakery; four of Betty's big chocolate chip cookies; apples and pears; a thermos, no doubt holding coffee; and two bottles of water.

She waved a careless hand toward the food. "Go for it," she said.

"You're not eating?"

She shrugged. "I'll eat." But she showed no enthusiasm for lunch. Instead, she kept looking back toward the building.

He didn't think he was hungry, but when he unwrapped a sandwich and discovered home-sliced ham and aged cheddar, his stomach growled. "Unwrap the other one and you can choose," he said, because he knew from his teen years that Betty never packed two of the same kind of sandwiches. And that no one could stay indifferent to food in the presence of Betty's lunches.

Sure enough, the one Deena unwrapped was peanut butter and banana and marshmallow fluff on whole wheat.

"Wow, they both look good," she said. "You decide."

"Let's each have half of each," he suggested. "Eat the ham first because the peanut butter is almost like dessert."

They ate for a few minutes. A little gray bird landed on the apple tree overhead and trilled out a song. The sun warmed his shoulders.

How long had it been since he'd relaxed like this? Lunch was usually a vending machine snack at his desk.

Sitting under a tree with a beautiful woman, eating wholesome, homemade food—not only was it healthier, but it was a lot more enjoyable.

He finished first and wiped his hands on a red-checked cloth napkin. "Now that you've seen inside the place, what do you think?" he asked. "Is it salvageable?"

"Totally," she said with confidence. "It's a mess, but I can envision the finished shop. It'll be amazing. A great addition to the town."

"I'm not so sure." He liked her confidence, but with his greater business experience, he wanted to manage her expectations. "It'll take a lot of cleaning, and that's just the start."

"I'm good at cleaning," she said.

He didn't want her using her energy that way, not when she had a business to start and Willow to care for. "If we do it," he said, "I'll hire a crew to get things off the ground."

"What do you mean, 'if'?" She whacked his arm. "We're doing it. You promised."

He grinned. He liked persistent women; it was something he'd liked about Tammalee.

For a second, he could picture the lively, high-energy woman with whom he'd shared a couple of very enjoyable nights almost three years ago. The thought that she was gone, that Willow would never know her mother, made his throat tighten.

Time to refocus. "We'll need to get a nice new sign," he said. "Something to draw people in. Like the old sign never did."

"And stuff in the windows. I loved making window displays at the bookstore where I used to work."

"Window displays don't work unless someone sees

them. We need a sign by the ferry landing, since we're at the edge of town. As soon as people get off the boat, or right before they get back on, they can know to head over this way."

She nodded almost reluctantly. "You're right. We can also get the other shops to help sell us, in exchange for us helping them. I met some shopkeepers when Betty and I went downtown on May Day. Learned some things about the retail environment in a place like this, too."

"Wait, you weren't just shopping with Betty?" He was deliberately baiting her and he wasn't sure why. Maybe he wanted to see how she handled it. "You came home with a few packages as I recall."

She mock-glared at him. "I'd think a businessman like you would know that you have to give to get. You don't walk into someone's shop and start asking a bunch of favors without buying anything." Her flush became genuine. "And I mostly bought stuff for Willow, not for me. I'm not exactly rolling in cash right now."

Whoa, whoa, whoa. "Don't do that again," he said. "If Willow needs something, let me know. I don't want you spending your own money on her." He should have thought of that before.

She lifted an eyebrow. "I've been buying her things since she was born. But, anyway, back to the bookshop and how to get things going on it."

Reluctantly, he accepted the change of subject after making a mental note to set up a household fund for Deena to draw from for Willow's needs. "Sounds like we have the beginnings of a business plan. We should write one up."

She pointed at him. "That's your arena. You have to have gone over a million of them in your work. Meanwhile, I'll look around to see if there are grants we can apply for. We might be able to get one, or at least a low-interest loan, if we include some ways to hype local history and serve the community. Or maybe it's a historic building, who knows?"

"I don't want to take free money and build up a lot of obligations," he protested.

She looked puzzled. "Wealthy people and corporations donate money to causes they believe in," she said. "Like preserving the history of an island that's slowly sinking into the bay."

"What?"

She shook her head. "You're the one who spent part of your childhood here. Don't you know more of the shoreline's eroding away every year?"

"Wait, I do, I do." Ryan was working on that. "And it's fine if you find us a grant, I guess."

"Thanks." She held out a hand as if she were going to smack his arm again.

He held his breath because he wanted her to touch him. Even briefly. Even as a joke.

But she didn't do it. She wrapped her arms around her upraised knees. "We need a new name for the shop," she said. "I can research what's out there, if we don't think of anything ourselves."

"Names are important." They both sat for a moment, studying the building and thinking.

Nothing came to Luis, but he found he didn't want the conversation to end. "Did you always like books?" he asked, leaning back on his elbows.

She smiled. "Always. I grew up right across the street from the big central library and I spent as much time as I could over there. It was an escape." Her face darkened for a moment, and her gaze dropped from his. "How about you?"

"I wasn't much of a reader until coming to the island as a teenager," he said. "Betty made us go to the library every week. She had us spend an hour in the living room with the TV off and a book in our hands every evening. We didn't have to read, but we all realized pretty quickly that she meant it and there was nothing else to do."

"She did you a real service."

He nodded. "Now it's about my only form of recreation," he admitted.

She tilted her head, studying him. "Really? I would have thought..." She broke off.

"Thought what?"

She shrugged. "I don't know, I guess I thought you'd... drive a big powerboat around, or go on safari. Or at least golf. Rich people hobbies."

He ripped out a laugh. "Not hardly."

"Why not? I mean...you *are* rich, right? From the research I did, you're one of the wealthiest men of your age in the District."

The fact that she'd researched him and discovered that gave him a warm feeling. A successful feeling. Women loved men who had money. *Everyone* loved men who had money. "Yeah, well, you don't get to be that way by running around on fancy vacations or joining the country club. You get it by working."

She nodded. "Because you didn't inherit wealth."

"I definitely did not." And he didn't want to go into his past, not on this warm, beautiful day. "Getting back to shop names... We should at least brainstorm a little."

"Sure." She nodded. "Maybe something about the Chesapeake, but Chesapeake Books sounds boring."

"Bayside Books? That's boring, too, isn't it?"

"Kinda. We want it to be a vacation kind of sound. Something cool and relaxing."

"What kind of books do you want to stock?" he asked. "Just a little of everything?"

"No," she said slowly. "Betty made the point that we should find a niche. I think we should specialize in vacation-type books. Beach books."

"Are there enough books about the beach to fill a bookshop?"

"No, no, no. Not *about* beaches, but the kind of books you read on the beach."

"Beach reads," he said. "The Beach Reads Bookshop?"

Her eyes widened and her mouth curved into a huge smile. "That's it! The Beach Reads Bookshop! Oh, Luis, I love it!" She stood and pulled him to his feet and threw her arms around him.

He laughed, delighted at her spontaneity, and returned her hug. Instantly, he was aware of her slender back, her curves, her sheer womanliness.

Heat and desire surged in him. He took a half step back, still holding on to her upper arms. Afraid that his expression was too intense—too much like a boyfriend than a business partner—he summoned up a smile. A genuine one, because he was enjoying her excitement and her personality in addition to her beautiful body and face.

Her delighted expression was still there, but it was evolving; evolving into a kind of awareness he liked. Awareness he wanted to cultivate.

His gaze dropped to her lips, full and pink, still curved into a smile.

Her eyes were hazy enough that he thought she might let him kiss her.

Caution fell away, was pushed away by his desire, and he leaned forward a few inches.

Her eyes narrowed and she bit her lip. Which just about undid him.

But no. Too much to lose. For him, and even more, for Willow. He dropped his hands and stepped back. "I'll take a few measurements while you write down some notes," he said, "and then we should be getting back."

"Right." She sounded the slightest bit breathless, but whether it was from the same kind of attraction he felt or something more complicated, he didn't know.

What he did know was that he was going to be working closely with this woman and, more importantly, raising a child with her, at least for now. And he couldn't ruin it, no matter how appealing those lips were, no matter how much he wanted to keep that delighted expression on her face.

CHAPTER SEVEN

EARLY ON MONDAY MORNING, Deena walked into the Bluebird Bakery, Luis at her side. Blue checkered café curtains, soft jazzy music and little ceramic bluebirds on each table made the place feel homey. Because of the steady rain, they'd driven here after dropping Willow off for her first solo morning at Miss Arletta's.

It was just the two of them. Which, after the way they'd bonded while discussing plans for the bookshop, was more than a little uncomfortable.

Deena never should have hugged him. There had been a hint of a romantic vibe between them throughout their picnic, which was concerning enough, but she'd hoped she was imagining it. After she'd hugged him, though, and he'd hugged her back, the vibe had gone from *maybe* to *definitely*. Man, she'd thought he was going to kiss her, and worse, she'd been about to let him.

That was something she had to nip in the bud. She had no intention of getting involved with Luis. Men were unreliable as romantic partners, and sometimes downright dangerous. Besides, Luis was her employer and Willow's father. They needed to keep things cool between them.

She'd managed to avoid Luis since that day, and thankfully, he had gone into full workaholic mode this weekend. Today, they both needed to be here. Since they were focused on Willow's needs, though, it should be easy to stay entirely on the professional level.

The smell of sweet baked goods, muffins and scones and coffee cakes, filled the steamy air, and there were people at most tables.

They merged into the long line, forced by the crowd to stand close together. Beneath the bakery smells, she caught a whiff of his cologne. It smelled good. And expensive. Of course. His arm radiated heat as he stopped a couple of kids from jostling her, and when she felt the touch of his hand on her back for just a moment, she sucked in air.

This close to him, every cell in her body sparked and crackled like fire. Her heartbeat went slow and hard and thudding, her breathing too fast.

Stop it! But scolding couldn't tame her hyperawareness of him. Which was a very weird thing. Deena was *never* hyperaware of a man.

They'd hammered out a schedule, at least for now, of who took care of Willow when. That had given Deena some time to spend at the bookshop making preliminary plans, and also to go to church, which had calmed her, reminding her what was important. The pastor was wonderful and people were friendly, and she'd ended up going out to brunch afterward with a singles group.

Not that she was interested in meeting other singles in a dating sense, no sirree. But the group was mostly women, and she did want to make friends if she was going to stay here. Since Tammalee's death, she really hadn't put any effort in that direction, and she knew being isolated wasn't good for her.

She needed friends, just not a boyfriend. She could

get along just fine without a man in her life, as long as she had good friends.

Having a bookstore was such a great opportunity. It offered up the possibility that she could stay on the island long term, which would allow her to stay in Willow's life. That was something she desperately wanted to do. *Had* to do, if she were to do any kind of justice to Tammalee's wishes. But no way, *no way*, could she get involved with a man, especially a man like Luis, and possibly ruin all of that.

Today, though, they couldn't avoid togetherness, because they both needed to be there for the initial meeting with the Early Intervention specialist. After this, the plan was to take the specialist over to Miss Arletta's house. They could all see how Willow was handling being there. Even though her visits to Miss Arletta's last week had gone well, one with Deena staying the whole time and one with Luis, Deena worried about how the child would do when cut loose from the only people she trusted and knew. Change, new people or anything unexpected could send her into a meltdown.

When they reached the front of the line, Deena saw why it had been moving slowly. A young woman with an obvious developmental disability, probably about thirty, was behind the counter. Taylor, whom Deena had met at the May Day cookout at Ryan and Mellie's house, was there speaking with the customers, taking orders and ringing things up. The other woman was carefully putting items into bags and handing them to the customers, most of whom had an encouraging word to say to her. Deena quickly picked up on the fact that the woman was named Ruthie and that she had recently been promoted to working behind the counter. She was still learning the ropes.

"This pace wouldn't be tolerated at a busy coffee shop in DC," Luis remarked quietly. "The island is kind to people who are different. So if Willow turns out to be—"

"She won't," Deena said uneasily. "Not forever." It was what Tammalee had always said, but Deena felt less certain. From what she'd read, she knew there was a chance Willow would always struggle with emotional regulation, if nothing else.

They'd just snagged a table after buying three coffees and a big bag of pastries when a middle-aged woman with a frenzied air came rushing in.

Luis stood and waved and she came over and shook their hands. "Hi, I'm Jovie! Jovie Johnson, but let's use first names. Thank you for meeting me here! I love this place, and when my mom heard I was coming here, she insisted I get her a teaberry pie. And then my kids wanted one, too. But first, let's chat."

Luis held her chair and Jovie sat down. Immediately, she was all business. "I did the preliminary interview over the phone with you, Luis," she said, "but just to confirm, the concern is that she may have FASD."

They both nodded.

"Deena, you've been caring for Willow for a long time. Luis, you're new to parenting, correct?" She'd pulled out a tablet and was taking notes, the ditziness gone. Maybe it had been an act to put them at ease.

"Very new. But I'm committed. I know I have a lot to learn, but I want the best for her."

"Of course. Getting her an Early Intervention assessment is a great step."

Relief washed over Deena as she listened to the two of them talk. She'd been carrying the burden of Willow's challenges alone since Tammalee had died. It was good to have more resources, more help.

She sipped coffee and took a bite of a teaberry scone. The buttery, slightly licorice-like taste of it exploded on her tongue. "Wow, this is so good!"

"That's why I got a bag of them." Luis took out another and held the bag to the social worker, who took one and bit into it.

"Such an unusual flavor," she said. "Minty and sweet." She turned to Deena. "Tell me your connection with Willow."

"Her mama was my best friend." Her throat tightened as she thought of Tammalee, how excited she'd been from the moment she'd delivered Willow, with Deena in the room coaching her. "She passed away three months ago."

"And Tammalee drank?" Jovie asked bluntly.

The question jolted Deena out of her memories. "She did. She wasn't an alcoholic, but she didn't know she was pregnant right away, and even after…there were a couple of binges."

Luis's head snapped around and his eyes narrowed. Jovie must have caught the movement. "You were unaware of this?"

He nodded. "I was. I…unfortunately, I didn't have a long-term relationship with Tammalee."

Jovie didn't express condemnation. She did, however, turn her body slightly toward Deena, as if to acknowledge that Deena was the one with the most answers. "I know you said Willow has the facial features, and from the photo you sent, I agree. How about her behavior?"

Deena spoke slowly, wanting to be accurate, not to paint Willow in an overly positive way, but not to seem too discouraged about her potential. "She can get pretty upset and it's hard to calm her down. Sometimes impossible. But she's still grieving the loss of her mom, I think."

"Right. Of course."

Deena went on to describe Willow's developmental levels, how many words she could say—not many, though she was learning more every day—and what she could do physically, which was maybe just a little behind other kids her age.

Jovie slid her tablet back into her briefcase. "It sounds like you're right to get me involved, so let's take the next step. I'd like to pay her a quick visit at her day care, as we discussed. If I agree with your assessment, I or a colleague could visit here once a week, sometimes at home and sometimes at her day care. And maybe you could bring her to the mainland for one appointment a week. After a while, we could get her involved in a playgroup there. We don't want her to stay just on the island."

"Is the island bad for her?" Deena asked, confused.

"No. No, not at all. It seems like an ideal environment. But too ideal and you end up with a kid who's inflexible, who can only make it here. We don't want that. We want her to reach her full potential."

"We absolutely do," Luis said. There was firm commitment in his voice and on his face, and it made Deena relax a little more. He was strong, and he cared.

And the way his hair curled off his forehead…those brawny forearms crossed in front of him on the table… Deena's mouth went dry. A completely involuntary physical reaction, of course. Most women probably had some reaction to a man like Luis.

She wished she wasn't having it.

From what she could see, she had been right to bring Willow to the island. There would be help and support here, a good environment.

But she couldn't let her softer feelings toward Luis show, or grow. Among other reasons, she knew she could never see it through, not with her background of mistrust. And men didn't tend to take well to relationships that stayed at the same platonic, friendly level rather than advancing forward.

Getting involved could blow up. And that would cause Willow harm, which Deena would never, ever do.

AFTER JOVIE HAD done her initial evaluation of Willow and made an appointment to return, it was midafternoon. They'd left the car for Betty, who needed it to bring home a few things while her own was being repaired, and walked to the day care. By the time they got there, Jovie had done her assessment and was gone. Miss Arletta told them that it would be best to take Willow home, that she was tired and hadn't napped well in a new place.

"But she did okay here?" Luis knew that making day care work was a crucial piece of the puzzle. He had Deena to be her caregiver, but Deena couldn't be on duty 24/7. She was strong, in fact almost ridiculously so, but she needed time to herself. And time to work on plans for the bookshop. The last thing he wanted was for her to burn out.

"She did just fine." Miss Arletta hesitated. "All the same, I do think it's good you're getting her some help."

Luis winced. "You noticed problems?"

"A couple of big meltdowns. And she's a little be-hind other kids her age."

Worried, he stroked back Willow's hair. "Were you a handful?"

Miss Arletta put a hand on his shoulder. "Don't worry, Luis. I specialize in handfuls. They're *all* hand-fuls in one way or another."

"Thank you for being willing to work with her." He picked Willow up and bounced her and cooed at her. She still wasn't as comfortable with him as she was with Deena, of course, but she was warming up.

He was, too. Every hour he spent with her made him more attached, more committed to taking the best care of her that he possibly could. He wanted to be a good father. To overcome his blood and do better than his own birth family had done.

Luis's father had died so young. Luis could barely remember him. His mother had struggled, and the rest of his extended family hadn't picked up the slack.

Arletta went back inside to tend to the other children.

Deena opened the stroller, and he set Willow down in it and fastened her in. "I'm going to order her a better one, or you can," he said. "These roads are too rough for this rickety little thing."

Deena opened her mouth as if she wanted to protest and then shrugged. "I mean…that seems like an ex-travagance, but sure. I'll look over some options and let you know."

It was strange, living together as they were, becom-ing an instant family. They'd moved in together and they ate most meals together. Now they were talking about family expenses.

He felt like he was playacting, but at something he'd always wanted to do, deep inside.

And something he knew wasn't for him. Time to get businesslike. "Let's walk home by way of the library," he said. "I want to pick up a couple of books. We could grab her some picture books, too."

Deena's eyebrows drew together. "She seems pretty tired."

"It'll just take a minute and it's not far out of the way." Luis began pushing the stroller in the direction of the library. Deena walked along beside him.

Making their way through town, with people greeting them, Luis again had that strange feeling that they were a family. It wasn't entirely unpleasant, either. Deena was a pretty woman to have at his side, which shouldn't matter, but Luis was enough of a typical guy to be proud to have a woman like her beside him. And Willow was adorable, earning lots of compliments and admiration. He liked being able to say he was her father.

Maybe he'd turn out to be better at this family stuff than he'd expected.

Inside the library, Linda the librarian was putting up a display. She nodded at them, preoccupied with her task. "Here we go with the shallow reading," she said, putting up a sign that read Beach Reads. "I can't wait until we can display some bigger, meatier books for the fall."

Luis glanced at Deena. "We're probably going to have the beach reads business covered, once we get the bookshop back up and running," he said. "We're going to focus on beach reads."

"That's the name of the shop," Deena said. "The Beach Reads Bookshop."

Linda rolled her eyes. "Are you serious?"

He nodded. "That's what the tourists want. And a lot of the locals, too."

"It's what they *think* they want, because they don't know any better."

Luis laughed. "You can teach them, Linda, but meanwhile, we'll make the sales."

She shook her head like he was hopeless.

Willow dropped the stuffed frog she'd been holding and started to fuss. Deena knelt to get it for her, shushing her, pulling her a little away from Linda and Luis.

"Speaking of beach reads, I should have a couple of bestsellers waiting for me," he said to Linda.

"Let me get them." She headed toward the circulation desk. "You know, you're a smart man," she said over her shoulder. "You need to read more than spy novels and business books."

Deena had taken Willow out of the stroller and was jostling her around, taking her to look out the windows of the library. The place held a few other patrons: a man reading a newspaper, and a couple of women browsing the shelves.

"I read deeper things, too," he told the librarian. "A little science, a little history."

"You're going to need to keep that up. You need to set a good example for the little one."

"Of course. You're right." That hadn't even occurred to Luis.

As Linda located his books and checked them out, Willow's mild fussing rose to a wail. That particular keening wail that Luis already knew meant they were in for a long night.

I'll be outside, Deena mouthed from across the room, and carried the stiff, writhing baby out of the library.

It didn't look like they'd have the opportunity to browse the picture books, not today.

"Let me hurry this up." Linda stamped old-fashioned checkout cards quickly. "You need to go help her get the child under control." Linda spoke more gently than when she'd scolded him about bestsellers.

It stung, though. He was the one who'd insisted they come to the library, even though Deena had warned that Willow was too tired. And he'd done it for selfish reasons, so that he would have something to read tonight.

Obviously, he wasn't doing as well as he'd thought at fatherhood. He had a lot to learn.

CHAPTER EIGHT

JUST TAKE ANY JOB, Carol counseled herself as she walked into the island's small market on Wednesday at 4:00 p.m.

The place was basic, and that was putting it kindly. One wall held produce, surprisingly fresh looking, but the section was about a tenth the size of the produce section she'd frequented at her big chain supermarket back home. A deli counter, an aisle of canned goods, some baking supplies...that was about it, aside from the small freezer half-full of vegetables and the other half holding all kinds of teaberry ice cream items. The rest of the place looked like a combination tourist shop and hardware store.

Carol had found the market charming when they'd come here as a child, had loved getting her teaberry ice cream cone every day. Now that it was going to be her main source of groceries, she was less impressed.

The upside was that she could wander back and grab a pair of gardening gloves and some WD-40. In some ways, the market's selection was broad, indeed.

She picked up a handbasket and started shopping, the better to scope the place out before asking for a job.

"You're the new lady who lives out on Sandy Point, aren't you?" A woman about her age smiled at her. "I know your sister. I'm just down the road. I'm Peg."

"Carol Fisher." Carol held out her hand.

Two men, with similar salt-and-pepper hair and lanky builds, looked up from the small section of tables, where they were drinking coffee and doing some kind of paperwork.

Looking more closely, Carol realized the two men must be teachers—one was grading papers, and the other seemed to be making a lesson plan, from the way he kept flipping through a textbook and then typing on his laptop. She smiled and opened her mouth to say something friendly, but they ignored her and returned to their work, seeming to hunch away from her.

Carol blinked and turned back toward the woman she'd been talking to before.

"Don't take it personally," Peg whispered, gesturing her to the other side of the aisle, out of their earshot. "Israel and Gideon Bradshaw have been teaching elementary school on the island for years, and they also run a summer school for all ages, but they're not the most outgoing types." The woman waved at someone else across the store and bustled away, waving a response to Carol's murmured thanks.

Carol continued scoping out the store. After looking over her finances, she'd ascertained that she needed to get a job ASAP. Especially after she'd received divorce papers from Roger, which, admittedly, had sent her to her bed for a solid twenty-four hours. She'd really thought he would change his mind. But a conversation with him on the phone, in which Misty the Nurse was in the background, had confirmed it: they were going forward with the divorce, and Roger with his new relationship.

Just the thought of it made her stomach ache.

She'd job-searched online, had contacted a couple

of friends and professional acquaintances to see if they knew of any openings. But if she lived anywhere but here where her family owned a house, she'd have to pay rent, quite expensive in Baltimore. One friend had suggested that she teach or tutor online—there were lots of opportunities for that, apparently—but the thought of trying to figure out the technology, and then of trying to reach kids through the medium of a screen, just didn't appeal to her.

For now, she'd decided, she'd aim for a more basic job. Like working in a market.

And she was dithering now, something she never did. She marched up to the deli counter, where a woman was scooping a container of what looked like crab salad.

"Help you?" the woman asked.

"Yes, I'd like a pint of that," she said. "And I'd like to speak to your manager, if he or she's available."

"Hang on," the woman said, wrapping up her container and putting a price on it, then handing it to Carol. She turned to another customer and got into a discussion of the two types of pasta salad available.

While she waited, Carol realized that even here, she'd need to learn new things. How to operate a scale, how to ring things up, what was available each day. Her stomach tensed, but she told herself to buck up. *You've worked at a college, you can be a cashier.*

The woman who'd waited on her at the deli counter came around, wiping her hands. "I'm Betty Raines," she said. "I own the market. How can I help you?"

Carol was glad to see an older lady, not someone who would expect her to be a tech wizard. "I'm looking for a job," she said. "Are you hiring?"

"There's a chance I might need some summer help.

Not sure. Are you familiar with digital cash registers and computers?"

Carol's insides quivered. Was there no place on this earth where a person didn't need to be computer adept? "I've worked with computers a fair amount," she said, which wasn't a lie. "But it could take a little time for me to learn a new system."

"Understandable. People skills are important, too. And I'd need references."

"Of course." That was one thing Carol had done right; she'd contacted people in her old job who liked her and asked if they were willing to provide a reference, and every one of them had said yes.

Though if Betty asked to speak with her supervisor, things could get dicey.

In the table area, a mother and teen son seemed to be arguing.

"I'll take your name," Betty said, and Carol wrote her name and phone number on the pad of paper Betty handed her. Good. One possible option, at least.

She turned away in time to see the teen throw his textbook to the floor and stomp out, his mother yelling behind him. An idea formed in her mind, and she walked over and introduced herself, though the quivering, red-faced lady didn't reciprocate.

"I'm an experienced tutor," Carol said. "Sometimes a parent isn't the best person to help a kid with academics. Let me give you my phone number." She fumbled for a scrap of paper in her purse, noticing the flash cards strewed across the table. "If your son is struggling with flash cards, I could introduce him to some other strategies."

The woman stood, banging into the table in her haste,

slopping coffee over the flash cards. "Who are *you* to tell me how to raise my son?" she asked. "The nerve!"

Then she flounced out.

Carol winced. So she'd been a little forward, maybe. And...she looked around. Yes. The two teachers had watched the whole exchange, as had Betty.

People skills are important, too.

Her own big mouth might have lost her the opportunity for a job. When would she learn to keep it shut?

ON SATURDAY NIGHT, Deena was heating up leftover macaroni and cheese for her and Willow when she heard a vehicle pull up outside. A moment later, Luis came banging through the back door.

Rain dripped off his dark hair and his face wore a big grin. "Where's my favorite little girl?" he crowed as he headed toward Willow, who was on the floor banging a wooden spoon onto a big soup pot. She shrank back from Luis, looked up at Deena and started to cry.

Deena picked her up and propped her on her hip. "It's okay, it's Daddy," she said. Inside she was thinking, *It's about time.*

Luis took off his raincoat and hung it on a hook by the door. "Where's Betty?"

"Her book club went to some event on the mainland," she said. She checked the temperature of the mac and cheese, then set the microwave for another minute.

Willow continued to cry.

"What's wrong with her?" Luis asked.

"She's hungry," Deena said, "and she may be a little bit scared of you."

"I thought she was used to me." He'd modulated his voice and sat down, giving the toddler a chance to get reacquainted. Deena could swear that his expression held hurt feelings.

"You're big," Deena explained. "And you were gone for a while."

"Yeah. Sorry about that." He held up a bag. "I picked up some hard-shell crabs, already cooked. Do you mind if we eat together?"

"Of course not!" Deena was astounded he asked a question like that. He had more right to be here than she did.

Moments later they were at the table. The sun was setting, visible through the window, making the bay glow golden. Luis opened a bottle of wine, and Deena accepted a glass and served up food. Willow had little pieces of mac and cheese on her tray. She got progressively happier as she ate and enjoyed attention from the both of them.

"This is good," he said, holding up a forkful of mac and cheese. "Homemade?"

"Yes, although it's a day old."

"Beats eating out," he said. Then grinned. "Especially when the eating out is fast food. I know I'm supposed to give it up, but I got busy. And I do love it."

Deena shook her head. "With your medical issues, you should be eating healthy home cooked food all the time."

"You're not wrong." He took another bite and then unwrapped the crabs he'd brought home. Deena had never eaten hard-shell crabs before, so he found Betty's mallets and showed her how to break them open. He gave Willow a mallet, too, and she pounded it on her high chair tray with obvious delight.

"Don't beat it to death," he explained to Deena. "Just

crack it a little, and then use your fingers to pull out the meat." He demonstrated, then held out a morsel of crabmeat on his fork.

On impulse, she leaned forward and took the piece of crab from the fork he was holding. Her cheeks heated at the intimacy of the moment.

And then she tasted the crab. "That is *good*," she said, glad to focus on something other than the intensity of his gaze. "Wow, I've really been missing something all these years."

"You have." He seemed to recognize the need to pull back. He got busy cracking crabs again. "Who hasn't ever had fresh crabs?"

"Poor people," she said, rolling her eyes. "They're expensive. When was the first time you had them?"

He looked thoughtful. "It was right here, or rather, out in the yard," he said. "Wayne and Betty got a mess of crabs and we had a feast. The three of us boys probably ate a couple hundred dollars' worth of crabmeat, but they didn't mind. They said it was an experience we needed to have, if we were to live on the island."

"Sounds like they were good to you."

"They were." And they went back to eating.

It was nice. Willow was happy, and when Deena looked inside, she recognized that she was happy, too. This life, this island, this family—they were sweet. Just what Willow needed.

What Deena needed, too, or at least, what she craved. *But you can't have it, not permanently.*

And with that thought, she decided not to just keep the peace anymore. "I was surprised you took off without telling me Monday, right after the appointment with Willow's therapist," she said. "I didn't know when you'd come back, and neither did Willow. I thought you were supposed to be staying around the island most of the time."

"I said I was sorry."

"Yeah, but what does that mean? Are you going to keep doing it? Because if you want to have a good relationship with this daughter you just discovered, you need to be there for her."

"I *need* to earn a living." He hit the crab with the mallet, hard.

"Don't you have more money than the king of England already?"

He opened his mouth, shut it and then finally burst out: "I stink as a father, okay? I couldn't tell that Willow needed to go home right away on Monday night. I'm never going to be any good at anything but making money."

She gaped at him.

The kitchen clock ticked. Outside, a tree branch scraped against the window.

And suddenly it was all clear to Deena. He wasn't being a jerk. He was just insecure.

He seemed to know he'd revealed something significant, because he stood abruptly. "I'll clean up later," he said. He headed for the stairs.

"Luis, wait."

He stopped but didn't turn around.

"Would you like to put her to bed with me?"

"I don't…" He turned back, and she was surprised at the torment on his face. "I…sure. Okay. I'll help you put her to bed."

Too late, Deena realized what an intimate and family-like act that would be. She needed to stop being attracted to, or sympathetic with, Luis.

Doing something so sweet and intimate wasn't the way.

LUIS PICKED WILLOW UP. Apparently she'd gotten used to him again as they'd eaten dinner together, because she leaned her head against his chest, her dark violet eyes blinking closed, her long lashes dark against rosy cheeks.

Emotion swelled Luis's heart, a surge so intense he lost his breath.

He'd done nothing to earn Willow's trust, not yet. And yet she trusted him.

He had little experience with good family connections. But he was going to figure it out enough to take good care of this child. *His* child. She'd lack for nothing, including a father's love.

But you don't even know what a father's love looks like.

From his work in business, he knew that negative thinking was something to dismiss.

It was true that he didn't know what a father's love looked like. Wayne had been great, but as a mentor to the teen boys he'd fostered, not a daddy nurturing a young child. But he had two good examples he could watch and emulate: his brothers. Ryan and Cody were excellent fathers. If he had to, he'd mimic what they did. He'd fake it until he made it.

He followed Deena upstairs to the room where they'd set up Willow's crib. He noticed for the first time that it was decorated with the same curtains and mobile that had been in Willow's room back in DC, in that run-down apartment.

"You brought the stuff from her room," he said.

"I thought it would make her feel more at home. Here, I'll change her and then I bet she'll go right to sleep."

Luis put her on the changing table. "I admit, I'm thankful you're doing that. I haven't developed the knack. I always make the diaper either too tight or too loose."

"You'll learn." Deena was done in record time, and she lifted Willow into the crib.

"Mama." Willow lay on her back, looking up at Deena.

Luis raised his eyebrows. She called Deena Mama?

"Daddy is here, too," Deena said in a gentle, singsong voice, stroking the child's hair. "See? This is Daddy." She took Luis's elbow and pulled him closer.

Her touch burned. When she pulled her hand away quickly, he wondered if she'd felt the heat, too.

"Da-da," Willow said.

Luis's heart melted into a squishy puddle, and he blinked back sudden, surprising tears. Deena stepped aside and Luis reached down into the crib, stroking Willow's hair as Deena had been doing.

"Da-da," Willow murmured again, her eyes closing. Soon her breathing was steady, sleep breathing, but he stayed there a long time, stroking her hair.

When he finally stepped away from the crib, he looked at Deena. She was folding laundry, tucking little shirts into a drawer. "She called me Da-da," he said, still marveling over it.

Deena nodded. "Pretty powerful, isn't it?" Her voice

was pitched low, and the room's twilight darkness created a mood. Not romantic, exactly; more like a family mood. A loving mood.

You are losing your mind.

"I worry about her calling me Mama," Deena said. "I mean, it's inevitable she'll forget Tammalee, I guess, but I'm not her mama." Her voice seemed to choke up just a little on the last word, but she cleared her throat, and when he looked at her face, it was smooth and calm.

Maybe Luis had imagined her emotions around the idea of being, or not being, Willow's mama. Or maybe not. "You're the closest thing she has to a mother," he said quietly. They were living here like a family, him and Deena and Willow. They even had the doting grandma in the house, for Betty had assumed that role, buying Willow little treats and babysitting her at every opportunity.

No doubt it was good for Willow. If Luis had done one thing right as a father, it was bringing Willow here to the island and convincing Deena to come along. "I guess we could ask the Early Intervention people about her calling you Mama," he said. "Or Miss Arletta. She's pretty wise about kids, I think."

"Good idea."

They peeked in at Willow one more time and then walked out of the room together. As they headed downstairs, Luis was getting images of spending the evening with Deena. Drinking wine and maybe watching something on TV.

At the bottom of the stairs, she turned. Was it possible that she had the same idea? His heart pounded.

"Can we talk about the bookshop?" she asked.

"Uh…sure." He hadn't expected that shift in gears

and her businesslike tone disappointed him. But at least she wanted to spend time together. "I'll open a bottle of wine and we can sit on the porch," he suggested.

"I'll get my laptop." Her voice was still firm, but her quick glance told him that she wasn't unaware of the romantic overtones. A glass of wine on the front porch after the kid was in bed… Yeah. Anyone would notice that.

By the time he brought out the opened bottle of wine and two glasses, Deena had her laptop open. "Thanks," she said when he poured her a glass and handed it to her. She took a sip and set it down. "Do you want me to read you my to-do list for the shop?"

He'd listen to her reading an electric bill, just now. "Sure," he said. He sipped his own wine and looked out over the island, trying to settle into the role of business partner rather than romantic partner.

"Okay. Obviously cleaning is first. I might get started after church tomorrow if you'll be here for Willow."

For the first time, he realized that when he'd left the island on Monday to go work in the city, it meant that Deena couldn't spend much time doing her job at the bookshop, here on the island. "I'll take charge of her for the rest of the weekend," he said.

"That's great. Can your brothers help with the heavy cleaning, do you think?"

The idea had its appeal. It would be a good time to implement his plan of picking his brothers' brains about how to be a better father. "Maybe," he said. "Although it might be easier to just hire some cleaners."

"Either way. And then we'll need to either buy or build some shelving. Get a new sign made. And then we need to announce an opening date and get people excited about it."

"Good." He kind of wanted to just focus on Deena, but the business talk was fun, too. "I'm wondering when to open," he said. "Could we be ready by Memorial Day? It's the start of the tourist season."

She stared at him. "That's in two weeks! No way!"

"I can get a crew in. They'll work fast."

"But..." She frowned. "I want to make some of the decisions myself, and I imagine you do, too. Plus, how fast can you really get a work crew here and up to speed?"

Obviously, she didn't know what money could do. "It won't be a problem."

She tilted her head, then shook it. "I don't see us being ready that fast. Maybe, if we work really hard, by July 4."

"No. We'd miss too many sales."

She opened her mouth as if to argue and then shrugged. "You're the boss," she said.

He didn't want her to lose interest. He wanted her to stay invested in the bookshop, so that she'd stay happily on the island and continue to be one hundred percent committed to Willow, who really needed her. "I need your skills at ordering books and equipment. The crew can make a lot of the shelving and construction decisions, if we give them basic parameters."

He leaned back and sipped wine, swinging the porch swing with his foot. "We'll get it worked out. First things first. I'll hire a crew and have the place inspected on Monday."

"And I get to order stock," she said. "That's going to be so much fun. I've sent away for all the publishers' catalogs, just so I can look through them on paper. I'm excited!"

And you're beautiful when you're excited, he wanted to say, but didn't.

He liked being with her. It was fun and energizing, but also strangely calming. The doctor's "you should get married" comments came to mind.

Which was ridiculous; he couldn't do that. Didn't have it in him, not after the way he'd grown up.

She was chattering on about the bookshop, what she might want to order for it, whether to make a seating section or an actual café. He just nodded and smiled, enjoying her enthusiasm.

Finally, she wound down and looked at him inquiringly. "So what do you think?"

"I think," he said, "I'm glad you're here." A long curl fell into her face, and he couldn't help himself: he tucked it back behind her ear.

Her lips seemed to get even fuller, her eyes wider. Man, was she pretty. He leaned a little forward.

All his senses were thrumming.

She stood suddenly, the porch swing shaking, chains jangling. "Well. I'd better get to sleep. See you tomorrow, Luis." And she nearly ran inside, laptop clutched to her chest.

What had he done? He hadn't *done* anything, had he?

But inside, he knew. It was how he'd looked at her, the nonverbal message he'd sent.

It had scared her away. Which was a good thing. Wasn't it?

CHAPTER NINE

ON MONDAY AFTERNOON, Carol trudged up to the door of the library and took in a deep breath. This was her last chance for a job on the island, or so it seemed. Betty from the market hadn't called, and when Carol had followed up, she'd said she didn't have any openings right now. Some fishermen needed crew members for the boats, but that work seemed too physical for Carol. There were no other options.

Unless she wanted to take Luis up on his ridiculous offer of working as an employee in her own family's bookshop, the bookshop she should own.

Be positive. She opened the door and walked in. Immediately, she felt better, immersed in the fragrance of old books, surrounded by quiet.

The librarian, Linda, was at the front desk, straightening things up. "Hi, come on in. We're closing in ten minutes, though, so you'll have to browse quickly."

Carol approached the desk, opened her mouth to ask about jobs and then saw the book Linda was tucking into her bag, a bookmark in the middle. "That's a great book," she blurted out.

Linda smiled. "I like it. I'm not always so big into science fiction, but this is really thought-provoking."

"It was." They talked about the book for a minute, and it transpired that there was a book group that met here once a month, and that they were having a year of science fiction focus. "I'm trying to steer them away from aliens and interplanetary warfare," Linda said, her voice wry, "but it's an uphill battle." She glanced at the clock.

Carol realized she'd better get to the point of her visit. "I'm looking for a job on the island," she said. "I have experience working at a university, and I'm pretty familiar with books. I'm a hard worker. Any chance you have an opening?"

Linda sighed and smiled. "I wish I could help," she said. "But we have no budget for hiring anyone. The library's a one-woman show. Unless you'd like to volunteer. Volunteers make up a big part of our workforce, such as it is."

Carol felt herself deflating. "I wouldn't mind volunteering once I'm established here," she said, "but I do need to earn a living. I have to focus on that first."

"Of course." Linda stretched her neck from one side to the other as if it were stiff. "I want to retire sometime soon. At that point, there'll be an opening. But unfortunately, it won't happen within the next year."

"Don't be too quick to retire," Carol advised, then pressed her lips together. She didn't need to be telling anyone she'd been forced to "retire," aka been fired.

A couple of school-age girls came up with books to check out, and Carol stepped back and looked around the library. The old-fashioned circulation desk stood on one side, and there was a display case of summer books near the door. In the back was a colorful room that looked like it was for children. A couple of comfortable-looking easy chairs seemed to beckon readers to settle in with a good book.

"What are your skills?" Linda asked when she'd finished with the checkout. "Maybe I can help you connect with someone on the island."

"Tutoring," she said. "And…and caregiving." It was true, she'd cared for Roger.

Look where that had gotten her. Then again, maybe she could become a caregiver to a rich man here, wear a skimpy little nurse costume and charm him into leaving her his fortune.

It was a thought.

Linda nodded toward the only two patrons in the library, the two men whom Carol recognized as the austere brothers who'd been at the market. "The Bradshaw brothers are teachers," she said. "They might know of some tutoring opportunities. Come on, I'll introduce you."

"I already met them. Or saw them, at least. They didn't seem interested in being friendly."

"They bark, but they don't bite." Linda walked across the room, leaving Carol nothing to do except follow in her wake.

"We're not deaf," one of the brothers said irritably as they approached.

"Nor are we dogs," the other said.

Linda looked blank.

"So we neither bark nor bite," the first brother explained.

Carol started to smile. She couldn't help it. The way these two men finished each other's sentences was funny.

They were dressed similarly, in the sort of short-sleeved white shirts Carol hadn't seen anyone wear since her father had passed away. One wore a tie, while the other simply wore his shirt buttoned to his throat.

"This is Carol," Linda said. "Carol, meet Gideon and Israel."

Carol smiled at the two men but didn't offer to shake hands. They didn't look like they'd welcome it. She studied them to try and detect a difference that would help her tell them apart. This close, she saw that Gideon was the bulkier of the two. Fitting, since Gideon in the Bible was a soldier. She also noticed that his hand was missing two fingers, causing him to hold his pen awkwardly.

"She's looking for a tutoring job," Carol explained. "Do you know of any possibilities?"

The brothers glanced at each other. "Almost all of our students could use some tutoring," Israel said finally. "But the island people are independent."

"So I gathered." She reminded them of her effort to help the mother-son pair in the market.

"That wasn't surprising, given the personalities involved," Gideon said. "We'll keep our eyes open. We may have some kids in our summer school program that need extra help. But even if you took on a couple of students willing, that's not enough to make a living."

Carol sighed.

"Sit down," Gideon suggested, "so we don't feel unmannerly not standing up for two ladies."

Carol looked at Linda, who shrugged. "May as well. Just let me close up."

She walked to the door and flipped the sign to Closed. Then she flicked off most of the lights, leaving only a couple on in the part of the room where the brothers sat.

Carol settled into the chair beside Israel, and Linda sat across from her. The library's shelves of books, the dim lights and the smooth old wood of the table felt somehow soothing.

Up close, the brothers didn't seem so intimidating, despite their old-fashioned clothing. And it had been cordial of them to invite her and Linda to sit down.

"So you're looking for work," Israel prompted in a rumbling voice that no doubt intimidated students at the elementary school.

"I am, and I'm getting discouraged," Carol said.

"Not many options on the island. The market, the bakery…"

"Tried both of those," Carol said. "I even asked at the restaurants, but no openings."

"And I have no funding for extra staff at the library," Linda said.

"I do have a potential offer at the new bookshop," Carol said. "But I can hardly stand to see my family's shop turned into a 'beach reads' bookshop." She put the words in air quotes.

The men gasped.

Linda nodded grimly. "It's true," she said. "That's the actual name of the place, and they're focusing on the kind of books you read on the beach."

Israel shook his head, the corners of his mouth turning down. "That's a sad thing."

"It is," Carol said, glad to find some kindred spirits. "Do either of you remember when my grandfather ran the bookshop?"

"Yes, indeed," Israel said. "Focused on island history, wasn't it?"

"It was." Carol sighed. "I'd like for it to stay that way. I'd like to bring it back."

The brothers looked at each other, clearly communicating, although no words were exchanged. "We would like to help with that project," Gideon said finally.

"I would, too," Linda said.

Until that moment, it hadn't been a project, just a wish. But the way the three of them looked expectantly at her, she had to smile. "I don't have any idea how we'd do it," she said slowly, "but I would love to try."

ON WEDNESDAY, LUIS ARRIVED back from an unexpected early morning work meeting on the mainland. Betty was available to babysit Willow, so Deena hurried to the bookshop.

"Wait up!" Luis ran after her, still in his suit.

"I thought you wanted to change clothes first. I can get started."

"No, I'll just...go like this." He was unknotting his tie as he walked.

"Why?"

"Because there's a surprise for you."

She cut her eyes at him. "I like surprises." Then she blushed.

He raised an eyebrow, a slight smile tugging at his mouth, but didn't speak.

They walked the rest of the way to the bookshop without much talk. Deena was trying not to think about the last time they'd spent time together, Saturday night when they'd put Willow to bed, and the romantic vibes had gotten intense, and she'd felt like kissing him.

That just never happened to her. She didn't trust men, not since that awful incident in high school, and then her stepfather's abandonment. Mistrust had always bred distaste, at least before. Now it wasn't as if she trusted

Luis…but what she felt certainly wasn't distaste. She was attracted to him. Big-time. *Really* big-time.

They were approaching the bookshop now, and Deena felt a thrill. This was her shop. Or at least, she was running it, managing it, in charge of it. She'd just leapfrogged way up the career ladder and was doing something better than she'd ever dreamed of.

Not only that, but she loved the bookshop already. Its history seemed to radiate from the weathered floorboards and from the boxes of old books and papers they'd put in the back storeroom. Its walls seemed to whisper: *Come in, visit, read.*

The sun made long shadows and seabirds called as they got closer. "Go ahead," Luis said, stopping to tie his shoe. There was something funny about how he'd said it.

She opened the door and walked in.

And gasped.

She'd left a clean but basically empty place. Now, shelves had been built along the walls and in the middle of the store. There was a counter and even a chair behind it, and it looked like the electrical wiring had been done.

"Luis?" she asked, her voice squeaking. "Did you do this?"

He came up behind her. "Yes. Or rather, I hired a crew to do it. Like it?" He was smiling, confident.

"Uh…yes. Sure."

Her response clearly wasn't what he'd been expecting and now he looked like a little boy whose gift had been rejected. "What's wrong?"

"I mean…it's great. I just kind of wanted to be consulted. Make some of the decisions."

"What would you do differently?" he asked.

She looked around and had to admit that they'd done a great job. "Nothing, really. I don't know. It's…it's really nice, it is."

And it was. She wasn't sure what her uneasiness was about. Having this much done meant that there was a place for the books that were starting to arrive. And that they had the possibility of opening up on Memorial Day weekend, as Luis had wanted.

"It's all moving so fast," she told him, wanting to explain her reaction. "I'm a cautious person. Takes me a little while to make a decision. Clearly, you're different. And it's resulted in a lot of progress."

He studied her face for a moment and then lifted a shoulder. "If you're sure, then let's talk organization," he said. "Since everything is beach reads, how are you going to do it? One big section?"

"No. I've been thinking about that." She pulled out her phone to consult her note-taking app. "I'm thinking, general fiction, romance, thrillers and mysteries, science fiction and fantasy, and young adult. And then a kids' section."

"I think we should also sell other stuff. Beach-related loot."

"Well, a little bit of that. But the focus should be on books."

They walked around, haggling, arguing, agreeing, and soon they'd figured out the basic layout of the bookshop.

"Wait," Deena said. "I'd like to reserve a space for some used books."

He frowned. "That doesn't sound focused. And

where are we going to get used books? They don't make any money, do they?"

"It'll take a while to build up a collection," she said. "But people on the island will bring in books they've finished reading and don't want to keep. We'll give them what money we can for them, then sell them at a little more."

He shook his head. "That'll take up space we could be using for full-price merchandise. Which will cut into our profits."

"Maybe? But there are people who can't afford a new book but might be able to afford a used one."

"They can go to the library," he said. "You don't stock things based on what your poorest customer can afford."

"But you need to be aware of the area you're in," she said. "Back at the bookshop in the District, we had a lot of hardcover history and biography and political books because we were near the Capitol with so many lawyers and such. Here, it's a different clientele."

"Right, but—"

"It's probably hard for you to understand," she interrupted gently, "because you've never been poor. You could always buy a hardback new book, but other people can't."

His forehead creased. "You've got it wrong. I haven't always been wealthy."

Based on his designer suit and high-end leather shoes, she had a hard time believing him. "I know your childhood wasn't perfect," she said, "but when did you not have everything you wanted?"

He knelt down to brush stray wood shavings off a shelf. "You know I grew up in foster care, right?"

"Right. I keep forgetting because…" She shrugged. "Because you're so successful."

He stood and brushed sawdust off his hands. "Me, Ryan and Cody are all successful. But that doesn't mean we started out that way."

She wanted to know, but she hated to ask. The wanting won. "How did you start out?"

"In a loving family until stuff happened."

"Like?"

"Like…" He moved his shoulders back and forth. "Like my dad passed away, and my mom did things her parents didn't approve of. Rather than toeing the line, she left. And rather than send me back to them when things got too hard, she placed me in the system."

"I'm sorry." She put a hand over his. "That must have been awful. How old were you?"

"I was five the last time I saw her. Most of what I just told you is what my social workers told me. I don't remember much from that time."

"Do you remember her at all?"

He shook his head. "Impressions. A few scattered memories."

She found a cloth and dusted shelves, just to have something to do with her hands. "Was your foster care experience good?"

"Once I got to Teaberry, it was great."

"And before that?"

He shook his head. "The system was overcrowded, and I wasn't very disciplined at first. I was angry and upset. I acted out and got moved around. Landed in a pretty good family for a few years, but then they got too old and sick to continue, so I had a few more years of bouncing around. I finally landed here." He gestured back toward Betty's house. "Best thing that could've happened to me."

Imagining Luis as a young boy, torn apart from family after family before finally finding a home on Teaberry, brought a lot of things into perspective. No wonder he'd wanted to raise Willow here. No wonder he felt like this was home. "Where did you learn about money?" she asked.

"Kind of came naturally. In my first good foster home, I was encouraged. Dog walking, selling stuff, doing yardwork for the neighbors. They loved it when I could contribute." He shrugged. "I liked the feeling."

He sounded nonchalant, but looking into his deep brown eyes, Deena saw more. She saw a young boy who'd lost his loving family bringing home earnings from mowing the neighbor's yard, offering it up to his foster mother and letting her smile or praise fill what must have been a great big hole in his heart.

She swallowed hard. "And that's why you want to do your best by Willow, I'm guessing."

"Right." His smile was a little crooked. "And that's why I get that not everyone can afford brand-new books, but come on. We're carrying paperbacks. They're not that expensive. Price of a coffee."

"Coffee *and* a pastry at the Bluebird Bakery," she corrected, glad they were back to business. "Island prices aren't the same as DC prices, remember?"

"Let's get the main part done and then decide," he said diplomatically. "If after we open you see that there's a need for used books, we can talk again."

She frowned, then shrugged. "I guess that's fair. And we do need to focus. There's a lot to get done by opening day." Hands on hips, she did a slow 360 spin. "There are a lot of books to get on the shelves."

"You can just label each box of where you want it to go. My people will come in and do it." Luis was already tapping out a message on his phone.

"No, I want to." Deena wasn't used to having someone else take over the physical work. Even back in DC, she'd often stocked shelves. The chance to touch the new books for the first time, to snap photos of the covers she wanted to read—mostly checked out from the library because she couldn't afford to buy new books— it had been a delight.

"Why?"

How to explain that desire to be hands-on and in control? "You said I could run it," she said, realizing even as she spoke that she sounded petulant, childish.

"Run it, not do the grunt work."

"But the grunt work's fun."

"But we need to open by Memorial Day. And besides…" He looked rueful.

"What?"

"I already scheduled my people to come in and finish up. They'll be here later today."

She slammed a book onto a shelf harder than she needed to. "Am I just a figurehead, running this shop?" She liked Luis, but the fact that he didn't seem to trust her to get things done meant that she didn't really trust him, either.

Not that she'd ever trusted a man in her life.

"No. No, Deena, not at all."

She didn't believe him.

CHAPTER TEN

LUIS COULD TELL that Deena didn't believe him, not entirely. And he couldn't blame her.

She *wasn't* just a figurehead to run the shop. He wanted her to do it and believed she'd do it well, with guidance from someone who knew more about business, aka him.

But the truth was, the big reason he wanted her to stay was so that she would help him take good care of Willow. That was paramount.

If there was another, emotional reason he wanted her to stay on Teaberry Island, well, he had no intention of telling her what it was, because he hadn't even put a name to it himself. It was just a warm feeling he got when he looked at her.

His team arrived not long after their little spat.

Eight of them, with their big-city attitudes that were at odds with the more measured island pace of life, but oh, well. Within half an hour, he'd gotten them up to speed on where the project stood, and they were adjusting shelves and unloading boxes and setting up the cash register.

He stood directing things, loving the rush of a new project. He tried to keep Deena in the loop, but she backed way off when she heard him barking orders.

The next time he looked over at her, she was holding Willow and a diaper bag and talking with Betty. What was Willow doing here? He went over and held out his arms.

When Deena handed Willow over, when she smiled and said "Da-da," delight swelled in his heart and nothing else mattered.

"Sorry, but we have an emergency at the market, and I have to go in," Betty said. "Luckily it's a nice day, and it looks like you're getting a lot done. Would you rather I run you back to the house with the baby, or do you want to stay here and watch the progress with her?"

"We'll stay," Deena said without consulting Luis.

"I have a blanket in the trunk," Betty said, and went and got it. As she drove off, Deena spread the blanket in a sun-dappled spot under a budding apple tree and gestured for Luis to put Willow down on the blanket.

He did, kneeling to tickle her chin, making her laugh. Then he looked up at Deena. "I'm sorry the way I took over. And how they're taking over. But you can see how efficient it is to get a big team in here to knock out a lot of the prep work."

"Uh-huh." She didn't seem impressed.

That disappointed Luis. But she turned and focused on Willow, and someone called out to him for direction on a wall repair, and the chance to discuss the issue was lost. He ran a hand over Willow's soft hair and went to join the workers.

As he consulted about the wall, he fumed a little. He got that Deena wanted to be in control. Man, did he get that, because he was the same way.

But she wasn't an expert on starting a business; he was. And he really wanted this particular business to be a success.

Not so much to prove something, although that was always humming in the back of his mind. But because he wanted her to stay, and he knew that having the opportunity to run the bookshop was a key part of that.

Didn't she understand that he was doing this for her?

As he walked around, checking each team member's progress, he kept an eye on Deena and Willow.

She turned the pages of a board book, pointing, making Willow smile. She showed the toddler the sky, lying back and pointing up. When Willow got fussy, she stood and walked her around until she settled.

He wasn't the only person who admired the pretty picture of slender blonde Deena and cute little Willow. He noticed several of his workers watching her, too.

Which he didn't especially like, but he tried to stifle his caveman "she's mine" instincts. She *wasn't* his.

And she was awesome with Willow. Even though she was annoyed with Luis for taking over something she'd wanted to control, she didn't let her mood infect her time with Willow, didn't take it out on her.

Luis had experienced more families than most during his growing-up years, and he knew that taking your moods out on your kids was common, the rule rather than the exception. He admired that Deena didn't do that.

He also admired how pretty she was. It was as if there were a magnet inside her, drawing him to her.

He forced himself to work for another forty-five minutes and then gave up. He had to check in with her and the baby. His emotions, his sense of responsibility and his hormones all insisted on it.

She looked up at him, her face quizzical. "Do you want to sit down?"

He wanted to, more than anything. But, keeping his goals in mind and exerting major self-discipline, he shook his head. "Gotta keep pushing."

"Really?" She raised an eyebrow. "Willow craves your attention more than your money and success."

That was one of those ordinary but brilliant observations Deena tended to come up with. He wasn't used to considering things from a kid's point of view, but Deena was right. To Willow, the fact that he was the boss and financier of the little bookshop and the crew mattered not a bit. What mattered was that he was Daddy. So when Willow held out her hands to him and said "Da-da," he sat down on the blanket, took Willow in his arms and lay back, flying her over him in the classic superkid move.

Willow chortled, her dark curls swirling around her head like a halo, the crisscrossing apple tree branches above making a lacy pattern against the blue sky.

Once again, he felt lost with love, like nothing else mattered.

Deena was laughing, but after a moment, she put a hand on Luis's shoulder. "She just ate a snack," she said. "Might not want to jiggle her too much."

That made him sit up quickly. Kid throw-up was no joke; he'd just cleaned up an episode of it last night. He settled her into his lap and reached for the book Deena had been reading her. "Does she like that one?"

"Uh-huh. Especially if you make all the animal noises. Try it."

Why did he have the feeling Deena was trying to trick him into playing with and loving his own kid? On the other hand, maybe he needed that. Needed instruction on how to do it, at least.

Deena led the way, making the farm animal sounds as he read the text, and when he saw how that made Willow laugh, how she tried to imitate Deena's sounds, he couldn't resist joining in. She thought the "moo" especially hilarious when they both did it and she joined in as best she could.

He looked over at Deena, laughing, her head thrown back, and a wave of longing hit him with the force of a spring thunderstorm. What would it be like if they were really the family they appeared to be here? What would it be like to hold this woman in his arms?

She caught his eye and her face got somehow both serious and wise. Maybe she could read minds, or his at least.

And he didn't need to be making a fool of himself, mooning over a woman who deserved a man who was good at family stuff, not just at making money.

"I need to get back to work," he said, and this time, she didn't stop him.

He stood and started walking, determined not to look back at the beautiful tableau of Willow and Deena.

Nausea and dizziness rushed at him and he staggered and reached around for something to catch himself on.

Like happened so often around here, there was a dog beside him, one of the island dogs that roamed the place freely. He grasped the big creature's fur and steadied himself. He stood for a minute while his stomach and mind settled.

Then he looked around. None of his coworkers had noticed, fortunately.

He needed to take it easier.

"Are you okay?" The voice behind him was Deena's. Willow was in her arms.

"Sure. Fine. Stood up too fast." He let go of the dog and rubbed its ears in silent thanks.

He *wasn't* okay. There was still something wrong with him. And to keep up his responsibilities, he needed to find out what it was.

CAROL LED HER three coconspirators through the moonlit night. They were headed toward the bookshop, where work had been going on all last week. Even today, Saturday, the workers, plus Deena and Luis, had been busy all day.

"Are you sure this is wise?" Israel asked. He was breathing hard. He wasn't in as good of shape as his brother, Gideon, who kept up easily with Carol's fast pace.

"We're just checking things out," Linda said in a soothing voice. She'd fallen back to keep Israel company.

As they approached the bookshop, the bay behind it shone silver. Trees starting to leaf out cast spidery shadows, and a soft salt smell filled the air. Except for the occasional cry of a loon, the island was quiet.

Maybe they should just stay out here, enjoy the pleasant evening.

But no. Their mission was important.

She and Gideon slowed down as they reached the door, waiting for the others to catch up. Carol's heart pounded. She hadn't had an adventure in a really long time.

"There should be a loose brick right up there," she said, pointing above the door. "See if there's still a key." The chances of it being there after all these years, and working, were slim, so she had a plan B of climbing through the window. That might be tough athletically. Gideon would have to boost her, a thought that sent a tiny thrill through her body.

Stop it, you're a married woman. But not for long. She'd signed the divorce papers and sent them to her lawyer. She was on the road to becoming a single woman. A divorced woman.

But you're not there yet, she reminded herself.

"Got it," Gideon said, coming down from his tip-toes with a dusty, old-fashioned key in hand, the one Carol remembered. Hands shaking just a little, she fit it in the door.

"It works!" Carol was amazed.

"What kind of businesspeople leave the same lock on the door of a newly purchased property?" Israel shook his head.

"People on Teaberry Island, that's who." Linda shrugged. "Half the people in town know where the key to the library is. If I'm running late, I can always get Mrs. Tanner from the post office or Hector Lozano to run over and open it up."

"Come to think of it, Deena mentioned they had a locksmith scheduled," Carol said as she stepped through the door first, the others crowding after her. "Guess they didn't hustle fast enough." She reached for the light switch.

Gideon put a hand over hers, stopping her. It was the hand that had missing fingers, and when he noticed she was looking at it, he pulled it back. "Sorry," he said.

"Why? I have no problem with your hand."

He smiled, crinkles forming at the outside edges of his eyes. "Don't turn on the lights. We don't want to call attention," he said. "Israel and I have flashlights."

"Me, too." Linda pulled a small one from her jeans pocket.

They flashed their lights on and Carol looked around. The walls were painted a deep turquoise blue, the shelves that lined them white. The floor was light refinished wood, and small tables stood in the middle. About half the shelves were lined with books, and boxes stacked along the back wall looked to be full of more.

"Wow," Linda said. "Makes the library look shabby."

"Definitely more upscale than when my family was running it," Carol admitted reluctantly, a wave of jealousy flashing through her.

"That's what happens when you throw the big bucks at something," Gideon said briskly. "Luis Dominguez seems to have more money than sense."

Israel nodded. "I like a bookshop that smells like books, not paint, and one that looks old, not shiny new."

The men's words made Carol feel better.

Linda was walking around. "Look at the labels," she said. "Mysteries. Science Fiction. Romance." She shuddered a little. "Where is the *literature*?"

Gideon had picked up a fat science fiction novel and was paging through it, but at Linda's words, he put it down.

"Is there anything we can do to stop this train?" Carol asked. She hadn't expected things to be this far along, this fast. She'd never have believed it possible, but it looked like the bookshop would be ready to open on Memorial Day.

Israel was examining the boxes. He pulled out a stuffed figure from a recent Disney movie and waved it over his head. "We could decapitate all the unfortunate creatures in this box," he said. "They don't belong in a bookstore."

Carol and Linda stared at him, then looked at each other and cracked up. "Good idea, but too violent," Carol commented.

"He's joking, ladies," Gideon said. "Vandalism isn't the answer. How about we sneak in a bunch of classic, old, seafaring books like your folks used to stock?"

Carol squinted at him, saw that he was joking, too, and laughed.

"I say we put up signs directing people to the library," Linda said.

"Set up a booth outside with real books," Gideon suggested. "A...what do they call it? Like a bookmobile, but—"

"A pop-up!" Linda and Carol said simultaneously. They high-fived each other.

Israel still held the Disney toy, tossing it from one hand to the other.

Carol looked around at these people she hadn't known a month ago and a bubbly feeling filled her, like champagne.

She hadn't had this much fun in a long time.

A series of beeps and honks sounded, so loud they all jolted. It sounded like a car alarm and didn't stop.

Israel pointed at a blinking sensor in the corner above the cash register. "We triggered an alarm," he yelled over the din.

"Obviously!" Gideon started for the door. "Let's get out of here."

Carol was frozen. "What if we're on camera?"

"If we're not now, we will be when the owners come!

Come on!" Linda grabbed Carol's arm and started pulling her toward the door.

They all rushed out of the shop and raced across the street. Behind them, the alarms stopped, but now they could hear a car coming from down the road, its motor gunning. Then the alarm started up again.

"This way!" Linda gestured. "We'll hide out at the library."

"They'll look for us there." Gideon frowned at her. "You've been vocal in objecting to the bookshop."

"My place, then," Carol said. "Come on!"

They turned and raced toward Carol's place as fast as the arthritic Israel could go. Behind them, they could hear shouting.

They didn't stop running until they reached the house and collapsed inside. Carol fell on the couch, laughing. Once again, she realized that she hadn't had this much fun in a long time.

CHAPTER ELEVEN

On the Thursday before the Memorial Day weekend, Deena trudged home from the bookshop, exhausted. The grand opening was Saturday, and she wasn't ready.

It didn't help that they'd had an intruder a few nights ago. Neither she nor Luis, nor any of the work teams, knew how someone could have gotten in. The person hadn't done anything, at least not that any of them could tell, but the front door had been swinging open, the alarm blaring, when Luis had gotten there.

They'd changed the locks, advancing the previous appointment. Luis had waved aside the extra expense of a rush job.

He waved aside every expense, which was a little disconcerting. But not as disconcerting as his dark, penetrating eyes that seemed to follow her a lot of the time.

Now she needed to relieve Luis or Betty, whoever had been taking care of Willow. She straightened her shoulders and climbed the front steps of the farmhouse.

"Wait! Don't go in!" A car pulled up, brakes screeching, the sound of female laughter spilling from the open windows. "Come on, Deena. You're going out with us!"

She turned, and there were Mellie, Taylor and Taylor's sister, Savannah, spilling out of the car. Mellie, who was driving, looked like her usual steady self, but the two sisters seemed to have had a drink or several.

They were laughing and leaning on each other as they approached the house.

"Come on," Mellie said. "We're headed to the Dockside Diner, and you need to come along."

"Can't," Deena said regretfully. "I need to get inside and take care of Willow."

The sisters made their way up the steps and peeked in the front window. "She's fine, she's with her daddy," Savannah said.

"But—"

"You're not her mom," Taylor said. "You don't have to spend every minute you're not working with her."

Taylor didn't mean anything bad with her casual words, but nonetheless, they stabbed into Deena like tiny, sharp knives.

She loved Willow so much, more and more every day. She wanted to raise her. *Wanted* to be her mother.

But it wasn't to be. Other people saw it, and she needed to get on board and remember it herself.

"Betty sent us to make sure you take a break," Mellie said. "She says you've been burning the candle at both ends and you need to get out."

"But I told Luis and Betty I'd take over—" She checked the time on her phone. "Half an hour ago. I'd better get inside."

Taylor banged on the front door. "Luis! Hey, Luis!"

He came to the door, shirt open, dark circles under his eyes. Willow was in his arms, her face puckering up in the familiar "I'm about to cry" expression. "What's up?" His eyes widened when he saw the four women.

"We're taking Deena out. Just wanted to let you know." Taylor patted Luis's arm. "Bye, Dad."

"Luis, I—" Deena looked at him helplessly.

Mellie took one arm, Savannah took the other, and they turned her around. "Betty's orders," Mellie called back over her shoulder. "We're walking to the Dockside, but we might need a ride home later, okay? Ryan's home if you need anything."

"I'm sorry…" Deena called as the other two women propelled her forward. She looked back in time to see Luis shutting the door, laughing. Good. He wasn't mad.

As soon as it was clear she wasn't going to resist further, the other three women started lecturing her. "Why are you sorry?" Taylor demanded. "You're working two jobs for the man, and how many hours have you already put in today?"

She thought. "I got to the store about nine this morning."

"And it's 8:00 p.m. now, so eleven hours," Savannah said. "But how much time did you put in beforehand, getting Willow fed and dressed and to day care?"

"A couple," Deena admitted.

"So you feel guilty about *only* putting in a thirteen-hour day." Taylor shook her head. "I mean, it's good you're working hard, and retail is tough. And knowing Luis, he's probably paying you well. But you have to give yourself a break or you'll burn out."

"That's right." Savannah gave a little skip. "And working for someone in his home, it's hard to ever get any time off."

"Especially when your boss is hot." Taylor elbowed her sister. "Then, you don't even want time off, right, sis?"

"Oh, shut up." Savannah's smile was small, but very satisfied. Having seen her with her former boss, Hank, now her husband, Deena could see why. They seemed blissfully happy together.

They were approaching the diner now, and the outdoor deck was at least half-full of customers laughing. Little lights were strung over it and a guitar-and-drum pair in one corner gave it a festive air.

"Hey." Mellie slowed down and came to Deena's side. "Maybe *you* find your boss hot, eh?"

Deena's eyes widened. What had Mellie seen in her? "I mean," she said, stumbling over her words, "no one can deny that Luis is good-looking, can they?"

"Nope," Mellie said promptly.

"Nope."

"Nope." Savannah smiled. "Even us happily married women can see that. But what do *you* think?"

"I think," Deena said, deliberately drawing out her answer, "I think… I'd like one of those Orange Crush drinks I've heard so much about." She'd have a fruity drink, maybe learn something interesting about Luis, like how to resist his charms, and then go get some much-needed rest.

Minutes later, they were at a table by the railing, with a perfect view of the fading sunset sky, purple and blue, cloud-scudded. "Does it ever get old?" Deena asked, gesturing toward it.

"Nope. This island gets its hooks into you and you can't leave."

"I don't want to leave," Deena said, surprising herself. "I love it here."

"Already a goner." Taylor looked up at the waiter who'd approached. "Four Orange Crushes, please."

Deena *was* a goner.

She'd never felt like she belonged anywhere the way

she belonged on Teaberry Island. All those years with no father and a busy mother, who'd then married Andrew, who wasn't crazy about her…she'd never felt quite secure in the knowledge that she had a family who loved her. She'd had friends growing up and as an adult, most notably Tammalee, but she'd always been so busy working and taking care of her mother and then helping with Willow. When she'd seen groups of women friends drinking and partying in DC's trendy neighborhoods, she'd felt…not jealous, exactly. Just that she'd never have that.

And yet now, she looked around at the three women who'd spirited her away from an evening of childcare and felt a warmth and kinship she'd never known before. Never known she'd longed for.

Oh, she was getting attached to Teaberry Island. Too attached, maybe.

As they waited, they talked to a few other people at nearby tables. Between the three women, they seemed to know everyone. And everyone was friendly, laughing, having a good time. The smell of fried seafood wafted their way, and Deena suddenly realized she hadn't had dinner. She waved a hand and ordered a fried seafood appetizer platter for the table.

"You're going to be the death of my diet," Taylor said.

"Don't diet. You don't need to." Savannah, a model-thin and gorgeous woman who, Deena had heard, actually had been a model, whacked her sister on the arm.

"Okay, I won't." Taylor grinned. "I'm fine with how I look, and I do love the Dockside's fried oysters."

Deena figured it might be the right time to try to learn something about Luis. "So," she said, "what's the story with the three brothers, Ryan, Cody and Luis?

They're closer than most brothers, or at least it seems that way, but they're not actually related."

Mellie and Taylor glanced at each other. "They *are* brothers, in every way that matters," Taylor said. "They love each other and they have each other's backs. When Cody's younger siblings were basically dumped on him, Ryan and Mellie were there to help him figure out how to raise them."

"And they all came to our wedding, even though it was a last-minute trek for them," Mellie said. "They're all so different, but they mesh really well. My Ryan, he's the quiet one." She smiled. "Quiet but brilliant."

"Cody's the wild one," Taylor said. "He came to Mellie and Ryan's wedding from a helicopter, in a Santa suit. Christmas wedding," she added.

"So…what's Luis, if he's not quiet or wild?"

"Luis is…complicated," Mellie said. "I grew up next to the farmhouse, so I've known all three of them since they came to live here as teenagers. They all had a lot of issues, but Luis was the hardest to get to know."

"He's known as the moneymaker," Taylor said, "and he *is* that, but he's also totally guarded. I think he had things pretty hard, growing up."

"Well," Mellie said, "I do know that he had a real good early childhood and then it was ripped away. Unlike Ryan, who had a horrible life from the get-go, and Cody, whose mom loved him but was totally neglectful."

"Luis dates, but he's never had an actual girlfriend, according to Cody." Taylor wrinkled her nose. "Well, I mean, he has a kid, but—"

"But Tammalee wasn't a girlfriend," Deena said.

"She was maybe a three-night stand. Which was all she wanted to be, so it wasn't like he took advantage."

"He wouldn't," Mellie said. "But I think that's his pattern. Find women who don't want anything more than a fling."

Deena was grateful that their food came then so she could take a break from talking and think about what the other women had said.

She'd kind of known from Tammalee that Luis was only the short fling type. But to hear the other women confirm it was daunting, given her own feelings.

After the glimpses she'd seen of his difficult childhood, she admired the way he'd made a success of himself. Watching him with Willow, she saw his capacity for protectiveness and deep emotion. That was echoed in his obvious love for his brothers and their children.

She was starting to care for Luis, more and more as they got to know each other. And that was not wise, given what she knew about his background in regard to women and dating.

He might be the type for intense but short-term relationships, but she wasn't. The truth was, she'd only dated a little after the one early disaster, and never seriously. She'd grown up feeling that men weren't to be trusted, and so far, no one had proven her wrong.

She didn't want to test it with Luis, though. Didn't want that disappointment.

"Hurry up and finish," Savannah urged. "I want to dance!"

"I can't," Deena protested, but against her wishes, they pulled her out onto the dance floor. And maybe it was the drink she'd had, unexpectedly strong, but she soon found herself dancing her heart out.

It was better than breaking her heart over Luis.

At first, it was the four of them dancing together. But soon enough, several men about their age were on the dance floor with them. The other women welcomed them in for the fast dances and flashed their wedding rings when the slow dances came on. Deena followed their lead, minus the wedding ring, and they all sat down and had another Orange Crush.

This had been a good idea. Deena needed to make friends and get out of the work rut she'd gotten in. The work rut she'd been in for several years, come to think of it. She didn't have to keep her nose to the grindstone that hard. The salary Luis was paying her was more than generous, and she'd already made a big payment toward her credit card debt. She was getting her feet under her. She could relax, enjoy, dance.

A fisherman tapped on her shoulder, and she shrugged and danced with him. Apparently single women were in short supply, because several other men followed suit.

She'd just finished dancing to a lively rock and roll song with a boat captain and was trying to explain to him that she didn't want to slow dance when she saw Luis striding toward them. He did *not* look happy.

All the emotions rose at once in Deena's chest. Smug female satisfaction that he looked so possessive. Relief that he was going to rescue her from the boat captain. Annoyance that he seemed to think he had a say over how she spent her time and whom she danced with.

It was going to be an interesting end to the evening.

LUIS SET THE fisherman straight, collected the other women and drove them all home. His pulse rate was up and he was fuming but he managed to hold it together until they were alone in the car.

Then he turned to Deena. "What were you thinking?"

"What do you mean?" She leaned back in the passenger seat and stretched. "Wow, I'm tired. I don't think I could've walked home. Thanks for coming to get us."

"You couldn't walk home because you're drunk," he said. "You got drunk in a strange place with strange men around you. Putting their hands on you."

She tilted her head at him. "I'm not. I had two drinks. I definitely felt them, which is why I switched to water after that. So don't judge me."

"Even two drinks can impair you. Those guys were all over you." Just seeing that fishing captain, his hands on Deena's hips, pulling her closer, had made Luis furious.

Deena laughed, a sound like holiday bells. "Believe me," she said, "I know how to take care of myself. I've been out in the world for a while, and men never take advantage of me."

Did her expression darken for a moment or was he imagining things? "You're a stranger here," he said.

"With three protective friends who would have smashed anyone who tried anything against my will."

"That's true," Luis conceded. He definitely wouldn't want to mess with Taylor, Mellie and Savannah.

"And besides," she said, glaring at him as they pulled up to the farmhouse, "what business is it of yours who I'm dancing with?"

"True again, except..." He trailed off. What could he say? That he couldn't have her himself, but didn't want anyone else to have her, either? That *he* wanted to be the one dancing with her?

"Except what?" She was looking at him, half turned in the seat; he could feel it even when his eyes were on the road.

"Never mind." He pulled into the driveway and got out quickly. She was looking and smelling too good. He came around and opened her door.

"Such a gentleman." She wasn't slurring her words, but there was a slight inflection to them.

"Want to sit outside for a bit?" he asked impulsively. Then he could have kicked himself. *You can't have her, you can't have her.*

"Um, I guess?" She looked up at him through her lashes, and he smelled her perfume, a faint hint of honeysuckle that both turned him on and made him jealous. Why had she worn perfume to the bar? Did she always wear it? He didn't think so.

"Down here." He led the way to a couple of Adirondack chairs that faced the bay, now silvery with moonlight. "I'll run in and grab us something to drink. Do you want me to open a bottle of wine, or something else?"

Again, she gave him that look that might be sultry, but might just be normal. "I think I'd better stick to water," she said. "Don't want to lose my inhibitions."

As he walked inside to grab a couple of water bottles, her words echoed in his mind, again and again. What would happen if she lost her inhibitions? And what had she meant by saying that? Did she have feelings for him that she was keeping to herself?

He really wanted to know.

Back in the chairs, he handed her the cold water and

sat down next to her. He'd brought out a blanket, too, in case the night got chilly, and he handed it to her.

"Won't you get cold, too? Want to share?"

Why was she saying things like that? Was she hitting on him, or at least, showing that she was open to him hitting on her?

His competitive and testosterone-driven instincts wanted to push forward. If she'd been his usual type of seemingly willing woman, he would have.

But this was Deena. Deena, who was caring for his child. Deena, who was running a business with him.

Deena, who wasn't the no-strings-attached type. "So," he said, looking out at the bay, "how did things go at the shop today?"

She leaned her head back against the chair, looking up toward the stars. "I *think* they went well, but I'm nervous about whether we'll be ready for Saturday's opening. I still haven't figured out how to run the cash register. And I don't know about hiring people, aside from Carol."

"Did she take the job?"

"She's coming in tomorrow to talk with me about it. Which is another stress. She's not exactly friendly. I don't know why she wants to work at the store."

"Because I offered her the job? Dumb move on my part, I guess." He shrugged. It was hard to stay focused on business, and Luis *never* had a problem staying focused on business. Teaberry Island, and this woman, were changing him.

Maybe he was changed enough for a woman like Deena. Was that possible? Could he commit?

Would she like him for anything other than his money? Could he be valuable to her another way?

He sighed, and stretched, and his hand bumped hers. And suddenly, their hands were interlaced. He didn't know quite how it had happened, who had initiated it, but he knew he didn't want to let go.

She didn't tug away, either.

He felt like a middle school kid holding hands with a girl for the first time. His heart thumping, his body wide-awake, his eyes on her face, trying to gauge what she was feeling.

The difference was, when their hands started to get sweaty, he didn't just cling on like he would have as a young boy. Instead, he leaned forward and then slid onto his knees beside her chair. "C'mere," he said. He held out his arms, but didn't touch her. Not until she showed for sure she wanted him to, even though it would kill him to hold back if she turned away.

She looked at him, her eyes a little confused, but a little knowing, too. She leaned forward, her gaze flicking to his lips and then back to his eyes.

It was all the invitation he needed. He reached up and cupped her face in his hands and kissed her.

CHAPTER TWELVE

DEENA WASN'T A complete innocent. She'd kissed and been kissed before.

But not like this. Nothing like this.

Luis's lips on hers were so warm. He was so knowing. There was none of the awkward "where do I put my nose" business. He simply took charge and kissed her silly.

He wasn't acting, either. Luis was into it. When she came up for air, he made a little growl in his throat that told her he didn't want her to pull back, that he wanted more of her.

He smelled of some kind of shaving cream, something clean and old-fashioned, at odds with his trendy image, but she liked it. He was careful not to let his heavy beard stubble scratch her. He tasted of butterscotch.

He touched her like she was rare and precious, his hand stroking her hair. He took a strand of it and inhaled, closing his eyes. "You smell so good," he said, his tone deep and husky.

Part of her stayed guarded, waiting for the moment when he'd start to grope her and she'd have to make a decision. Here in the moonlight, under his expert touch, his husky praise, she wasn't sure what her decision would be. Not an automatic "no way" like she usually did, that was for sure. She wanted him. Every part of her heated and tingled and longed for more from this man.

But he kept his hands above her shoulders and didn't try to push things too far, too fast. That was comforting in a deep way. She didn't have to be the chastity police. She could relax and enjoy his kiss.

Some fairy-tale part of her brain, a part rarely activated, started to dance. Maybe this could work.

Wouldn't it be wonderful? A girl like her getting a guy like him?

"One for the record books," he murmured against her neck, and she froze.

That was something Tammalee had used to say. Had he heard it from her?

Remember how he treated Tammalee. He'd shared a few nights of intense passion, according to her roommate, and then it had been over, poof, as if it had never been.

Except it *wasn't* over, because Tammalee had been left carrying his child.

And Luis hadn't even bothered to check in with her.

Seeming to sense her distraction, Luis stroked her cheek and looked deep into her eyes. "You're something else, Deena. Something different." He lowered his head and took her lips again.

And it was wonderful, but not quite as wonderful as before. She could take abandonment, she was used to it, but it couldn't be allowed to happen to Willow. She couldn't put Willow's well-being at risk.

She pulled away and he resisted, just a little, keeping her close. And heaven help her, she didn't want to move away from him, to *be* away from him. She turned her head to one side, resting her cheek on his chest. She needed to catch her breath, and then she'd put a stop to this. To this experience she unfortunately shared with her late friend and roommate.

He'd kissed Tammalee like this and what's more, he'd made a baby with her.

She jumped up and backed away from him. It was like ripping herself out of a magnetic field, hard to do. Once she was out, she forced herself to keep moving.

He stood looking at her, a question in his eyes.

"That shouldn't have happened," she said. "I'm sorry. The moonlight must have gotten to me. It won't happen again."

He blinked, like he was trying to process what she said. His deep brown eyes looked hurt, and she had a flash of feeling like she'd kissed, and then kicked, a puppy.

Although Luis was more like a big bad wolf than a puppy.

And she couldn't look at him anymore or she'd rush back into his arms. She gave a silly little wave, spun and half walked, half ran into the house.

LATE FRIDAY AFTERNOON, Luis logged into his video meeting with his assistant, Gunther, early. Work was the way to forget about his problems.

Like that problematic kiss.

It hadn't actually been a problem for him; it had been great. Mood boosting, soul stirring, potentially life changing.

Except Deena had said it was a mistake.

And she was right. Somehow, she'd discerned that

Luis wasn't the real deal, and she'd instantly backed off. She'd followed up by avoiding him all day today. Well, granted, she'd had to work at the bookshop, but still. She'd barely said a word to him when she'd seen him.

Women had often proclaimed that Luis was a good man, a great kisser, a desirable partner. But those were women who wanted access to his money. Deena hadn't had those blinders on. She wasn't materialistic, and she wasn't impressed by Luis's early success.

She'd seen right through to his true self, and she'd backed off.

Of course she had, and Luis needed to return to what he was good at: making money.

Gunther hadn't shown up on the call, even though it was 4:01. Impatient, Luis sent him a text reminder.

Be right there, sorry.

No problem. Luis stood and looked out the window, knowing the bay would distract and calm him.

Except that there, kneeling beside the bay, was Deena. Willow stood in front of her, and they were picking up rocks and shells and throwing them into the bay.

Deena wore cutoff shorts and a T-shirt, her hair, or most of it, caught up in some kind of clip. Her slender build and long, tanned legs hit him square in the gut.

Instantly, the way she'd felt in his arms came back to him. Small-boned, but with muscles in her back and shoulders. She wasn't soft.

And those lips, their fullness, their natural pink color even with no makeup. Movie star lips.

He forced his mind back to the present and watched

Willow throw something into the water. Apparently, her previous efforts hadn't gotten that far, because she jumped up and down. Deena clapped and hugged her. Even from here, Luis could see Willow's wide smile.

Emotion gripped him, warming his whole chest. He'd do anything for that sweet child.

"Luis?" Gunther's tone suggested it wasn't the first time he'd spoken. "Is your volume turned down?"

"No, I'm here." Luis tore himself away from the window and sat back down in front of the computer. He needed to keep a lid on those softer feelings and focus on business. That was his skill set, that was how he could do good in the world, that was what people loved him for. "This new proposal is going to take a lot of work. Let's go at it throughout the weekend and we'll be the first to get something to the client on Monday."

Gunther's face fell.

"What is it?"

The younger man hesitated.

"Go ahead, if there's a problem, tell me."

"It's just that…it's Memorial Day weekend and I, well, I had some plans."

Luis clapped his hand to the side of his head. "That's right. We'll get the initial phase done today and then you're off. I can finish up the rest."

"But aren't you supposed to take it easy?" Gunther's voice sounded warm and concerned, even coming through the computer monitor. "And aren't you opening your bookstore this weekend?"

With Deena? No, thanks. "My manager and employees will handle the bookshop." A slight wave of guilt washed over him, since he was the one who'd insisted on the early opening, and the truth was they hadn't yet hired a staff. Even if Carol took the job, she was only one person. Maybe he'd help some.

A noise from outside reached him, and involuntarily he half stood and looked out the window. Deena lay on her back on the grass now, propping Willow on her outstretched arms and feet in a Superman pose, putting good use to those muscles he'd noticed. The child was screeching with delight.

Getting more involved with the bookshop would be a mistake. Deena didn't want to see him, didn't want anything to do with him. So she'd either have to handle the bookshop herself, or they'd have to trade off shifts so they weren't working together.

"And your health?" Gunther's concerned voice prodded him. "If we preempt the other bidders and get the new project, you'll have to be in the office more. I thought you intended to mostly work remotely."

Luis waved a hand. "I thrive on work, you know that. And—" He made a snap decision. "It turns out to be fine for my health, spending more time in the office and commuting here on weekends."

Granted, that was a self-diagnosis. But doctors didn't know everything. Being here on the island would push up his blood pressure faster than working in the office, surrounded by his people who could distract him from, well, from the woman who was driving him into temptation on Teaberry Island.

He glanced out the window again, and there was Deena, standing up and holding Willow now, looking out toward the bay and the sky, scattered with gold-edged clouds.

She was lovely. Willow was lovely. This place was lovely.

An ache started up deep inside as he thought of leaving Teaberry, spending more time in the gritty, busy city.

But like he'd always said, Little League and lawn work weren't for him. He needed the bustle of the big city.

Gunther's phone kept buzzing, and Luis saw him scanning it. "Sorry," Gunther said, "I'll turn it off."

"No, go. You need to have a life. I'll see you Mon—" He broke off. Although Luis would go back Monday, maybe even Sunday, Gunther shouldn't have to work on a holiday. "I'll see you Tuesday. Enjoy the long weekend."

"Thanks. If you're sure you don't need me—"

"Go."

It was for the best, really. Luis would keep super busy working on this proposal tonight and tomorrow, and he'd head back to the city on Sunday.

He kept his gaze resolutely away from the window. He needed to get out of here ASAP, before he did something stupid.

Like walk down toward the bay and kiss Deena again.

On Saturday morning, Carol looked around The Beach Reads Bookshop and wondered whether taking the job here was a terrible mistake.

The store would open in an hour, and she and her new boss were already uncomfortable with each other.

"Did you finish the outdoor display?" Deena asked her as she came back in.

Carol stiffened. "I told you I'd do it."

"I'm sorry, I'm just nervous." Deena walked outside and looked at the tray of books that stood by the street. Deena had explained that this would draw people into the shop.

They were lucky to have a bright, warm day for the start of tourist season and the opening day of the new shop.

The old shop, really. Despite the renovation, sometimes she could catch the echo of what it had been, of her grandfather's deep laugh as he shared a new map or history book with his friends.

But those echoes were rare. The store was nothing like the place her family had run in the past.

Deena came back in, frowning. "I asked you to put out the latest bestsellers," she said, "but instead, you seem to have gathered the few local and historical books we have and put them out there."

Carol nodded briskly. "It shows character, what's unique about us," she said. "People can get those mainstream novels at any airport. Books about the bay are only available here."

"We need customers, not character," Deena said. "There's a reason all those books are at airports and in grocery stores. They're what people like to read. Redo it, please."

Carol blew out a noisy sigh. This woman was half her age, with, as far as she could tell, zero experience in retail. And yet here she was telling Carol what to do. "We always emphasized the science and history books when my family ran the store."

"That was then, this is now." Deena gave her a level glare.

Carol opened her mouth to protest further and then closed it again.

She could get fired from this job, just like she'd gotten fired from her previous one. When she thought about it, she'd lost her job because she couldn't take leadership from a younger and less experienced boss.

Even though she still thought she'd been right, it would be irrational to repeat the same mistake twice.

"Of course. I'll get on it." Carol grabbed an armload of bestselling fiction from one of the boxes under the indoor display tables.

She thought about the phone call she'd gotten yesterday from one of her former coworkers. Apparently, the university had already put the tutoring center online. They'd cut the in-person hours way down, and Evie Marie was being praised about her good budgeting.

Carol ground her teeth and lifted her hot face so the breeze could cool it. All those years she'd spent building up the tutoring center into a welcoming place where struggling students could feel comfortable dropping in…gone. Thinking of some of her favorites stopping by and seeing a Closed sign made her heart hurt.

She lined up the bestsellers so that the beachy-looking ones were face out. What did it matter, since they were only putting out all the same kind of shallow books?

She carried a stack of her thick historical favorites inside and started reshelving them. Thinking of her past professional life of course brought up thoughts of her personal life, and she remembered with annoyance her effort to call Roger yesterday. She hadn't been able to get through, which had worried her. What if he was sick, lying on the floor, unable to get up, abandoned by his silly nurse? So she'd called the neighbor, who had gone to check and come back saying that Roger was fine, that he and his "friend" were cooking fish on the grill.

Which, first of all, they hadn't even had a grill, so that was a new purchase.

Second of all, he hated fish.

And third of all, how dared he get domestic and cook when he'd never lifted a finger to help her in the kitchen?

"Oh, what an adorable place!" A couple, just a bit younger than Carol, had approached. The woman who'd spoken picked up a popular beach read and turned it over in her hands, then smiled at Carol. "Are you the owner?"

"No, I just work here. Can I help you find something?"

"I'd like to buy every one of these books," the woman said, laughing. She picked up another of the paperbacks Carol had faced forward, this one featuring a picture of a woman's feet in sandals on a lounge chair, with the ocean in the background.

"Do you have any other kinds of books?" the man asked.

"Absolutely. Thrillers, and science fiction. And some local history."

His face lit up. "I'll see you inside, honey," he said.

See, people like the history books. Carol wanted to stick her tongue out at Deena, but several other people were approaching. Most wore what Carol considered to be tourist clothes—brightly colored shorts and shirts, sundresses, hats, some with sweaters against the slight morning chill. The ferry must have arrived, bringing in the first batch of tourists. And Carol had to admit that

Deena and Luis had been smart, putting up a cute sign near where they disembarked, pointing the way here.

She directed people and spoke as perkily as she could about the books on the outdoor rack. Pretty soon, Deena asked her to come inside and help with ringing things up. That made Carol nervous, initially, but the cash register was actually pretty easy to figure out.

She was reshelving some fantasy novels someone had pulled out and then decided not to buy when she heard a deep voice beside her. "Recon going okay?"

It was Gideon. She put a finger to her lips and nodded, even though in truth, she'd forgotten about their group goal. They were all going to check out the bookshop independently and share impressions as part of their project to bring back depth and meaning to the place. Everyone was thrilled that Carol could get the inside scoop, as an employee.

He gave her a thumbs-up and wandered over to one of the tables in the center of the store, where many of the latest bestsellers were stacked. He looked back at her and rolled his eyes.

Emboldened, Carol walked over to a couple of women who stood in front of a rack of romances, chatting about something that seemed unrelated to books. "Are you interested in local history?" she asked them.

"Uh, well, sure," one of them said, smiling politely.

"Over here." She beckoned to the small shelf of books about the Eastern Shore and the Chesapeake.

"Nice," the other woman said dismissively. "Thanks. Barb, we need to get going."

The two of them walked out of the shop without buying anything.

Undaunted, Carol kept trying to interest people in

the more serious books. She also kept a tally in her head of what people were buying, for the recon. Unfortunately, people mostly did buy the lighter beach reads, but what could you expect when that was mostly what they stocked? She was too busy with other stuff—admittedly her actual job—to direct everyone over to the local history books.

Deena was no help, talking enthusiastically to people about the fluffy books she seemed to love, and also about what to see on the island. She was flushed and excited, it was clear. Even more so when Luis came in. Carol was pretty sure those two were dating or somehow involved.

When there was a lull, the three of them stood together, looking around the store. "How's it going?" Luis asked.

"Decent sales," Deena said.

"The bestsellers, everyone's already heard of," Carol said. "The more thought-provoking books, you have to hand sell."

Deena frowned. "That's not our focus, Carol."

"Of course there are some similarities to what other bookstores carry," Luis said. "People want that."

Carol started to argue and then pressed her lips together. She needed to keep this job.

Deena glanced at Luis, one eyebrow raised. It was a look Carol had seen exchanged between Bambi and Evie Marie, back at the college.

A look that both dismissed and excluded her.

Fortunately, another crowd of customers came in—probably another boat had just arrived—and Carol concentrated on being efficient rather than trying to direct people to her own favorite books.

"Excuse me, do you have any local history books?"

Carol looked up at the tall man across the counter and restrained a laugh. It was Israel, wearing sunglasses and a flowered tourist shirt. She'd only known him for a few days, but she knew the clothes were totally out of character for him. He was trying to be incognito. And because Luis and Deena didn't know him, not well at least, it might just work.

"Yes, we do, sir," she said, and led Israel back to the shelf of local history books.

She pulled out a volume to show him.

"How's it going?" he whispered.

"I'm doing my best." She looked up and saw that Deena was frowning at her. "Listen, can you buy a book from this shelf? Otherwise, I'm going to get in trouble for not selling the beach reads."

"Of course." He started to study the offerings.

Carol walked over to another customer and started chatting about what she liked to read, but the woman asked if they had any island souvenirs. When Carol said they didn't, and pointed out the books featuring the island, she left.

Deena came over. "Hey, are you deliberately turning people away from the beach reads?"

"No!"

"Are you sure? Because it seems like you're mostly showing customers the kind of books you want us to sell."

"I'm giving people guidance."

Fortunately, Israel came over with a guidebook in hand. "I'd like to buy this one. It looks really good."

"Thanks," she said under her breath as she rang it up.

Deena gave her an exasperated look and went over

to shelve something else. And Carol winced. The fun group project was one thing, her grandfather's legacy a more important thing, but right now, for the sake of her self-esteem and her wallet, keeping her job mattered the most.

She was pretty sure today hadn't been a move in the right direction.

CHAPTER THIRTEEN

On the Friday night after Memorial Day, Luis approached the farmhouse, shifting a giant stuffed bear from one arm to the other.

He'd gotten it at the toy store in Pleasant Shores. Had meant to get a small token gift—after all, Willow was too young to be greedy—but he'd seen the big floppy creature and bought it on impulse. If nothing else, Willow could climb on it and take a nap.

He couldn't resist. That was what was going on with him. Couldn't resist delighting in the sweetness that was Willow. Also couldn't resist Deena—thinking about her, yearning for her, wanting her. Even though those feelings resulted in him being a big, vulnerable goof carrying a five-foot teddy bear into the house.

He tapped on the front door and then walked in, eager to see both of them.

He needed to focus on Willow, learn more about how to raise her right. He'd lived the busy, stressful lifestyle he always lived in the past week, but he had to admit that its appeal had flattened. Even closing a major deal paled in comparison to getting a hug and kiss from his daughter. That was why he'd decided that this time, he'd stay on the island an extra day. He needed more time with Willow.

Not with Deena, he reminded himself. With Willow.

Dropping his small suitcase onto the floor, still carrying the bear, he walked around an empty downstairs. "Willow? Deena? Mama?"

All quiet. He looked out the window that faced the bay, now golden with the sunset.

There, in the dimming light, he could make out Deena and Willow. And...was that some guy?

He yanked open the back door, threw the bear down in a deck chair and marched toward the water. He and Deena had never talked through that kiss they'd shared last week, nor the way she'd quickly withdrawn afterward. Working together in the bookshop had been a little awkward, though fortunately, they'd been busy enough to smooth things over.

They didn't have any kind of agreement or commitment. They weren't dating.

But if she thought she'd go from kissing him to kissing some other guy, in the exact same place, in the space of a week—

"Hey, Luis." Deena's voice was perfectly pleasant. Happy, even. Willow and a similar-age boy were on a blanket in front of the pair, a bright plastic tool set between them. Both were busy banging the toys against the blue toolbox, and neither paid Luis any attention.

He saw the wine bottle between Deena and the guy and registered what else he heard in her voice. "You've been drinking!"

"Hey, hey now, she had one glass and so did I." The other guy stood.

"Chill, Luis," Deena said. "Want a glass?"

"No." He squinted at the other man. "Grant Mosely?"

"You're Luis, the money guy!" Grant held out a hand. "I heard you'd done well. Always knew you were going places." His grip wasn't overly hard. Why should it be? He had nothing to prove. He already had the woman. Luis was the interloper.

Grant turned to Deena, nodding toward Luis. "This guy took over the business club at our high school and made it so profitable that we got in trouble. Had to donate all our excessive funds to charity."

Luis snorted. "To the principal's favorite political charity, no less. Which wasn't *my* favorite."

Grant went over to the blanket and knelt down beside the children. "This is Cooper," he said, patting the little boy's back. "We lost his mom last year and now I'm raising him alone."

Willow reached out her arms toward Grant, and after a slight hesitation, he picked her up. She settled against his chest.

It gutted Luis.

To his credit, Grant stood quickly and carried Willow over to Luis, depositing her in his arms. Where she proceeded to scream and cry until he handed her to Deena. Sheesh.

"Coop and I had better get going," Grant said. He picked up the mini tool kit, and the little boy started crying, too, matching Willow's volume. Grant scooped him up expertly, slid a diaper bag over his shoulder. "Good to see you, man."

Luis didn't answer, nor did he offer to shake Grant's hand. He just slowly sat down in the chair Grant had occupied.

"What was that about?" Deena asked. "Were you guys friends in school, or not?"

He was trying to process the fact that Willow had been more comfortable with Grant Mosely, who'd been a gawky loner in high school, than with Luis, her own father. "I want to be the one down here, playing with Willow." *And drinking wine with you.* "Not Grant. Me."

"You weren't around, though. You haven't been around since last weekend."

"Did you and Grant get together every night?" The words seemed to burst out of him.

"No! Why would we do that?" She gave him a puzzled look that slowly turned into a frown. "Not that it's any of your business, but Cooper and Willow both go to Miss Arletta's. They seem to get along well, so we brought them here to play a little." She held up the wine bottle. "And to relax."

"Are you dating him?"

Deena rolled her eyes. "Exactly when would I find time to date, between getting the bookshop going and taking care of Willow?"

"You didn't answer the question."

She stood. "You know what, Luis, I don't like the way you're acting. I'm your employee, but what I do in my private time is my own business. You don't get to control my life."

She was right; he knew she was right. And the thought that she was probably telling the truth, that she actually hadn't had time to start dating Grant, helped to reduce his blood pressure.

"Wait," he said as she started to walk away, Willow in her arms. He scooped up the blanket, wine bottle and glasses, and followed her. "I'm sorry. I was being a jerk. Have you had dinner yet?"

"Nope. I was going to heat up some mashed potatoes and chicken left over from last night. Willow loved it. She's crazy about carbs, this one." She swung Willow up and blew a raspberry on her bare belly, causing Willow to burst out laughing.

The sound of it made Luis's heart melt. "I brought her something," he said as they approached the house. He gestured toward the bear, sitting crookedly in the chair where he'd tossed it.

Deena gasped. "Oh, my gosh, that's so cute!" She knelt down beside it with Willow and shook its paw. "Hello, Mr. Bear. What's your name?"

"Ted-dee!" Willow cried, reaching for it.

"Good talking!" Deena beamed. "I didn't know she knew that word. Probably learned it from Miss Arletta's." Gently, Deena sat her in the bear's lap and wrapped its plush arms around her.

Willow's smile melted Luis's heart. So did Deena's.

As Willow examined the bear, cooing with delight, Deena gave him a narrow-eyed gaze. "You know," she said, "having you around would be a much better gift for her than a hundred-dollar bear."

The bear had cost him two hundred dollars, but no matter. "Point taken," he said. "Do you mind if I join you two for dinner?"

DEENA TRIED TO hold on to her feeling of righteous indignation toward Luis. If she let it go, she'd risk swooning over him, so handsome in the tailored business suit that fitted his frame perfectly.

Having a drawn-out family dinner together was *not* the way to avoid swooning. She snapped her fingers. "I almost forgot. Grant said there's a family movie in the park tonight. I think I'll take her just to get us out of the house. We'll grab a bite there. But you help yourself to the leftovers. Top shelf of the fridge."

"I'll come along to the movie," he said.

"Oh, but—"

"Having me around is a better gift than an expensive bear," he reminded her. "Give me ten minutes to change."

He was in the house and headed upstairs before she could protest further.

Half an hour later, they were at the park. If anything, Luis looked more handsome in his faded jeans and short-sleeved green Henley shirt. Deena was aware that her own shirt was stained with the applesauce Willow had spilled on her, her jeans dusty from crawling around the floor of the bookshop painting a baseboard they'd forgotten to do in the initial renovation. She should have taken a minute to change her own clothes.

The park was moderately crowded with families clustered on blankets or in lawn chairs, facing a big screen. Off to one side, a row of long tables held hot dogs and baked beans and corn on the cob. The smell of burgers grilling made Deena's mouth water.

A sign beside a cash box read $5 Donation. Luis handed the woman tending it a twenty-dollar bill and waved off the change. "We'll settle in and be back for some food," he told Deena.

Having agreed that Willow was close to either sleep or a meltdown, they found a spot off to the left, a little sheltered from the noise of the crowd. Luis spread the blanket he'd been carrying and held out his hand for the diaper bag. "You go get something to eat," he said. "I'll start her off with a snack."

He really did seem to want to make up for his absence and bond with his daughter, she thought reluctantly. "You want a hot dog?"

No way. He's accustomed to caviar.

"Sure, I'll take two if they have enough." He pulled out a baggie of cheese and crackers and a small plastic container of strawberries. "Can she eat hot dogs?"

"If we cut them up small. I'll bring an extra one over."

Deena took her time wandering through the crowd, greeting the people she knew, a surprising number of them. There were Ryan and Mellie, and their son, Alfie, and Taylor from the Bluebird Bakery. Customers who'd visited The Beach Reads Bookshop waved and said hello.

It was amazing how quickly she'd begun to feel at home in the town. She was grateful. She'd never expected to build friendships here like she'd had back in the old neighborhood, but it was starting to happen.

She carried back a tray with hot dogs and drinks. As she approached Luis and Willow, she saw a couple of young women kneeling down beside them. One was fussing over Willow, and the other was looking with admiration at Luis, who was smiling in a friendly way.

Of course he was smiling. What man didn't like pretty girls fawning over him?

Her possessive feeling made her understand how Luis had felt when he'd come upon her and Grant drinking wine. It was a little ridiculous, just like his caveman attitude had been ridiculous. But seeing him smiling at other women didn't exactly make her trust him.

And why should she? Why should she think that their shared kiss meant anything to him? She was starting to think that he could learn to be there for Willow—clearly, he was coming to love his daughter—but as for his feelings about Deena, well, adoring, kissable women were a dime a dozen in his world, obviously.

She marched over and plopped on the blanket beside Luis. "Here, your hot dogs," she said, thrusting them at him and resisting the temptation to call him "honey."

Something in her demeanor must have scared off the younger women, though, because after a minute or two, they both got up and left.

"Friends of yours?" she asked him.

"Nah. They just wanted to meet Willow. She's such a cutie." He rubbed the baby's leg gently, smiling at her. "Aren't you?"

"Da-da," Willow said, smiling back at him.

They were bonding, and seeing that put everything into perspective. Her own fraught and ultimately temporary relationship with Luis wasn't important. Willow's growing connection with him was what mattered. Tammalee would have loved seeing that. Deena glanced up at the sky. Maybe Tammalee *could* see it. Deena hoped so.

The movie started, and they ate leisurely, and soon they were laughing at the silly jokes of the animated feature. Other families and groups of friends were settled in on chairs or blankets. Someone came around selling raffle tickets to benefit an organization making playground equipment more accessible, and most people bought several. When a little girl wandered off from her family and got lost, the movie was stopped, and her worried parents rushed to get her, causing a big round of applause.

Deena marveled at Luis. He had to be used to black-tie events, and she would never have guessed he'd be content watching a kids' movie and drinking red punch from a plastic cup. But watching his face, she could tell he wasn't faking it. He really was having a good time.

The fact that he could be flexible, could relax and enjoy a humble outdoor event with his newly discovered daughter, made him all too appealing. He was devilishly good-looking, his T-shirt snug enough to show his muscular chest and arms. Oh, those arms. A ribbon of desire twirled inside her.

She needed to ignore it. She would. Just not yet.

Willow leaned against Deena and was soon asleep. Deena and Luis lounged back against the bear Willow had insisted they bring.

They had Willow between them, all tucked close together, for all the world like a real family. Cicadas sung in chorus as the movie played, and the fragrance of new-mown grass wafted across and to her nose. The air was soft and warm. And she still felt that thrill of excitement in her middle. Her nerves seemed to spark when she looked at him and found his soft-as-silk gaze on her.

This is fine. This is normal. Life was good, at least at this moment, but Deena felt somehow panicky, like she was about to walk off a cliff. Which was ridiculous and negative. Tammalee would've scolded her, repeating her favorite saying: *You* can *have it all*.

A better person would simply enjoy an evening with an attractive man without trying to think ahead, without giving it any particular meaning, without worrying about the future.

But Deena had never been the carefree type. As a child, she'd had to grow up early to help her hardworking single mom cook and clean. Her unsupervised teen years had led to bad consequences. And then there had been her stepfather's abandonment just when she and her mother had needed him most. Hardest of all had been nursing Mom through those awful last days, so very glad she could be there for the woman who'd raised her, but hating herself for adding up the cost of lost work hours in her mind.

She looked up at the stars that were starting to appear. So many of them, so far away. So cold and so beautiful. She'd always found that coldness and indifference comforting. Not tonight, though.

"This is nice," Luis said. He reached over and squeezed her hand. His thumb caressed her knuckles for the briefest of moments before he let go.

It took Deena's breath away and melted her inside.

Not good. Deena had wanted to keep her distance rather than swooning over Luis, but she had failed. Instead, lying here on the blanket with him, she realized that she was rapidly losing another piece of her heart to him.

CHAPTER FOURTEEN

ON TUESDAY MORNING, Luis didn't return to the office as planned. He canceled his meetings to accompany Willow and Deena to an appointment with the developmental specialist in Pleasant Shores.

He was getting some flack about missing work today from his coworkers. Or not flack, exactly, since he was the boss, but questions.

He'd let people know he'd be back in the office like before, and now they expected it. Gunther wanted to know how to handle a potential client who was jittery about his deal. Mrs. Jackson had payroll forms for him to sign, something he'd always insisted on doing himself rather than handing it off to someone else. One of his board members had texted asking if he was okay.

He told all of them he was fine, he'd be back later this afternoon and would manage everything.

He shoved his phone into his pocket as they approached the specialist's office. He wanted to be a good father, present for Willow as much as was possible. Spending time with her this weekend had cemented that bond even further.

It had also made him conscious that he wasn't yet the father he wanted to be. Doubted he ever could be, but the desire to try was growing within him.

Was parenthood always a mixture of love and guilt?

He picked Willow up out of her stroller, savoring the sturdy weight of her, loving her smile as she studied him. Deena folded up the stroller, and they climbed the steps and entered a big room that looked to be a combination of an office and a playroom.

The specialist pecked at her computer for a few seconds and then came over, hand extended. "Marcy Wallingham. I'm assuming this is Willow?" She studied the child but didn't reach out.

"Yes, and I'm her father, Luis. This is Deena, who's cared for her almost since she was born." He didn't want to downplay Deena's role.

The woman greeted him and Deena, told them to call her Marcy and gestured toward a couple of couches arranged in an L shape, with a colorful carpet in front of them. "Can I ask why you're carrying her?" she said.

Luis glanced at Deena, who looked as puzzled as he felt, and then back at Marcy. "What do you mean?"

"Carrying her rather than letting her walk," the woman clarified.

Luis shrugged. "Because…we both like it?"

Marcy nodded. "Of course. It's good for a child of her age to be able to lengthen the tether a bit, though, so let's put her down on the floor and see how she moves."

She moves fine. Luis felt immediately on the defensive. It reminded him of every new school he'd attended as a foster kid. The teachers studying him, making notes, giving tests. Or, worse, just making assumptions based on his Hispanic last name and his identity as a foster kid. *Does he speak English?* he remembered one principal asking his foster mother as she got him registered.

Yeah, and I understand it, too, he'd snapped, adding an expletive and thus earning himself a reputation as a troublemaker on his very first day.

No need to get defiant now. He'd learned years ago to tame his emotions, and he'd do that for Willow's sake.

He set her down on the carpet and, when she reached for him, he settled beside her. Marcy nodded approval and set out a few different toys—a soft doll, some blocks and a "put the peg in the hole" game.

"Let's watch her play for a few minutes while we talk," Marcy said. She got a tablet and proceeded to ask them all kinds of questions.

Deena, of course, had more answers than Luis. She'd worn soft jeans and sandals with a little heel, a red shirt that contrasted with her pinned-up blond hair. She was beautiful whatever she wore, but Luis found himself wishing he could see her really dressed up. Wishing he could take her to some of the finer restaurants and clubs in DC, show her off.

Not that she was his to show off. If he'd ever had a thought of that, she had squelched it immediately after they'd kissed.

Willow was trying to put the pegs into the pegboard with limited success, and Luis's stomach twisted when he saw that Marcy was noticing. The older woman made a notation on her tablet. With her foot—Luis couldn't tell if it was intentional or not—she nudged the pegboard out of Willow's reach.

Willow crawled toward it and Marcy nodded with satisfaction. "Good. She's problem-solving."

However, now Willow was beside the pegboard and the pegs were out of reach. She looked from the board to the pegs and burst into tears.

Immediately, Luis shoved the pegs toward her. "Here. Go ahead." He tapped one of the colorful pegs against the board.

Willow stopped crying, grabbed the peg and started shoving it into place.

Luis felt good about his ability to calm his daughter. But Marcy was frowning. "You need to let her be frustrated and figure things out for herself," she said.

"What?" Luis stared at the woman, whom he was beginning to dislike. "If I can help her—"

"She needs for you to be there for her, but don't do everything for her."

Willow's attention flagged and she turned toward the cloth doll. Marcy slid to the floor and dropped a baby blanket over the doll.

Willow wailed. This time, she was winding up to a big meltdown.

Luis tried to restrain himself from helping her. He looked up at Deena, who was biting her lip.

Willow cried harder. Marcy made notations on her tablet.

Luis couldn't stand it. He scooted over to Willow, pulled her into his arms. When he saw that she was still reaching for the doll, he pulled it out from under the blanket and put it in her arms.

She stopped crying.

"Sorry," Luis said to Marcy, although he wasn't.

"We have work to do. But that's what I'm here for." They went through a few more activities with Willow, and a lot more questions from Marcy, and then their forty-five-minute appointment was up.

They walked out onto the street. "That was rough,"

Deena said. "I mean, I guess she's right, but I hate to see Willow get so frustrated and upset."

"Me, too." He picked his daughter up. "So there," he tossed back over his shoulder in the direction of Marcy's office, earning a snorting laugh from Deena.

Wanting to stay and talk it all over with Deena, he scoured the street, looking for a place they could grab some lunch. If he remembered correctly, there was a nice park somewhere near the downtown of Pleasant Shores.

His phone buzzed, stopped, buzzed again. When he pulled it out, he saw that he had a dozen or more messages. His work responsibilities couldn't be ignored any longer.

"You have to go back to DC, right?" Deena sounded resigned.

"Yeah." He put Willow into the stroller. "I'm sorry I couldn't stay. We can maybe talk about all of this on the phone tonight, okay?"

"Sure," she said, her voice offhand.

Willow reached for him, and he squatted down beside her. "Daddy's gotta go, cupcake," he said, tickling her arm.

He stood and faced Deena, awkwardly, feeling a strong urge to hug her.

"Go ahead. I'm going to stop a couple of places and do some shopping before catching the ferry back," she said.

"Sure. Talk later." He strode off toward where he'd parked his car, feeling like there were invisible bands trying to hold him together with his daughter and Deena.

Behind him, he heard Willow start to cry, and the bands tightened. He looked back.

Deena waved him away, turned and headed off toward a hardware store with a wailing, twisting Willow in the stroller, drawing raised eyebrows or sympathetic smiles from passersby.

The bright sun dimmed a little. His phone kept buzzing, but he couldn't make himself care about the latest office crisis.

He was failing at being a good dad, and he hated it.

ON THURSDAY, AFTER A slow morning of working on inventory, Deena beckoned to Carol, who'd just bagged a couple of books for the only customer in the shop. "Come on," she said, "I brought a peace offering."

Carol followed her toward the small office in the back of the shop. "Great minds think alike."

"Oh, no," Deena said, "you didn't bring lunch, did you?" She pulled a bag out of the minifridge and held it up. "Because I did."

"No, and I'm hungry, so that'll be welcome. But come see mine first."

They walked around to the back of the store. Carol had brought a window box, a couple of big planters and two flats of flowers. "I figured we could give the place a little face-lift," she said.

"Thank you so much!" Deena gave the woman an impulsive side hug. "I've been focused so hard on getting it up and running that I haven't had time to spruce up the storefront. This will look so pretty."

"It'll look more like how my grandfather had it," Carol said.

"Ohhhh." Deena nodded slowly. Maybe that meant

it wasn't really a peace offering, but an attempt to go back to the shop's past.

She and Carol had been operating on a polite but distant relationship that was a little uncomfortable. She decided she'd look on the bright side in the hopes that Carol really meant the flowers to be a goodwill gesture. And regardless, the red geraniums and white petunias would look really pretty.

"Plant first or lunch?" she asked the older woman.

"Plant. Work before play."

"I agree."

So they attached the window box to the front window—Carol proved to be handy with a hammer and nails—and arranged the plants so that the geraniums stood tall and the petunias spilled over the front. "Just give this a week and it'll look full and pretty," Carol promised.

They made quick work of the planters and set them on either side of the shop's front entrance. After washing up, they sat down on the porch steps to eat.

The sun was warm, but as usual, the breeze from the bay made things cool and pleasant. An oriole chirped and trilled overhead and a pair of squirrels ran up and down the apple tree, chattering at each other.

Deena figured that learning more about Carol would help their relationship. "Tell me about your grandfather, the one who ran this shop," she said as she offered Carol a sandwich and unwrapped her own. She hoped she wasn't opening a dangerous chest full of snakes, asking Carol about the past of the shop she'd wanted to keep in her own family.

But Carol didn't seem to take it amiss. "He was a wonderful man," she said. "Quiet, but brilliant. He never had the opportunity to go to college, but he taught himself everything—maps and science and even Latin, so he could understand old books better."

"That's impressive."

"He was. I admired him so much." Carol unwrapped her sandwich. "Yum, I love egg salad. Thanks for bringing lunch."

"Sure. So how'd he end up a bookshop owner?"

"He made his money in commercial fishing," Carol said. "Then he got hurt on the boat and couldn't do that anymore, so he bought this building. It used to be a fisherman's cottage. Read a couple of books about starting a business, and then went at it."

"Brave man." Deena smiled. She suspected Carol had inherited some of her grandfather's resourcefulness.

"He always did just what he wanted and found a way to make it work."

Deena tilted her head to one side and studied Carol. "It sounds like you and he were close. But you didn't grow up on the island, did you?"

"No." Carol wiped her hands. "My parents couldn't make a good living here, and they wanted me and my sister to go to college, so they left shortly after they got married. But my sister and I spent every summer here with our grandparents."

"Oh, how nice." Deena felt wistful, maybe a little jealous. Her own mother's parents had been estranged, and then had died young. She'd never had the chance to know them.

"How about you?" Carol asked. "What's your family background?" She took another bite of her sandwich.

Deena waved a hand. "Nothing so colorful. I was raised by a single mom in Baltimore. We never had much, but we were close. She passed away a few years ago."

"That must be hard," Carol said. "It was just the two of you?"

"Yes." Deena's heart rate increased a tiny bit, just as it always did when she thought about how alone she was in the world. "I've been lucky to make friends who are like family," she said firmly. It was a line she used when people started to pity her. Not just a line; it was true.

"Like Willow's mom?"

"Exactly." Deena smiled, relieved. They could enjoy their lunch without delving into Deena's background. She felt that she, as a boss, should know something of what made Carol tick, but Carol didn't need to know Deena's history and innermost thoughts. Hopefully their conversation would now drift into a new subject.

Except that didn't happen. "What happened to make you shy away from men?" Carol asked.

Deena blinked. "What?"

"You seem to like Luis, but you're skittish around him. And you're such a pretty woman, but you're not married and you never talk about a boyfriend." Carol clapped a hand to her mouth, her cheeks going pink. "Unless... Oh, my goodness, I'm sorry. Everyone doesn't have to pair up, or pair up with a man. I worked at a university and did all the diversity and inclusion training. I just fail to remember it sometimes, because I grew up thinking in stereotypes."

Deena tilted her head to one side, confused, forgetting to be uncomfortable with the personal questions.

"Although... I've never heard you talk about a special woman friend, either. Not that there's anything wrong with that. And not that you have to have a partner at all." Her face went even pinker. "My goodness. I'm really putting my foot in my mouth, aren't I?"

Light dawned. Deena laughed and waved a hand. "It's fine. And I'm straight. And..." Maybe it was Carol's awkwardness that made her feel okay to reveal more than she normally did. "Well, my father left my mom in the lurch, pregnant with me. I never met him."

Carol's expression softened. "I'm sorry to hear that."

Deena shrugged. "I didn't know to miss having a dad, not really. My mom married my stepfather when I was sixteen, and that was...fine. He wasn't ever going to be a father to me, but he made Mom happy and he treated us okay. Until she got sick."

"Uh-oh." Carol put down the rest of her sandwich. "What happened?"

Deena shrugged. "Mom got cancer, and he couldn't handle it. He left."

Carol frowned. "Just left?"

"Well, first he took all the money in their joint checking account."

Carol gasped. "How awful!"

"It was." Deena flashed back on that time, how Mom had made excuses and said he'd be back, grabbed her phone every time she got a call or a text, searched the news sites for any word about him. That had continued right up until she'd died. "I guess that just confirmed my opinion that men weren't safe to trust."

"You took care of your mom?"

Deena nodded. "I did, and I'm so glad, even though it put me in a financial hole that's been taking a while to dig out of."

"Oh, honey. That must have been so hard. But...and forgive me if this is a nosy question, but I have to ask.

Did you ever date much yourself, or are you basing your ideas about men on what happened to your mother?"

Deena blew out a breath. "You really don't want to know the answer to that." Deena's dating history was short, and pitiful, and made her look bad. She tried not to think about it herself.

"I *do* want to know, if you want to tell me." Carol patted her hand. "I worked with college students for more than twenty years. Believe me, I've heard every kind of 'my bad date' story there is."

Deena hesitated. The events that had put her off dating were long in the past, and maybe they should stay that way. But if she was ever going to talk about them, Carol was probably a safe person to share with. "Mostly, in high school, I was one of those anonymous kids. Did okay with classes, did a lot of babysitting, didn't socialize much. I was shy, and we didn't have money for the kind of clothes the cool kids wore."

Carol nodded. "I ran into a lot of kids who fit that description. A lot of times, they come into their own once they get out of high school, whether it's in college or later, in the world of work."

"For sure. High school isn't the pinnacle for most of us, thank heavens." She looked out toward the harbor. A couple of sailboats skimmed across the shimmering waters of the bay. "But when you're in it, the high school social structure seems all-important. So when a few of the popular kids started paying attention to me, I was thrilled. And when one of them, Timothy Bowers, asked me out, I was in heaven."

"I take it the experience wasn't what you hoped for."

"At first," Deena said, "it was. He took me out for a

couple of meals, and invited me to a bonfire, and told me how pretty I was. Heady stuff for a fifteen-year-old."

Carol lifted an eyebrow. "Fifteen's young for serious dating. How old was he?"

"Seventeen. Two years ahead of me in school, an older man. My bookworm friends were jealous."

"What did your mother think?"

Deena shook her head. "She didn't know. She worked a lot in those days, and I was kind of unsupervised. I'd never given her any reason to mistrust me. Mostly, I just did my schoolwork and babysat, so she was justified in letting me go my own way."

Carol's eyes narrowed, but she didn't speak.

"Anyway, it was good for a month or so, and then he invited me to a picnic in a waterfront park downtown. It was super romantic, secluded, wildflowers all around." She'd been so thrilled. Even back then, she'd been a big reader of romance novels, and she'd recognized the romantic nature of a picnic on the water. She'd felt like she was living in a dream.

"He pulled out a flask and tried to get me to drink some. I wouldn't do it. Not because I was some wonderful, perfect, law-abiding kid, but because the smell of it made me sick."

"Hard liquor," Carol said, nodding.

"Right. Whiskey, I think. Anyway, he drank a bunch of it and turned into a complete jerk. Pushed me down on the blanket and started pawing at me. It was like he was a different person from the nice boy I'd seen up to that point."

"That would definitely put you off dating for a while," Carol said.

"It did. The worst thing was, apparently he'd planned

the whole thing and invited a couple of his friends to come…I don't know, watch? Get involved? I'm not sure how much was premeditated, but when I fought him off, they came out of the bushes to help him." Deena shivered and wrapped her arms around herself. She tried to avoid thinking about the incident for this very reason: it made her insides crawl as if she'd been invaded by spiders.

But she'd gone this far. "I fought and screamed, and a really wonderful older couple heard me. The man waded in and started kicking and pushing the boys, and his wife called the police. Those horrible boys actually pushed him down—I think he sprained his wrist—but pretty quick, the police showed up and the boys ran away."

"Oh, honey." Carol put an arm around her shoulders and gave her a quick squeeze. "I'm so sorry that happened to you. It sounds awful. Did you press charges?"

She shook her head. "I thought about it, and the cops tried to get me to do it, but all I could think of was how to survive the year and a half until they all graduated. I just kind of went back into my shell, and hung out with my couple of safe, bookish friends, and…didn't date after that."

"Not ever?"

"Not seriously." She shrugged. "That's so far in the past. I've moved beyond it, and I almost never think about it, but… I guess it did put me off guys for a long time."

"Like, until now?"

Deena didn't want to explore the reasons why her period of avoiding men might be coming to an end. She also didn't want to keep talking about herself, so she brought up a question she'd been curious about. "You said you were married on your job application," she said. And stopped.

"And you wonder where my husband is?" Carol shook her head. "He's head over heels in love with his caregiver. He's disabled," she added.

"Um, a little crush?"

"Nope. A full-blown affair, and we're getting divorced. I just signed the paperwork." Carol bit her lip and looked away.

"Oh, Carol, that's awful, that he betrayed your trust like that." Not surprising, given how men were, but awful.

"You know, I was mad. I was ready to exact all kinds of revenge on him." Carol looked thoughtful. "But now? I forget about him for hours at a time, and I'm enjoying my life here."

"That's good. I think you can have a really good life without a man."

Carol lifted an eyebrow and seemed about to ask her to expand on that comment. But to Deena's relief, a car pulled up and four people spilled out: Betty, her friend Peg and a couple Deena didn't know.

"Sitting down on the job, are you?" Betty teased. "We've come to buy books, give you some business."

The couple, who looked to be in their eighties, was approaching the porch. "Why, this looks the same as the day you proposed," the woman said to the man. "The very same type of flowers."

Carol smiled at Deena. "See, I told you the flowers would be a good touch."

"You were right."

"And you're Tom's granddaughter, aren't you?" the woman asked Carol.

"I am." She stood and helped the couple up the stairs, chatting with them. Apparently, they had gotten engaged right on this porch more than sixty years ago.

Betty sank down on the steps beside Deena while Peg followed the older couple and Carol. "Wayne proposed to me here, too, you know," Betty said.

"I didn't know. Was this the place to do it?"

"It was. Being on the edge of town, close to the harbor—it was very romantic," Betty explained. "People would sit here and, you know, get affectionate. I guess proposing was a natural progression." Her eyes were shiny. "We were married thirty years. I still miss him."

Peg came back out in time to hear the last statement. She sank down beside Betty, smiling. "Don't forget, it wasn't all roses between you and Wayne."

"No, it wasn't. No marriage ever is, and I regret the time I lost to mistrusting him. Life is short."

Deena studied the two women. Betty had lost the man she loved, but at least she had loved. Would Deena ever work up the courage to do the same?

She lifted her face to the Chesapeake breeze and let herself long, just a little, for Luis.

CHAPTER FIFTEEN

On Friday afternoon, Carol walked out of the Teaberry Island School feeling somehow lighter than when she'd walked in. Lighter than she'd felt since being let go from the university.

She'd tutored two high school students from the summer classes the Bradshaw brothers taught here. It was a different experience than tutoring college students. A little scary how far behind the high school kids were.

But it was motivating. If these boys didn't get through high school, their opportunities would be severely limited in today's world—much more so than a kid who failed a college class. What she was doing felt important, really important.

Plus, she didn't have to be in charge of the paperwork nor go to endless meetings. She was just a contract tutor, and as such, she had only one responsibility: get these students through, respectively, geography and English.

It was a beautiful June afternoon, the cool island breeze blowing in off the bay, the sun warm on her shoulders. A few younger kids ran past her, shouting their joy at being released from summer school. Due to the dedication of Israel and Gideon, there were summer classes for all grades, tailored and individualized, in the island's little elementary school.

"You did a good job in there," said Israel, coming up behind her. "I'm glad we hired you."

"Thanks." She waited while he fell into step beside her. "I liked it more than I expected, working with high school instead of college students." The brothers had managed a quick hire, pegged temporary casual, which was how she was already working. They needed the help and the candidates were few and far between. And of course, she had all her clearances from working at the university.

She still missed her old job, when she thought about it. Missed some of her former colleagues. Missed the salary and benefits, for sure. Most of all, she missed the students.

But working part-time on Teaberry had a lot to recommend it. It allowed her to get off early on a Friday, and to emerge into soft-smelling island air instead of the exhaust fumes and street noises that had always surrounded the college.

Gideon came up on the other side of her. "Can I help you carry that?" he asked, indicating her book bag.

"Well, sure. Thank you."

Israel glared at his brother. "I could have done that."

"But you didn't think to offer, did you?"

Carol tilted her head to one side and drew her eyebrows together, looking from one to the other. Were they fighting over who could carry her book bag? Seriously?

Take that, Roger.

That thought took her aback. She wasn't even divorced from Roger yet, though it was in process. She had no call to get interested in someone else, didn't want to. She wanted to be independent and spread her wings.

A little attention from the two men was flattering, but no more. "Do we need to pick up Linda for our strategy session, or is she meeting us?"

"Too nice of a day to meet in the library," Gideon said. "I texted her and told her to meet us downtown."

"Hey, guys." Linda came up behind them, breathing hard. "Good idea. It's too nice of a day—"

"To meet in the library," the three of them chorused, laughing.

Why did Carol feel like a young teenager, newly hanging out with peers, glad to have escaped from the oppression of home? Had she really been oppressed with Roger? With her job? "Look," she said, pointing to a colorful ice cream cart with a big plastic ice cream cone twirling slowly on top. "Let's get ice cream!"

Israel winced.

"What is it?" she asked.

He waved a hand. "Nothing, nothing. It's just a bit… tacky, that's all."

Carol laughed. "Oh, Israel, ice cream isn't supposed to be classy."

As they approached the cart, Betty came out onto the porch in front of the market. "Get your classic teaberry ice cream here, folks," she brayed.

"Stop stealing my customers, Betty Raines," the woman running the tacky ice cream cart yelled in an irritable voice. "Hi, folks, what'll it be? We have chocolate, vanilla, strawberry, mint chocolate chip and butter pecan."

Betty had strolled over in time to hear what the other woman said. "Same thing you could get anywhere else in the USA. Teaberry's exclusive to our island."

The rivalry was obvious, but Carol didn't think it

was anything serious. "I'll have a chocolate cone," she said to the cart woman.

"Same for me," Gideon said.

"I'll stick with teaberry." Israel veered off from the group.

"I'll come with you," Linda said, and Israel chivalrously held out his arm for her.

Carol had the absurd urge to giggle. Were they pairing off now?

She and Gideon took their cones to a bench at the edge of the park. Some of the kids she'd seen running from the school were now engaged in a complicated game that looked like tag. Younger kids climbed the play structure at the center of the park, and a small group of parents stood nearby, watching and chatting. That always-fresh breeze cooled Carol's face.

"So, do you think you'll stay on the island?" Gideon licked a drip from his cone.

Carol wiped her mouth and shrugged. "I don't know. My sister and her son will be back for the summer next week, and we'll see how we all get along. Depends on whether I can support myself, too."

"No chance you'll go back to your other life?" He didn't look at her as he asked.

"You mean my husband?" She'd never talked to the brothers about her divorce, but she hadn't hidden it, either. He'd probably heard her mention it to Linda.

"That, and your job." He still wasn't looking at her. *Why does he want to know?*

"No chance of my going back," she said, figuring there was no point in hiding reality. "The divorce papers have been signed, and my job at the university has disappeared. If I leave here, that's not where I would go." As she said it, she realized it was true. She didn't want to return to a big, crowded city.

"Well. You have added a lot of interest to island life," Gideon said. "Israel and I hope you'll stay."

"Thank you." Carol was touched. "I'm afraid I've been a bad influence on you two, with all the bookshop shenanigans."

"We've all been a bad influence on each other," he corrected. "Although it's true that you're the catalyst. Israel and I have known Linda for several years, but we never did any breaking and entering before you came along."

A catalyst? Her?

Thinking of herself as an agent of change—which in this case was the same as saying she was a troublemaker—was alien to Carol. Her old self reared up and scolded her, telling her she'd better settle down and behave.

A cautious person would cut off all efforts to defy authority and change the bookshop she no longer had any ownership in, especially now that she and Deena were getting along better. But thoughts of her grandfather—always a maverick who didn't care what anyone thought, and one of the most interesting people she'd ever known—kept rising up in her mind.

She shouldn't do anything to change Luis and Deena's vision for the bookshop, but then again, she'd stood up for herself at the university all the time. And while she'd gotten dinged for it, ultimately lost the job, she'd also been propelled into making a major change in her life, one that was turning out great.

The other two came up, both scooping bites from dishes of pink teaberry ice cream.

Gideon stood, and Linda sat down on the bench beside Carol. The two men sprawled awkwardly on the grass in front of them.

"So where do we go from here?" Linda asked. "We haven't given up on at least improving the tone of the bookshop's offerings, have we?"

"No," Israel said. "We need to offer a source of culture here. The reading and understanding level of today's students is plummeting."

"I have to admit, I was surprised about the kids I tutored today," Carol said. "They were pretty far behind."

"It's our society," Gideon said. "Always looking for the quick, easy fix. No attention span."

"Fine, but I don't see what we can do." Carol took her napkin to the trash can and came back. "I need to be clear—I can't do anything out in the open again. I need the job. And to be honest—" She broke off.

All three of the others looked at her. "What?"

"I don't understand why you're so concerned about the bookshop. I mean, it's my family business. But what's your motivation?"

Gideon and Israel looked at each other.

"We made a promise," Israel said.

"To your grandfather," Gideon added.

Carol's jaw about dropped. "You knew him that well?"

"He mentored the both of us," Gideon explained. "We lost our parents young, and though the island people helped us, it seemed like there was no place to go except fishing for a living. Your granddad saw our academic sides and encouraged us into the teaching field."

"Wow." Carol stared at them. Her grandfather had been a good man, bookish, even more so after Grandma had died. He'd been lonely no doubt when one family member after another left to spread their wings, but he'd always encouraged them to go.

"Even though he couldn't go to college himself, he inspired a lot of academic sorts on the island, through his shop," Israel said. "We told him we'd try to keep it going, even though he knew it was doubtful that we could. It would be giving back if we could help restore it to its former glory."

"Always said we should buy it," Gideon added, "but the time was never right."

"Because you're busy mentoring the next generation through your teaching," Linda said. "But with the four of us working together, surely we can make *some* improvements."

"How about if we sneak in good books?" Gideon suggested. "Carol, you're always shelving things. You could slip some better books in between the beach reads, couldn't you?"

"Maybe," Carol said. "If they didn't look too classic, I could slip in a few."

"Where would you get the books?" Israel asked. "Can you order them?"

"No way. Deena or Luis has to approve everything."

"The library!" Linda said. "We get book donations we don't have room to shelve, and some are like new. If we sold those, we could use the money to order more books."

"But what about when they get rung up?" Gideon shook his head. "They wouldn't be in the system."

"If you're handling it, Carol, can't you just not record the sale?"

"Sounds dangerous," Israel said. "The last thing we want is to get you in trouble."

"It wouldn't be stealing if we bring in the books ourselves," Linda said.

"We could try a few and see if it works," Carol said doubtfully. She felt excited at the prospect, but also worried. She didn't need to further alienate Deena. "If people go nuts over the classics, if we're able to hand sell them, maybe I can gradually order some books and bring the operation aboveboard."

"We're like a bunch of kids. We have no master plan," Linda said. "We need to figure out what we're doing."

"Pizza tonight at my place?" Carol said. "It's my last time to host since my sister will be back soon."

"I'm in. We could watch a classic movie."

Carol started to wonder, was this about the bookshop, or was it about four people who wanted to hang around having fun together but couldn't admit it?

Should she call them on it? But no, she had the same mix of feelings. She did want to fix the bookshop, but more than that, she was enjoying the friendships.

She thought of the novel she'd purchased during her shift yesterday and was eager to get into. Hmm, it did have a beachy, romantic cover. She'd have to make sure it was out of sight before the group came over.

"You're sure you'll be okay with Willow?" Betty asked Luis on Saturday morning. She had her purse and keys in hand, headed out to open the market before the first ferryboat arrived.

"Of course—" Luis began, but before he could finish saying that taking care of Willow would be easy, Deena trotted down the stairs. She wore some kind of lightweight, baggy pants and a fitted, rose-colored shirt that somehow looked incredibly sexy on her.

She must have noticed him looking, because her cheeks went as pink as her shirt. "What?"

He forced himself to quit his teenage-boy-style gawking. "Nothing. Nothing, I was just thinking...maybe we should get bookshop T-shirts for everyone."

"Great idea," she said, brushing her hands together. Then she looked from him to Willow. "You know, if you don't feel okay having her by yourself, I can take her to the shop."

Thanks for the vote of confidence, ladies. Seriously, Deena thought having Willow at a busy shop where no one would have time to watch her was better than leaving her at home with her father?

Luis forced himself to relax, leaning back on his arms beside Willow, who was attempting to put her doll headfirst into a big plastic car. She wore a red-and-white-checked shirt and shorts, and she hunched over her project with complete focus, her tongue sticking out one side of her mouth. Involuntarily, he reached out and ran a hand over her dark, messy curls, and she looked up at him and smiled briefly before refocusing on her task.

That was good. Focus was good, and he'd be sure to tell the developmental specialist about it the next time they met with her.

"Her snacks are set out on the kitchen counter," Betty said.

"I just changed her, but she'll probably need changing again in the middle of the morning," Deena added.

"Got it." He tried not to take the two women's doubts personally, but it was hard to avoid when their views coincided pretty closely with his secret fears.

He *could* manage Willow for a rainy morning on his own, couldn't he?

He'd had her alone before, but not for long. He usually went over to Ryan and Mellie's, right next door, if he was in charge of her and got into a tight spot. But Ryan and Alfie were at a summer league basketball practice. Who'd have suspected his geeky brother would volunteer to coach, or that his geeky nephew would play, for that matter? And Mellie would be at the market, since it was all hands on deck on a summer Saturday.

"Call us if there's any problem," Deena said.

"I will. We'll be fine. Get outta here." It was an effort to keep his voice calm and relaxed, but he did it. This was where years of doing deals with a poker face came in handy.

As the door clicked shut, he looked at Willow to find her looking at him, her little face doubtful. Uh-oh. What if she started to cry?

His concern must have been reflected in his face, because hers scrunched up a little. She looked at the door where Deena and Betty had just exited.

Yep, she was about to lose it.

Stay calm, solve the problem.

Two-year-olds didn't interact with each other a lot when they played, he'd read on one of the multiple parenting websites he'd been visiting lately. They didn't have the social and communication skills yet. They liked to be side by side, though.

He wasn't a two-year-old, but he couldn't think of another solution. He lay down on his side, making himself smaller, and started playing with a set of colorful blocks. He didn't look at her nor invite her to join in; he just built a little tower, whistling.

From the corner of his eye, he sneaked a glance at her. No more scrunched face. Instead, she was looking from him to the blocks with a speculative expression.

He built the tower up higher.

She leaned closer and *whack*! She knocked the tower down, causing all the blocks to bounce and bang onto the floor. She burst out laughing.

He laughed, too, relieved that at least one meltdown had been averted. He started to build another tower, and she quickly knocked it down. "More!" she demanded.

So they continued playing with the blocks, and he loved watching her laugh each time she knocked his tower down. He tried moving the tower to a different spot, and she gamely crawled over to destroy that one, too.

"You want to try?" he asked, pushing some blocks toward her. Was that something a kid her age could do? He was tempted to pull his phone out and check, but he didn't want to be that dad who was always on his phone.

Willow delicately picked up a yellow block and placed it on top of another yellow block. Then she placed a third on the top—also yellow—and looked at him.

He blinked. Not only could she stack blocks, but she could sort them by color. "Smart girl," he said, and a little of the weight of his worry about her lifted. He didn't doubt that she had issues from the FAS and needed help, but she seemed to him to be…well, brilliant.

She leaned forward and pushed herself to her feet. "Juice," she said.

"Sure, you can have juice." They went into the kitchen and he carefully poured apple juice into her sippy cup.

She downed it quickly and held it out to him. "More!"

He frowned, wondering if more juice would upset her stomach.

Was parenting an endless series of decisions and problem-solving? And he'd thought running a business was challenging. But it couldn't even compare, because nothing mattered more than a child, her health and happiness.

He took the cup and filled it with water. She tasted it and frowned and held it out to him.

He took it. "Yum, water," he said, and pretended to drink, making loud slurping sounds.

She giggled, and when he handed the cup back to her, she drank from it and seemed to forget her dislike of the substitution he'd made.

He felt a rush of pride. He was doing okay with her. And she was growing in her ability to calm herself down.

It was still rainy outside, so they went back into the living room. He was tempted to turn on the TV, but he knew it wasn't good for young kids. He'd save that as a last resort. He grabbed a ball and rolled it to her, and she clapped and batted at it. As they rolled the ball back and forth, he was amazed at how much work it was to keep a little one entertained.

He was up for it, though. He wanted to do it. He wanted to do everything for her. To be here for her.

His stomach growled and he thought about grabbing some chips and a soda, but didn't do it. He'd need to take care of himself so he could take care of her. He'd fix Willow an apple soon and have one himself.

On the weekends, here on Teaberry, he'd been eating pretty well. It was during the week that he resorted to the vending machine or drive-through. He was more active here, too.

He loved to swim and he used to hit the pool at his gym a few times a week, but in the past couple of ultra-busy years, he'd gotten out of the habit. And now, with commuting back and forth from DC to Teaberry, it was out of the question. He just didn't have time.

Plus, fighting for a lane at the crowded gym pool didn't appeal. He wanted to swim in the bay, like he and his brothers had done as teenagers, pushing each other out of boats, dunking each other, fooling around outside.

Despite their bad backgrounds, those had been good days. A lot of them.

Willow sprawled on her back and kicked her heels. "Ma-ma," she said, her voice a little fretful.

Did she mean Deena or Tammalee? Either way, he needed to distract her. He looked around for entertainment they hadn't already used, saw the big bear he'd bought her and grabbed it. He held it in front of him, hiding behind it as he walked toward her. "Willow," he growled in a deep, bear voice.

She burst into hysterical tears.

Oh, no. He thrust the bear aside and picked her up and cuddled her. "It's okay. Daddy was being silly."

"Bear," she said, pointing at the stuffed animal and then burying her face in his chest, still crying.

He murmured comforting words and then, when she didn't settle, he took a risk and carried her over to the bear. "Look, Teddy is crying," he said, and made loud boo-hoo noises. Propping her on one hip, he eased to the ground and used one hand to make the bear wipe his eyes.

She looked doubtful, but she did stop crying.

"Sad bear. So sad." He patted the bear.

"Sad," she agreed, and patted it, too.

Whew. He'd calmed her down and it felt good.

Maybe he wasn't a genius at fathering, but with practice, he could do okay. And it was important. The most important thing.

"Come on," he said, "let's go play in the puddles outside." Yeah, he'd have to change her clothes, and yeah, Betty and Deena might not appreciate it. But it would be a good experience for Willow and that was what mattered.

He could make decisions about how to care for his daughter. He could add something to her life that no one else could. But to do that, he had to be here for her, more than just sometimes.

As they splashed in the puddles, Willow clapped and laughed. He showed her how to stomp her foot and splash him, and then she did it over and over again. "Da-da wet!" she shouted.

Which might not be the right lesson for her to learn, except that she was so happy.

Manners could be taught later. For now, the important thing was Willow's heart. If she was relaxed and happy, she'd learn better, make friends better, have a better life.

Luis knew that from experience. He knew that those early, happy times with his birth family were what had kept him from going into a deep, dark place later in life.

He wanted to give that to Willow. Wanted to convey the unique lessons only he could offer her.

That was more important, by far, than making more deals, no matter how lucrative.

Luis kept thinking. And by the time they went inside, he knew what he had to do.

CHAPTER SIXTEEN

ON SUNDAY AFTERNOON, Deena headed across the yard to Mellie and Ryan's house. She was moving at a slow pace, holding Willow's hand, letting her walk rather than carrying her, because that was what the specialist had recommended. In her other hand, she held a bag containing the fixings for a fruit salad.

Thank heavens, they'd been invited to Sunday dinner with a big crowd and she wouldn't have to spend more time alone with Luis. And she wouldn't have to think about him leaving for the week.

Her feelings were in a knot. Ever since they'd kissed, the air had been heavy between them. Heavy with meaning, with tension, with a magnetic pull together. Oh, she'd run away when it had happened, but she hadn't wanted to. And then they'd done movie night in the park with Willow, and he'd held her hand for five seconds... and she'd relived the moment twenty times since. Which was wrong. Totally wrong.

Doing the right thing these days was diametrically opposed to doing what her heart longed to do.

"Look at how well she's walking!" Mellie came out the back door of their house to meet them, drying her hands on a dish towel. "Come on in and I'll put you to work. Taylor and Savannah ran home to get something, but they'll be right back. Nadine—that's Savannah's stepdaughter—said she'd keep an eye on the kiddos while we cook."

"Sounds good to me."

Nadine, a pretty teenager, was ushering Mellie's son, Alfie, along with Taylor's two kids out the door behind Mellie. When she saw Willow, she smiled and sank down onto her knees. "Hi, sweetheart! Want to come play with us?"

"Play," Willow said, and she toddled determinedly toward the small cluster.

Deena's heart warmed. Having these connections— basically cousins since they were all related somehow to Luis's brothers—was such a great thing for Willow.

She made sure that Nadine had both her and Luis's cell phone numbers, even though the kids were just going down to the edge of the bay to play. "Sorry, I'm a little overprotective," she said.

"Hey, you're a mom." The teenager smiled and started ushering the kids toward the bay before Deena could clarify that no, she wasn't Willow's mom, she was just a caregiver.

She didn't feel like just a caregiver, though. She felt more like a mother every day. Not wise.

Back in the house, Mellie set out a cutting board and sharp knife for Deena and then returned to the counter, where she was stirring up some kind of dough. "I'm probably wrong to try baking anything when our bakery experts Taylor and Cody are coming, but I saw a great recipe for cheese scones and wanted to try it."

"Sounds really good." Deena started chopping strawberries. "Thanks for having us over."

"It's fun. And Ryan is happiest when his brothers are

around. It's been a while since the three of them could spend this much time together."

"They really seem to love each other." Deena hesitated, unsure of how to phrase what she wanted to ask. "Is Ryan…was he able to, you know, connect, pretty easily?"

Mellie glanced over at her. "He can connect, really strongly. But there were some barriers to break through first. Why do you ask?"

Deena shrugged, then when Mellie didn't fill the silence, she put down the knife and turned to face the other woman. She opened her mouth to say "just curious," but the compassionate expression on Mellie's face stopped her. "I…well, I was wondering about Luis. Whether he—"

"Did I hear my name?" Luis's voice came from the back porch.

Heat flooded Deena's face as Luis walked in the door.

"Skedaddle, Luis," Mellie said. "Stop eavesdropping and go find Ryan. He needs you to help him fix the dock, and you can help Nadine keep an eye on the kids while you're at it."

"My brother picked a bossy one." Luis gave Deena a searching look.

She refocused on cutting up fruit.

"I'll talk to you later," he said, and headed out.

"That's what I'm afraid of," Deena muttered as the door closed.

Mellie came over to the other end of the wooden table. She sprinkled flour directly on the wood and then put a sphere of dough on top of it. "You and Luis are circling each other like herons doing a mating dance," she said. "Want to talk about it?"

"It's not a mating dance." Deena put down her knife. "Or at least… I don't know. I don't have a clue what's going on between us."

"Luis is a good guy." Mellie got a rolling pin and started rolling the dough into a thick circle. "Tries to hide it under all that money-hungry attitude, but he's a softy underneath."

Was he? Deena had seen hints of it, but she wasn't sure which side dominated the man. She drew up her leg under her knee. "Maybe."

"I see it in how he looks at Willow," Mellie said, and smiled. "And in how he looks at you."

That made Deena's heart jump. "Really?" She couldn't help but want to hear more.

"Uh-huh. He's got that helpless love look when he's around his child. Around you…it's a little more wolfish." Mellie smiled. "Which is to be expected. In addition to being a good, kind person, you're a beautiful woman. And the two of you are spending a lot of time together."

"Yes, we are." Maybe too much. In fact, definitely too much.

"Do you think it has a chance of becoming permanent?"

"Whoa whoa whoa." Deena put up a hand. "That's going way further than either of us has considered." Although, in her own case, that wasn't quite true. She *had* thought about having a family with Luis and Willow, but it was more like a daydream. A fantasy.

"Well, having a little fling isn't going to work very well, is it? Because of Willow if nothing else. And you don't seem like the fling type, either." As she spoke, Mellie cut dough into pie-shaped pieces.

"I'm not. I basically don't date. But Luis *is* the fling type. That's how Willow came to be."

"Well…" Mellie shook her head, her expression thoughtful. "He *has* flings, I'm sure of that. He's in his late twenties, rich and good-looking. I'm sure women throw themselves at him."

"Yeah." Deena picked up a kiwi and started peeling it. "I'm sure of that, too."

"He's not just a player, though. He has a soul. He's been rock solid for both Ryan and Cody. And I think he wants to settle down. Which leads me back to…any chance you and he will get together and stay the course? It would be great for Willow."

"I just…" She lifted her hands, palms up. "I just can't even think about that."

"Do you care for him?"

Deena kept her eyes on the fruit she was peeling. She didn't know Mellie well enough to go this deep. She also wasn't accustomed to this kind of probing from anyone but Tammalee. "I do. I care for him as a friend, and it could be more. But I'm not a real trusting person as far as men are concerned."

"Why not?" Mellie asked. "And feel free to tell me to bug off, of course."

This woman was relentless. "My stepfather dumped my mom and me when she became terminally ill," she said. "I never knew my dad. And there's more, but I'd rather not go into it." She definitely didn't want to dig into what had happened to her at fifteen, to turn her off dating and men. It was bad enough that she'd told Carol, but Carol was more of a mother figure, at least by age. Mellie was a peer, and more likely to judge.

"Oh, sure. I'm sorry." Mellie smacked the side of her head, an apologetic expression on her face. "It's not my business, but I really do like you, and I want the best for you and Luis and Willow."

"Thanks for that." Deena stood and started scraping fruit peelings into Mellie's kitchen compost bin. She was a little overwhelmed. She wasn't used to someone who pried into her business because she cared, rather than for gossipy reasons.

And the subject Mellie had raised was even more overwhelming.

Did Luis really look at her in some kind of a romantic way? What had Mellie called it...wolfish?

The thought gave her a thrill inside. That a man like Luis, so handsome, so sophisticated, would be drawn to her...well, any woman would be flattered. And Luis was more than just a handsome, wealthy face. There was a depth and a history there that *she* wanted to probe. She wanted to hug and kiss away the sadness that sometimes haunted his eyes.

She shook off her thoughts and helped Mellie finish the food and carry it outside.

They all sat at a long table covered by a red checkered tablecloth, in sight of the farmhouse next door and the bay off to the side. The air was soft, the sunshine warm, and laughter rang out often, mingled with the sound of children's voices.

Deena had never had an extended family to gather with. Mom had been an only child, and although there were distant cousins she'd met once, and friends who invited them to join in their family celebrations, they'd usually spent holidays alone. Just the two of them, and later, when Mom had married Andrew, the three of them. Mom had done her best to make it fun, but Deena had always longed for a Hallmark Channel holiday and family.

All of a sudden, she seemed to have it. Looking around at the laughing, multigenerational crowd, she felt a mixture of joy and pain so intense that it hurt her chest.

She was here, experiencing that warmth that she'd always longed for.

But this group wasn't hers. She wasn't a true part of the family. And the route to being a part of it—Luis—was as risky as a narrow swinging bridge across a deep, dangerous chasm.

She looked at him, Willow in his lap, his head thrown back as he laughed at something Ryan had said. It wasn't just that she wanted him as a means to have a wonderful extended family, she realized. She wanted him for himself.

Her feelings were growing, and if she didn't do something about it, they'd blaze out of control.

As soon as people started getting up from the table, she stood and helped carry dishes inside. Luis helped, too—good on him—so she had the chance to speak to him in passing. "If you've got Willow," she said, "I'm going to go check on the bookshop." She tried to sound casual, businesslike, anything but conflicted and attracted and confused.

He must have heard something in her voice, though, because he stopped and studied her. "Is something wrong?"

"No! No. I'm sure Carol's been fine covering the

store today, but I want to see how we did for the week-end. And there's a new delivery to put away. Always more to do." She clenched her teeth together to stop herself from babbling.

"Good idea," he said. "I'll come with you."

How was Deena supposed to respond to that? "You don't need to."

"I want to," he said.

I tried, I really did. Putting distance between them was the wiser choice. But for Luis to want to spend more time with her sent fireworks shooting off inside.

LUIS HAD TO get his feelings toward Deena back on a businesslike footing, and a visit to the bookshop should help do that. They were together to take care of Willow and build a retail shop, and he just needed to remind himself of that.

He'd thought it might possibly be fun, too—business-like fun—but that wasn't happening. Their walk over here had been nearly silent, with Deena responding in curt monosyllables to his attempts at conversation.

Which was probably just as well. He didn't need to have fun. He needed to make a success of this business, which was a world he understood.

He wasn't like his brothers. He couldn't overcome his past and build a family life.

When they reached the bookshop, Carol was carrying the folding sign inside. She seemed to jump when they called out to her. "How'd today go?" Deena asked, her tone friendly, nothing like the way she'd sounded talking to Luis.

"Fine, good. We had a lot of customers. Kept me

busy." Carol stowed away the sign behind the counter. "I put the deposit in the safe."

Luis frowned. "Deena, aren't you supposed to count the drawer with her? Or isn't someone?"

"We talked about that. It's best practice, but for such a small business, it's not always practical."

"Why not?"

"Because you're gone five days a week, and the shop closes about the time that Willow needs to be cared for," she said, her voice impatient. "Do you want to hire someone else just to double-check the cash drawer?"

"No." Leaving the business's cash in the hands of a single employee was asking for trouble, but with the plan he was in the middle of executing, that wouldn't be a problem much longer.

Inside, there were still a couple of customers. "Best not to cash out until everyone's out of the store," he said quietly to Carol.

"Oh, they're friends," she said.

He opened his mouth to comment on that—it was highly irregular that friends would be in the shop while she counted the cash and closed up—but Deena elbowed him. "Don't insult our employee," she said in a stage whisper. "We need her." And then, louder: "Hi, Israel. Linda. Find anything interesting?"

She was every inch the cordial businessperson, brisk, smiling, energetic. A different woman from the quiet, withdrawn person with whom he'd walked over here.

And a different person from the sexy woman you kissed.

Oh, yeah. That.

"Uh, no, didn't find anything today," the man named Israel said, forking his fingers through his thick shock of graying hair. "Beach reads really aren't my cup of tea."

"Nor mine," Linda said quickly, no doubt to explain her own empty hands.

Deena glanced at Luis and communication arced between them: *If they don't like beach reads, what are they doing at a store called The Beach Reads Bookshop?*

"Better be going," Israel said. "Later, Carol." He hurried out, not even holding the door for Linda, who scuttled after him.

Deena shrugged and walked along the shelves that lined the shop's walls. Then she studied the tables in the center of the store. "Looks like we'll have room for our new shipment, after all," she said to Carol. "You must have sold a lot of books today."

"A big crowd of folks came in with an hour to spare before the ferry left," the older woman said. "Money to burn, apparently. They bought a lot."

"That's what we want to hear." Deena rubbed her hands together, smiling.

"I, ah, I can work on shelving the books tomorrow," Carol said. Her hands were gripping the edge of the counter.

Luis was accustomed to reading body language in his business of making deals. What was Carol nervous about? "It's okay," he said. "We'll do at least some of it tonight. I'm sure you want to get home."

"There's plenty to do for everyone," Deena said, and now she sounded tense. "You can stay, work a couple extra hours if you'd like."

Luis could guess exactly what her tension was about. She didn't want to be alone in the shop with him.

"I guess I *would* like to catch up with my friends

and grab a bite to eat," Carol said. "If you're sure you don't need me?"

"We're sure," Luis said quickly, just to be ornery.

Deena shot him an irritated look as Carol headed out the door.

"I'll start bringing the shipment out and you can shelve them," Deena said as she disappeared into the back of the shop.

He followed her. "How much background research did you do on Carol?" he asked.

"Well, considering that you offered her the job twenty minutes after you met her, not much." Deena knelt down by a big carton and used a box cutter to open it, a little too violently for Luis's taste. "I called her references and they had good things to say about her. Couldn't get a hold of her former supervisor, though."

"Hmm." Luis frowned in the direction Carol had gone.

Deena sat back on her heels and studied the boxes. "Oh, this is great. New releases. Can you grab that dolly, please?"

He did, and together they loaded four boxes of books. The space was small, and there was no choice but to brush against each other. Luis breathed in the smell of Deena's light, honeysuckle perfume.

She must have noticed his pause because she looked over at him. His face was close to hers.

He glanced at her lips, full and pretty. If he took one step to the side, he'd be close enough to kiss her.

He wanted to kiss her again. He *really* wanted that.

She sucked in an audible breath, glanced at his lips, blew it out. Then she scooted away. "No, just...no."

Left hanging, he felt his face redden. He opened his

mouth to say he hadn't been going to do anything, that she'd misinterpreted. Plausible deniability.

But that would be pushing the embarrassment back onto her, and he didn't want to do that. He straightened, tilted the dolly onto its wheels and pushed it out into the middle of the store. He started placing books on shelves, taking deep breaths to calm down.

Okay, maybe he was a little random about where he was putting things. But her snapping "Don't just throw books anywhere!" seemed overly harsh.

He bit his lip so as not to respond in kind.

It hadn't been easy, but he'd taught himself to be the calm person in the group. At work, when one of his supervisors yelled at an employee, he took them aside and counseled them on anger management. When a board member got irate, or a deal negotiation got heated, he was the one with the cool head. The go-to man in a crisis. It was a hard-won skill he was proud of.

So why did being with Deena seem to push him over the edge so easily?

She drew in a breath. "Sorry. You have to arrange the books thoughtfully, that's all. People who are just stepping in the door might want to grab the latest bestseller. People who have time to browse along the different sections can get interested in a wider variety of books. So let's make a display of these new books right here in front."

"Aye, aye, captain," he said.

She rolled her eyes. "Uncomfortable with a woman telling you what to do?"

"Hey, I've had female bosses!"

"Uh-huh." She moved a small table to the front of the store. "Maybe I'd better work on this display. You can shelve the third box down in mysteries and thrillers. Alphabetically, please."

"Fine." But the truth was, her cranky bossing of him made him feel better after his faux pas in the back room, when he'd nearly kissed her.

Fifteen minutes later, as he was fitting a couple of mysteries into the cozy section—he'd quickly discerned that "cozy" meant cats or witches or knitting on the cover—he came across an already-shelved volume that didn't seem to fit. It was a book that looked like it belonged in the classroom, with a stolid gray-and-white cover. Edgar Allan Poe. Hmm. He'd ask Deena about that.

Moments later, he found another one. *The Scarlet Pimpernel*? Definitely not a beach read. "Hey, let's talk about ordering strategy," he called across the store. "You've got some mysteries in here that seem like they're off-brand."

"Everybody's a critic," she muttered from the front of the shop, where she was breaking down an empty box. She walked over. "What's the problem?"

He showed her the two books he'd identified. "Nothing wrong with the classics," he said, "but they don't fit with the shop's theme. I doubt they'll move, at least not to the summer tourists."

She looked at the two books and frowned. "I didn't order these."

"Hey, it's okay. We can send them back. Everyone makes mistakes."

"No, I mean it," she said. "I didn't order them."

"Well, I certainly didn't. Did Carol?"

"No, she and the other part-timer aren't involved in making orders."

"Then it must have been you."

"It wasn't me," she insisted. She glared up at him. "And you can stop accusing me of it."

A smile tugged at the corner of his mouth. He tried to keep it from showing without success. She was just so cute when she was mad, but she'd probably kick him in the shins if he told her that. "Maybe the bookshop has a ghost?"

She looked up at the ceiling, shaking her head. "Why do I have to put up with you?" Then her eyes twinkled. "Maybe it's Carol's grandfather, old Tom, who started the bookshop. Maybe he's a fan of the classics."

He laughed. Involuntarily he reached out a hand toward her. Then, quickly, he pulled it back, hoping she hadn't detected the motion.

This wasn't good. Far from keeping this a businesslike visit, he'd gotten even more attracted to Deena, enough so that he was having trouble hiding it.

And if, somewhere inside, he'd been testing the waters with her, they'd proved to be cold. Not icy, but definitely not warm and welcoming. It was good he'd made plans to be back in DC bright and early tomorrow morning.

CHAPTER SEVENTEEN

ON MONDAY MORNING, everything went wrong. Starting with Deena's own mood.

She hadn't slept well, between Willow fretting and waking up several times and her own thoughts about Luis. The man was so attractive and so infuriating. She wasn't sure if he had intended to kiss her or not, last night in the back room of the shop. And she wasn't sure whether she was glad she'd backed away, or not.

This morning, Willow didn't want to get into any of her clothes. Finally, Deena stuffed her into a pair of overalls and T-shirt against her wails and thrashing. Sometimes, taking care of a two-year-old was a contact sport. She didn't like to manhandle the child, but she was going to be late opening the bookshop, and she hated to neglect her responsibilities.

"Can I help?" Betty said at the door to Willow's room. She wore flannels and an old T-shirt, and she was yawning.

Poor Betty. She hadn't bargained for such noisy houseguests. "I'm sorry we woke you up."

"No problem. Want me to try to get her socks and shoes on?"

"No!" Willow said, clinging to Deena, looking over her shoulder at Betty as if the woman were some kind of monster.

"I guess not," Deena said, though she would have welcomed the help.

"I'll make a quick breakfast, then. Everybody feels better with something in their tummy."

"Thank you. That would help a lot." Deena had planned to go the granola bar route, but something solid was better.

"Where Mommy?" Willow asked as Betty turned away.

Deena froze. It had now been four months since Tammalee had died, and Willow hadn't talked about her in weeks. She called Deena "mama" more and more often.

But this was different. Somehow, she knew that today, Willow was talking about her actual mommy. About Tammalee.

"Want Mommy."

Deena sucked in a breath. Maybe this was what Willow's poor sleep and volatile mood was about. In her reading about childhood grief, she'd learned that these kinds of important moments tended to come at the most inconvenient times. But it was important to talk to a child, communicate that it was okay to bring up the missing parent, let her feel her feelings. Both Jovie and the developmental specialist had said that for Willow, maybe more than most babies, it was important to let her work through whatever came up.

Deena scooped up a photo of Tammalee and Willow from the shelf and hauled Willow into her lap. "Mommy died," she said, something she'd told Willow multiple times in the days following Tammalee's accident. It never got any easier to say, though.

As she had in the past, Willow looked confused. According to the experts, a two-year-old couldn't really comprehend death or "never coming back."

"Her body stopped working and she died. She can't

play with us or hug us anymore." Deena recited the phrases she'd learned from websites focused on helping kids deal with death. She would have said Tammalee was in heaven, but that was another concept too complicated for a two-year-old. Deena didn't want to hold out hope to Willow that they could go to a place and find her mother.

"Want Mommy," Willow said, her voice forlorn.

"I do, too." So much. Mostly for Willow, but also because she missed her friend's ready laugh, sense of fun and loyal friendship.

Willow looked up at Deena. Then she swung out her arm and hit Deena in the face, hard.

"Ow!" Deena couldn't help screeching. She nearly shoved Willow off her lap, but she stopped herself and instead, held her at arm's length while she flailed, trying to hit Deena again. Tears were rolling down her round, scrunched-up face.

Deena's cheekbone throbbed. She was going to have a bruise, if not an entire black eye. But Willow didn't know what she was doing. She was angry about a loss that would make anybody angry, and the common wisdom was to encourage her to express her feelings.

"Shh," she said as Willow wound down a little. "Sometimes I feel angry, too. We can hit a pillow but we can't hit a person." She reached over and grabbed a pillow off the bed. "Want to hit it?"

Willow looked puzzled.

"Like this." She set down the pillow and punched it, gently. Then a little harder because she *was* angry. Angry that Tammalee was gone. Angry that Tammalee had left her alone and in charge of a child she felt totally inadequate to help.

Leaving her to deal with Luis, whom Deena never would have met if not for Tammalee's fling.

Willow hit the pillow, too, but without a lot of steam. Then she reached up and touched Deena's face. "I sorry," she said. "No hit." She smacked herself on the arm.

"Oh, no, honey, don't hit yourself. Remember, we don't hit people, even ourselves." Could Willow understand that? "Come on, let's go get some breakfast and then we'll go see Miss Arletta and your friends."

She carried Willow down the stairs, plunked her into her booster chair and sank down at the table. "Feels like we've already been through a whole day," she said. She told Betty an abbreviated version of what had happened.

Betty put a plate of eggs in front of her and another in front of Willow. "You're going to have a nice shiner," she said to Deena.

Gingerly, Deena patted a couple of fingertips on her cheekbone. Ouch.

"I heard some of it," Betty said, her expression sad. "You did a good job. But still…" She trailed off.

Deena took rapid bites of egg and looked over to make sure that Willow was doing the same. She was, though in a messier way than Deena. Oh, well. Miss Arletta was used to messes. They had to get going. "But still, what?" she asked Betty as she stood.

"Do you think I should call Luis? If he knew Willow was having a serious flashback, I bet he'd come home."

Deena hesitated. "I know he's super busy," she said, "but…I have to admit it. Having him here would be a big relief."

ON MONDAY AFTERNOON, Carol stood on the dock waiting for her sister and nephew to arrive, practically jumping up and down as the ferry slowly chugged into the harbor. The breeze here on the water was brisk, making little whitecaps in the bay. The gulls seemed to like it, cawing out their opinions as they swooped overhead, undoubtedly hoping for some of the fish Carol could smell from the crabber that had just docked.

She was glad to see her family, of course. But her eagerness was about something else. She needed their help if she wanted to save her job.

The phone in her pocket seemed to burn with the message she'd gotten from Deena last night: do you know anything about the additional books we found here? She'd sent along a photo of a couple of the classic books Carol and her friends had planted at the shop.

They'd been discovered. They should have waited to put them out until closer to the tourist-heavy weekend.

She'd told Israel and Gideon at tutoring today. They'd consulted Linda by phone, and they'd all agreed they needed to get at least the most visible of the books out of there, either hiding them in the back or removing them entirely. The others had offered to help, but Carol was the one with a reason to be in the store. She wasn't scheduled to work today, but her family's arrival made the perfect excuse for her to come in.

The cars rolled off the ferry, only three of them. Mary Beth's was obvious, piled high with suitcases. There was a kayak tied on top and bicycles on the back.

As soon as Mary Beth drove the car out and Pete walked off the boat, Carol hurried over and hugged them both.

"This is nice," Mary Beth said. "We usually don't have any fanfare when we come."

"I made brownies and put together a casserole to

bake tonight," Carol said. "That way, you don't have to rush into grocery shopping."

Mary Beth frowned. "I'm dieting."

"No way. You're gorgeous." Carol looked her sister up and down. "I envy you your figure. Now, there's another reason I'm here. I need your help." She gave them the bare outline of what was going on.

Peter didn't want to stop at the store; he wanted to relax, but Mary Beth scolded him and they all climbed out of the overloaded car. "I'm tired, too," Mary Beth warned.

"This won't take long," Carol said, "if you do exactly what I say."

After she'd explained the plan, they walked into the shop. "This is nice," Mary Beth said as she looked around. "Nicer than when our family had it."

"Definitely," Peter agreed. He headed immediately for the science fiction section.

"Where's the woman we're to distract?" Mary Beth asked.

Carol nodded at Deena. "She's busy now. Just keep her that way."

Deena waved.

Carol waved back and gestured at Mary Beth and Peter. "My family," she called gaily. "Wanted to show them what you've done. Go," she added under her breath to her sister.

Carol moved around the store, her large, empty purse over her shoulder. So far, Deena and Luis had only discovered a couple of the books they'd planted, but with it being Monday, a slow shop day, Deena would undoubtedly straighten shelves and discover enough more to rouse her suspicions.

Carol found a couple—*Emma* and *Jane Eyre*, in the romance section—and slipped them into her purse.

When she'd told Israel and Gideon that some of the books had been discovered, they'd agreed they should plant them at a different time and offered to help. But she'd discouraged them from being involved. They'd been in the shop last night when she'd been closing and Luis and Deena had come in. If they appeared again, it would be suspicious.

The customer had left, but Mary Beth was engaging Deena in conversation. "You've done a great job with the place," she said. "Does my sister get an employee discount?"

"Of course! What do you like to read?"

As the two women talked books, Carol moved toward her nephew in the SF section. "Cover me," she ordered, and collected Mary Shelley's *Frankenstein* and Huxley's *Brave New World.*

Then she moved on to the mystery section. This was dicey, close to where her sister and Deena were talking. But she had to get *The Woman in White*, *The Moonstone* and *The Hound of the Baskervilles* out of there before Deena's eagle eye saw them. She and Linda had covered this section and they had found a lot to include.

Moving carefully, she slipped more books into her tote. It was starting to get quite bulky. She couldn't get every single book they'd planted in here, but hopefully she'd gotten enough to allay Deena's suspicions. A few more wouldn't matter. She hoped.

Her heart was pounding, her hands sweating. She felt more alive than she had in years. Wait until Israel, Gideon and Linda heard about this! They'd have a good laugh. Maybe she'd have them over after dinner tonight. Having her sister here put a bit of a crimp in her entertaining style, but Mary Beth might enjoy getting to know Carol's new friends, even become part of their posse.

As she slid *The Maltese Falcon*—the last one from the mystery section—into her tote, she breathed a sigh of relief. She wasn't sure whether she was cut out for a life of crime. Probably not.

A hand gripped her shoulder. "What do you have in your bag, Carol?" Deena asked. Her voice was not pleasant.

"I… I didn't…" Carol's heart pounded so hard she could barely speak.

"Open it. Show me. Now."

Carol heard her own voice tremble as she said, "Please, don't fire me. I'm not stealing." Her words stumbled over each other as she explained that the books were classics that could add to the bookshop's reputation, and that she'd brought them in herself.

Deena shook her head. "You can't just do that without consulting me," she said. "I'm going to think about this rather than make an instant decision, but I'm very unhappy with what you've done."

Carol felt sick. She'd hoped to save her job today, but instead, she might have done exactly the wrong thing. And lost it.

CHAPTER EIGHTEEN

"I'M GOING TO get fired again, I just know it," Carol moaned an hour later. She and Mary Beth were sitting on the deck of the family home, looking out over the bay. A half-empty wine bottle and two glasses were between them.

Inside, Peter was unpacking his things. Music pulsated from the windows, too loud despite Mary Beth's hollering to "turn that garbage down!"

"She didn't seem mad as much as confused," Mary Beth said. "I'm confused, too, but I do know you. You've always done crazy things."

Had she? Carol didn't think of herself that way at all. "I had help," she said, "but the responsibility is on me." She poured Mary Beth more wine and told her about Linda, Gideon and Israel.

Mary Beth cracked up. "You're like the classics mob."

"Kind of." Carol sipped more wine. "I guess if I lose the bookshop job, I can always do more tutoring."

"I have to admit I'm impressed. You've only been here, what, two months? And you've already found two jobs. Pete struggled to find even one job last summer, but I don't think he was trying as hard as you."

"No bills to pay." Carol watched an osprey soar over the bay, then drop, dip and emerge with a large fish.

"Whereas I need to make a living. I was used to a pretty good salary and benefits."

"Yeah, and you used it to support Roger," Mary Beth said. "Which, I don't know if you've heard, but he and the nurse are having trouble."

"Oh, really?" Carol liked hearing that—she was only human—but she didn't feel avid the way she would have a few weeks ago. Roger wasn't quite as front and center as he'd been.

"Uh-huh. Apparently he was down at the Legion, complaining."

"Well, that's what you do at the Legion." She stood. "I need to check on dinner."

"Thanks for cooking, and for the wine. I'm glad you're here."

Carol patted Mary Beth's shoulder. "I'm glad, too. I like it here." She paused at the door. "Oh, I'll have some friends over later tonight. The classics mob, actually. We'll probably just sit out here if that's okay."

"It's your house, too," Mary Beth said, shrugging. "As long as I don't have to cook for them or clean up after them, I'm happy."

"Mom!" Pete called.

"I can't hear you over the music," Mary Beth yelled back.

"I'll go see what he wants." To Carol's surprise, she was enjoying having the family here. Of course, this was only day one.

She opened the oven to check on the crab casserole— a much tastier version of tuna noodle casserole, beloved on the island—and then headed upstairs to her nephew's room. "Hey, kiddo, what's wrong?" She shoved aside a pile of clothes and sat down on the edge of his bed, wondering how the room could already smell so distinctively of dirty socks.

"I forgot my books." He chewed his lip. "I can't pass my class without them."

"You're doing summer school?" Carol was surprised. "Online? Are you trying to get ahead for junior year?"

He looked away. "No. I flunked math last year."

She stared at him. "But how? You're so smart!"

"It was boring." His mouth twisted. "Plus, the teacher was a jerk. He made fun of me about Dad."

Carol stared at him. About his dad leaving the family? About his legal troubles? But she didn't want to probe and upset Pete more. "You've got to be kidding me."

"Nope." He shrugged. "I didn't pay attention for a few weeks because I was mad, and by the time I started trying again, I was way behind. Plus, he didn't like me so he wouldn't cut me a break."

Compassion twisted her heart. There was little emotion on her nephew's face but she knew there was a lot in his heart. "I can help you, if you want," she said. "Or you can get into a class here. A couple of my friends teach summer classes on the island, and they basically cover anything anyone needs."

"Mom won't let me do that. She's mad."

Carol shook her head. "She's tense. There's a difference. I'll talk to her." She stood and patted his shoulder. "Come down in half an hour for dinner, okay?"

"Okay. You're cool, Aunt Carol." He blushed and started digging through his big suitcases.

Carol's shoulders straightened as she left the room and trotted downstairs. This was something new: her teen nephew thinking she was cool.

Voices from the deck made her veer outside, where she found Israel, Gideon and Linda, all looking worried.

"Your sister's been telling us about the confrontation at the store," Linda said. "We should never have put you in that spot."

"We want to help assume the cost, whatever it is," Israel said. "If you lose the job, I'll work on getting you more tutoring hours."

"A good offer," Mary Beth said. "I like your friends. I'll go make a big salad so we have enough to invite them to stay for dinner."

"Good idea," Carol said. "Will you guys stay?"

"Of course." And they reached into a bag they'd brought, which held crackers and fancy cheese and a bottle of wine, plus Linda had made brownies that smelled heavenly.

Her new friends were sweet and, impulsively, she hugged each of them. "I'll be fine," she said, and realized it was true. She looked at the men. "Do you think we can get my nephew into your secondary math this summer?"

"We'll find a way. Send him over to the school tomorrow, or bring him by yourself."

"Great. Thank you." She appreciated their can-do attitude. She would try to emulate it in her work at the bookshop. She would find a way to make her way.

First on the list was talking to Deena and getting her to see what Carol had been doing, however wrongmindedly. She was beginning to realize that she had the serious potential to bring culture to the island, that it just might be her mission from here on out: to help others dig into the rich world of books and reading. Tutoring was important, too, because that world shouldn't be limited to those for whom academic things came easily.

She had a lot to offer, more than she'd considered before. She *had* to keep her job at the bookshop. She had to keep tutoring, too, including helping her nephew.

She looked out at the bay, ageless and endless. Then she looked into each of her friends' eyes. "We have to take ourselves more seriously," she said. "If not through the bookshop, then another way. It's important, what we're trying to do."

ON WEDNESDAY LATE in the afternoon, Deena went to Miss Arletta's to pick up Willow. The baby was sweaty and puffy-eyed, and Deena's heart lurched, even though she'd been expecting it. "She had a bad day?"

"She did." The older woman held Willow on her hip as if she were a small baby. Gently, repetitively, she swayed back and forth. "You spoke with Jovie?"

"Yes. She called me." As planned, the social worker had done a session with Willow at Miss Arletta's day care home, so she could see how Willow dealt with that lively environment and the other children.

It hadn't gone well, not because Willow didn't fit into the group at Miss Arletta's, but because she was going through an intense grieving process.

Deena held out her arms for Willow, but the baby twisted away, her face screwing up to cry some more. "Come on, sweetie," she said. "We're going home for dinner. Miss Arletta needs a break."

"I love her dearly," Arletta said. "But she's definitely high-maintenance this week. Where's her father?"

Where indeed. Although both Betty and Deena had called him, he hadn't shown up on the island. Short, cryptic texts were the only communication. "Your guess is as good as mine," she told Arletta, not caring if her frustration showed.

She needed Luis, and Willow *really* needed him, and he was AWOL.

In addition to Willow's obvious, pressing needs, there was the bookshop. Deena was stressed out because she was meeting with Carol to discuss her weird behavior. She might end up firing the woman. Before making a move like that, something she'd never done before, she really would have liked to talk it over with the man who was, at least nominally, her boss.

But that wasn't an option.

So, on her own, she had to figure out whether to fire Carol and what to do about Willow's sudden array of issues as she processed the loss of her mother. On top of that, Willow seemed to be getting sick—hopefully with just a summer cold, nothing worse.

It didn't feel right for Deena to be handling those problems alone, especially Willow's, considering that Willow wasn't, technically, her child.

She cared. She loved Willow so much, but she had no rights.

And beyond those practical issues, Deena had to get past the emotions that had sparked and nearly ignited between her and Luis when they'd been in the shop on Sunday night. No matter how smart and charming and attractive and successful, Luis was unreliable, just like every other man. Deena couldn't think him dangerous, now that she knew him. But he definitely had the potential to let her down. Was doing it right now, as a matter of fact.

She finally got Willow into her stroller, and the walk

toward the shopping district soothed both of them. Beach grasses grew beside the split rail fence that lined the road, tossing their tasseled heads. The salt breeze cooled her warm face and dried the sweat that had started to collect on her neck.

They'd almost reached the bookshop when Carol came out. She waved, flipped the door sign over to Closed and took the folding sign inside. Then she came back out, locked the door and turned to Deena. "Let's go to the diner," she said, "my treat."

Food sounded wonderful. Deena had forgotten to eat lunch, and she was starving. "Considering that we might be talking about terminating your employment with the shop," she said, "I'll pay my own bill."

She expected Carol to get weepy, like she had the other night when Deena had caught her putting books into her tote. Instead, she looked resigned. "You'd be well within your rights," she said. "I'd still like to buy you dinner."

"I have to bring Willow." Deena couldn't keep the bitterness out of her voice. "Her father was supposed to be here but he isn't."

Carol shrugged. "That's fine. We can sit outside. Maybe she'll like watching the boats come in."

So they made their way to the diner, walking slowly, both of them texting a little and chatting a little. Deena felt the pressure of having to make decisions, but, she figured, she might as well do it at the diner, enjoying the pleasant evening and some good food.

More than half of the tables were full, with locals having drinks and appetizers, and tourists killing time before the last ferry departed. They found a table by the railing where Willow could watch the boats, but she was still fussy.

Their waitress was a pretty woman named Tiffany who was married to Pastor David. She came toward them carrying menus, took one look and turned around. A moment later, she was back with several packages of crackers and a little plastic spinning toy. She handed all of it to Deena. "Don't worry, I washed the toy. And crackers always make my kids feel better."

"Thank you." Deena's shoulders relaxed, just a little.

"Should we have a pitcher of sangria?" Carol asked.

"I'd better stick to iced tea. This little one sometimes requires me to be alert." She rubbed Willow's arm.

As the waitress left with their drink orders, Deena explained, "She's going through something. She lost her mom and she's kind of cycling through her grief. This seems to be an especially tough time for her."

"Poor kiddo." Carol nodded. "I've read about trauma in my work with college students. Good you're getting her to process it now so it doesn't come back to haunt her. What's her father's take on it?"

The million-dollar question everyone seemed to want answered. "Like I said before, he's supposed to be here but he isn't. But that's my problem. We need to talk about what you were doing at the bookshop."

"Right." The waitress brought their tea then, and they both sipped and let her get out of earshot.

"Can you explain what you were doing again? I'm still confused."

Carol nodded. "I can imagine. You thought I was stealing from the shop, but I was only taking back the extra stock I'd put out myself."

"Which is better than stealing," Deena said. "But

still, it's undermining my authority. Undermining our brand." She paused. "You want us to carry the classics, highbrow literary books and serious nonfiction. I understand that, but Luis and I made a different business plan. If you can't sell beach reads—"

"I can," Carol interrupted. "I'm an employee, and I can get behind your vision for the store."

"Can you, though?"

Carol looked rueful. "I'm going to try harder."

"I need you, Carol, and I hate to fire you, but what you did was out of line."

"It was," Carol said. "I made a mistake."

"*We* made a mistake." The voice came from a man behind her. And then the two men who taught summer school, plus Linda the librarian, surrounded the table, making Willow wail again.

Deena's stress level went up. She shot Carol a "deal with this" look and then stood and walked away from the group, trying to calm Willow's cries.

"Thanks, guys," she heard Carol saying over the din, "but I'll handle this."

The group of four talked for a few minutes more and then the others made moves toward going back to their table.

Deena walked down the steps and toward the docks, not wanting to take a squalling baby back to the dining area. Sunshine slanted over the water and the boats, a mixture of commercial fishing rigs and pleasure boats. People called to each other, most of them working on their boats in one way or another. Water lapped against the rocks that lined the shore and pelicans perched on the pilings.

Willow relaxed in her arms, and Deena took deep breaths and relaxed, too. There was something spiritual about the waterfront. The vast bay reminded her that her problems were small.

Willow was safe and well-fed; she had people who loved her. Losing her mother was a trauma, of course, but she was small enough that love and care could see her through it to a better tomorrow. And she had fetal alcohol issues that made her fly off the handle easily, yes, but the counselor was clear that, with help, she could learn to calm herself as she matured.

No matter how unreliable Luis was, he did love Willow. He would be a good force in her life, as long as he wasn't her only caregiver.

Deena looked upward and thought of Tammalee, her laughing attitude, her trust that things would work out. In many ways they'd been opposites, but that had made their friendship stronger. Their strengths compensated for each other's weaknesses.

Deena breathed deeply, savoring the soft, fresh air. Willow yawned in her arms. She recommitted herself to raising Willow, caring for her in every way possible, as best she could. No, she wasn't Willow's mother, and being technically the hired help still stung.

But nothing was ever perfect. Maybe Luis's tendency toward overwork was God's way of allowing Deena to get more time being Willow's unofficial mother.

Feeling better, she climbed the stairs to the deck and returned to the table where Carol sat, now alone.

"She's settled now?" Carol stood and pulled out Deena's chair. "I'm sorry my friends upset her."

"She was already upset. It happens." Deena took a sip of her drink and eased Willow into a more comfortable position in her lap. If she fell asleep there, Deena would have to eat her dinner with one hand, but that was fine if it meant a few minutes of peace.

She felt like she should follow up on the conversation with Carol, try to understand the woman better. Not that she'd studied business management or served as a leader, like Luis did. She was feeling her way, using her instincts. It was all she had to go on in Luis's absence. "So, Carol. Can you tell me about the reason you were doing what you did?"

"Oh." Carol looked surprised. "Well, I just think it's wrong to focus on shallow books that leave people empty. I was trying to introduce a little culture into the shop."

"Wrong, like morally wrong?"

Carol shook her head. "Wrong like my grandfather wouldn't have approved."

"And what about your friends? They felt the same way?"

Carol nodded. "Israel and Gideon, they're teachers and they think we've declined from the days when everyone read the classics," she said. "And Linda, you know, she's a librarian. She studied literature, serious literature, in school."

Deena thought about the difference between the bookstore where she'd worked in DC and The Beach Reads Bookshop. "I guess I get that. To tell you the truth, I didn't give it a lot of thought in the way that you mean. Luis is a businessman, and I want the business to succeed. Beach reads are something that will sell, for sure. Especially in a vacation spot."

"Sales and money aren't the only things that matter, are they?" Carol clapped a hand over her mouth. "I'm sorry. I told myself I wasn't going to be antagonistic."

"It's fine." Deena shrugged. "I'm beyond getting upset about stuff like that. What bothers me is that you didn't talk to me about it. You just assumed I'd say no and went ahead and did it."

"I *did* try to talk to you about it," Carol said. "You discounted what I said. Which is fair, I'm just an employee, but it left me with no other option."

You could have just done your job. But Deena didn't want to be that kind of boss. "Look, it messes with the bookkeeping if all these uninventoried books are included with the regular stock. That's not the way to go about it."

"I see that now. We were being silly. It was almost… a lark." She glanced over in the direction of her friends, who were laughing and talking. "No more larks at the bookshop, I promise. I really do want to keep my job if that's possible, and I'll stick to the job description."

She sounded sincere. And she was a good employee when she wasn't trying to undermine the whole business plan.

Deena hadn't wanted to make this decision without Luis, but she did feel she'd handled the conversation well. A little wave of pride washed over her, a sense of accomplishment. "If there are other incidents like this, I'll have to let you go. But for now, you can stay."

"Thank you." Carol clasped her hand. "I appreciate that."

"And," Deena said, thinking as she spoke, "maybe you can find beach read classics, if there is such a thing. Books that are lighter, easier to read, but that also count as good literature. Maybe books about the beach and vacations. We can try setting up a special shelf, and you can curate it, and we'll see how they sell." She hoped

Luis wouldn't mind her working with Carol like this. But since he wasn't around, he left her no choice.

"You would do that?" Carol looked thrilled. "I would love that so much."

"Let's make it happen, then. But I really do mean you're in charge. You come up with the book list, and make room in the shop, and hand sell the books."

"I will." She hesitated. "I like you, Deena. You're doing a noble thing with that baby as well as managing the bookshop with smarts and kindness. If there's any way I can help, I hope you'll call on me."

To her own shock, tears welled in Deena's eyes.

"Hey, hey," Carol said. "Are you okay? Did I say something wrong?"

"No, no." Deena grabbed a napkin and wiped her eyes. "You know I lost my mom. You're about the age she would've been, and it's nice to hear a compliment from you."

Carol patted her arm and ordered her another iced tea and beckoned her friends to come over. Willow woke up, and the elders entertained her. Carol told Deena about her nephew, who'd struggled some in school but was supersmart and responsible otherwise, and pretty soon Deena had agreed to give him a trial run as a part-time worker at The Beach Reads Bookshop.

They stayed, chatting, until the last ferry chugged into the harbor. Deena hoped against hope that Luis was on it, because despite the successes of today, she was oh so tired.

But all the passengers disembarked, and she watched, and he wasn't among them.

Of course he wasn't. She should never have hoped otherwise.

CHAPTER NINETEEN

LUIS FURTIVELY CHECKED his watch and winced. He'd missed the opportunity to head back to the island tonight, even if he could find someone to charter him.

All for a good cause, though.

Farewell and Best Wishes, Enjoy Your Retirement, and similar signs decorated the offices of Dominguez Enterprises. His staff had thrown together a surprise party for him, and his plan to slip away with no fanfare had been pushed to the side. No way could he hurt them by leaving, or even leaving early, when he was the guest of honor.

He was touched enough that he didn't mind the change of plans.

"We're gonna miss you, man!" Gunther's voice was slurred as he threw an arm around Luis. Alcohol fumes nearly knocked Luis over.

Luis took a step back, put a hand on Gunther's shoulder and studied the man. "You have a ride home, right?"

"Yeah. See, you always take care of us." Gunther gave him a sloppy kiss on the cheek and staggered off to get another drink.

Luis shook his head, laughing. His uptight assistant almost never let loose, but he definitely deserved it this week.

With Gunther's help, Luis had pulled off the fastest

deal of his career, selling his business to a competitor, a good woman he'd always liked and respected. She would take the business to the next level if anyone could.

Gunther had been involved in the negotiations and was now going to have to learn to manage a new boss. Plus, he'd helped Luis through another little health crisis, which hadn't turned out to be serious, but which had meant a visit to the ER, where he'd been told, yet again, that he needed to reduce stress in his life.

That had just sealed Luis's belief that he was doing the right thing.

He was going to live on Teaberry full-time, do some consulting and help Deena manage The Beach Reads Bookshop. But his main focus would be on being a good father.

He hadn't wanted to spring it on Betty or Deena until he was sure the sale would go through, and so he'd been noncommunicative in responding to their texts and messages. They'd wanted him to return, but they'd been vague about why.

He knew without them saying it that Willow needed more of him. So he'd figured out a way to make that happen. Now that everything had been straightened out, he couldn't wait to get back there and tell them. To start living the life he'd never dreamed he could live.

He'd intended to go back tonight, but then his people had sprung this party on him. Everyone was hugging him and wishing him well, a few even crying about how much they'd miss him. People had made funny speeches, with Mrs. Jackson's roast, slyly depicting all of Luis's little quirks, stealing the show.

Now, even though it was late, nobody seemed to want to go home.

Luis wasn't even paying for this party. He'd told Gunther to put it on his tab as soon as he'd grasped what was going on, but Gunther had refused. Everyone had chipped in, he'd said. They'd wanted to give him a send-off he didn't have to pay for. They'd split up the shopping and Gunther and a couple of the staff who were skilled in the kitchen had done the food. Others had brought in paper plates and cups and bags of chips.

That touched him. Not because he couldn't afford to pay for an office party with a keg and boxed wine and grocery store snack items, but because it meant they cared for him. They valued him for more than his money. They weren't just doing this for a free party.

That was a revelation. It melted a little of the ice that had formed around his heart when he was a kid, impressive only for his early moneymaking acumen.

Joyce, who was buying the business, came in then—he'd called her when he'd realized what was happening, and she'd managed to get away and, he assumed, taxi across town—and he introduced her. A fiftysomething widow with grown kids and a Caribbean accent and silver dreadlocks, she couldn't be more different from Luis on the surface. But underneath, she had a similar view of business and a similar skill set. She would look out for the bottom line, but she'd always be ethical and treat people right.

She gave a charming speech, and Luis could see that people were going to love her.

The business was in good hands. Now everyone started talking to her, welcoming her, and Luis backed off and took a bunch of pictures on his phone. They cut the cake.

Finally, Steve, one of the building security guards, came in and told them they'd have to shut it down. He was good-natured about it, turned down a beer but took a piece of cake and some cookies to share with his kids. The group wound into "For He's a Jolly Good Fellow."

And Luis joined hands with everyone and swayed and accepted their final good wishes. He stood with people for pictures and made sure everyone knew how to stay in touch, and that those who'd had too much to drink had rides. As he helped the main organizers clean up the mess, he couldn't deny that the moment was bittersweet. He loved the work he'd done here, the team he'd built. He would miss the pace and the people.

But here, in the business, he could be replaced. Not so with Willow. He was the only father she had. To her, he was irreplaceable.

The same thing wasn't true for Deena, since plenty of other men would vie to be with her. But maybe, if all these people could love him for who he was rather than for his money and status, she could come to care for him for who he was, too.

He sure hoped so because he'd gotten more attached to her with each passing day.

He couldn't wait to get home and live his new life, starting tomorrow.

DEENA HADN'T EXPECTED the Teaberry Island Clinic to be this crowded on a Thursday afternoon, but apparently something was going around. Maybe a lot of things, judging from the sneezing family with an infant, the white-haired couple who looked like tourists, and a woman Deena vaguely recognized as Carol's sister.

Lord help them if Carol got sick, too.

She shifted Willow in her lap and swayed with her, praying that she wouldn't have a meltdown.

Even more, she prayed that Willow's illness wasn't serious. The poor kid was hot and miserable, coughing, her nose running.

This morning, Deena had made the decision to take Willow to Miss Arletta's, despite the fact that she seemed a little congested. She'd told Arletta about it and asked her whether she should take Willow back home.

Arletta had looked Willow over then laughed and said that if every sniffly kid stayed home, she'd go out of business.

Deena had been relieved. She had to open the bookshop, Betty was busy with the market, and she had no other options for childcare. That was something she needed to work on, she realized now.

It would be nice if Luis was an option, she'd thought resentfully.

By afternoon, Arletta had called telling her she needed to pick up Willow. Her cough had worsened and she'd developed a fever. Luckily, Carol had been able to come into the shop right after her tutoring gig, and Deena had rushed to pick Willow up and take her home. A brief consultation with Betty confirmed what Miss Arletta had suspected: Willow should see the doctor, who was here at the clinic on Tuesdays, Thursdays and some Fridays.

Deena was unaccustomed to such limited medical services, but the thought of not having professional help with Willow until next Tuesday had sent her hightailing it to the clinic in Betty's car.

Her phone buzzed with a text, and she glanced at it. Luis. Again.

Like before, she paid it no attention. Let him see how it felt to be ignored.

She was being petty, she knew it, but come on. He'd

had all kinds of chances to be involved and he'd blown it. As a result, Deena had been dealing with Willow's grief meltdowns alone. No wonder the poor kid had gotten sick.

Of course, that wasn't fair. Deena hadn't really been dealing with all of it alone; Betty and Miss Arletta had been wonderful. Mellie had sat on the porch with her one whole evening while she rocked Willow, and she'd brought out Doughnut the dog, who had done more than anything else to calm Willow down.

Deena was becoming a huge fan of Teaberry Island as a place to make friends and raise kids.

She shifted Willow in her arms, which were starting to ache. Willow looked up at her as if for reassurance, then leaned the side of her head against Deena's chest and stuck her thumb in her mouth. Her eyes fluttered closed.

Deena felt a surge of love for the little girl, so sweet and affectionate despite her challenges. She stroked Willow's damp curls and studied her flushed face. Her breathing was a little more rapid than usual.

It was probably nothing, a simple virus, but Deena's chest still ached with worry.

The door of the waiting room burst open, and Luis rushed in. "There you are! You haven't been answering my texts." He knelt in front of Deena and Willow, ignoring the other people in the room. "How is she?"

He wore slacks and a dress shirt with the sleeves rolled up. His hair was slightly mussed, as if he'd been running his fingers through it. He reached out for Willow, brushing a hand over her arm and then her face.

Deena hated herself for the way her pulse leaped at his closeness. She pressed her lips tighter together, determined not to reveal that she still had feelings for him.

He glanced around the room. He nodded at the other family with the infant, then looked back at Deena and Willow. "Busy in here."

"We've been waiting about half an hour," she said.

Willow must have felt the tension or else heard her father's voice. Her eyes fluttered open and she looked around, reached out for Luis and then turned her face into Deena's chest.

Luis eased into the chair next to them, graceful as a big cat. "How long has she been like this?"

Enough with the interrogation. Luckily, the door to the back offices opened at that moment. "Willow?"

Deena stood, tottered a little under Willow's weight and started walking back. The slap of those expensive Italian shoes on the tile floor told her that Luis was right behind her.

Of course he was coming in. Now he was going to play the concerned father, and she couldn't object. He was, after all, Willow's father. It was good that he was here.

But the thought of being in a small exam room with him, when her own emotions were running so high and conflicted, made her break out into a cold sweat.

They sat down side by side, and the nurse who'd brought them back perched on a stool in front of a computer. "So this is Willow. You're Mom and Dad?"

"He's Dad. I'm the caregiver." It never got easier to say.

"What's been going on?" The nurse looked expectantly at Luis.

But of course, he didn't know what had been going on.

"She's been a little congested, but today at childcare

she developed a fever, as well," Deena said. "It came on quickly."

The nurse took Willow's temperature, checked her weight and noted her symptoms. "The doctor is finishing with another patient and then he'll be in," she said.

And then they were in the office, just the three of them.

Willow reached out for Luis again, and he took her, cradling her against his broad chest. "You're gonna feel all better soon," he crooned at her, his voice gentle. He stroked her hair and rocked her a little.

Deena tried hard not to melt. She did *not* want to give in to how appealing Luis was, taking care of his daughter. That was just a thing, a big man and a little child. Tammalee had had an entire calendar of Hot Dads that had been full of similar photos.

Luis looked over at her. "I have good news," he said. "I sold the business."

"What?" She blinked. "Why would you do that?"

A strange expression flashed across his face and then was gone. "The time was right," he said with a shrug.

Deena didn't get it. "So…what are you going to do now?"

The door opened then, and the doctor came in, and they were all taken up with his examination of Willow. He listened to her breathing and heartbeat, coaxed her into opening her mouth so he could look at her throat, and pressed gentle fingers on her neck.

Deena helped coax Willow into cooperating, but inside she felt more and more confused.

Luis had quit his job, really? Or no, that wasn't what he'd said. He'd said he sold his business.

That was surprising, considering the bustling office where she'd first met him, the office that bore his name. But she supposed he could do that, he was wealthy enough. He'd no doubt start another venture soon.

It didn't explain why he'd been so unavailable to her and to Willow's needs.

They were all standing around the examining table, looking at Willow. "Looks to me like she has RSV, but I'm going to do a nasal swab just to confirm it," the doctor said, matching words to action so quickly that Willow didn't have time to get upset. "She has all the symptoms—cough, fever, runny nose, sneezing."

"What's RSV?" Deena and Luis asked almost at the same time. Which would have been funny if they were on better terms and the situation wasn't so serious.

"Respiratory syncytial virus. It's common, and usually not serious, but we want to be alert. In some cases, it can cause inflammation in the airways and result in pneumonia."

He recommended children's acetaminophen and lots of fluids and explained how to use nasal saline drops— that was going to be fun—to help clear her stuffy nose. The doctor glanced from Luis to Deena. "The two of you are likely to get it, too. No return to day care until she's done with the fever, and you may need to stay home from work, too."

Deena blew out a breath. She'd been hoping to be able to stay entirely away from Luis, but it looked like she was going to need him.

The doctor gave them things to look for and instructions for if it got worse, patted Willow on the head and walked out of the room, telling them to stay until his assistant could bring in printed instructions.

Being in close quarters with Luis felt more and more uncomfortable, at least to Deena. "Look," she said, "why don't you just leave? I probably have the virus, but we don't want you to catch it."

He shrugged. "If it happens, it happens."

"No," she said. "You need to be able to run the bookshop while I stay home with her. You haven't been there for either of us, but surely the business is of interest."

He had been playing with Willow's little stuffed monkey, evoking her laughter by making it dance in front of her, but at Deena's words he looked up quickly. "You're upset."

She barely restrained herself from rolling her eyes. "Of course I'm upset. But the longer you're in this little room with us, the more likely that you'll catch this RSV and be completely useless."

"Useless?" He opened his mouth as if to say more, then closed it again. His forehead was wrinkled.

"I'm sorry, that was harsh. You'll be out of commission, that's what I meant."

"No, it's not." He looked at her and then at the floor.

She wanted to comfort him, but where was the use in that? "Go on," she said. "Take off. Get out of the contagion zone," she added, trying to make it feel like less of a rejection.

He tucked the stuffed monkey into Willow's arms and backed away.

Willow started to cry.

Deena felt awful, physically and emotionally. Which

was no surprise. She was almost certainly catching what Willow had.

But there was more to it. She felt like she was back in her childhood, with her mother, who was always mourning the loss of one man or other. Deena had mourned some of them, too, but as often as not, she'd had to be the strong one.

Men. You couldn't count on them. And even when they came back with smiles and excuses, it did no good to make up with them. They would just let you down again.

Or worse.

"Go on, I wish you'd just go," she said over Willow's cries.

Luis frowned, hesitated.

"Seriously." She reached for an excuse that would get him out of here fast. "You'll be more help to her running the business than you will getting sick. Betty and I can take care of her without you."

"Right. Okay." The nurse came back in then and handed them a sheaf of papers, and they walked out together. Luis wanted to drive them, but Deena shook her head. "It's not necessary. I have Betty's car."

"Then I'll see you back at the house."

She wanted that. Wanted relief from caring for Willow, wanted someone to share the worries and fears of a sick child with. But she shook her head. "I'm just going to put her to bed and then go to sleep myself," she said. "The bookshop opens tomorrow at ten. It would be great if you could take my shift."

"Right." He turned on his heel and left.

And Deena swallowed hard and tried to tell herself she was doing the right thing, the best thing, the only thing she could do for this beautiful, sick baby she held in her arms.

Only she knew in her heart that rejecting Luis's help wasn't for Willow's well-being. It was for her own emotional survival.

CHAPTER TWENTY

BEHIND THE BOOKSHOP the day after arriving home to Willow's health scare, Luis was finding it surprisingly satisfying to demolish the dilapidated shed.

He swung the sledgehammer he'd borrowed, his muscles straining at the unaccustomed exertion. Then he used a big metal claw to pull apart the boards. The hot Chesapeake sun beat down on his back and sweat poured off him, soaking his T-shirt.

The sound of the hammer and the gulls and the chattering group of customers heading into the bookshop couldn't drown out his thoughts. Why was Deena so angry with him?

Worried about Willow, he'd knocked on Deena's door last night, but she'd only opened it a crack, her finger to her lips, and told him Willow was in the room with her, asleep. This morning, she hadn't even answered his tap on the door. Maybe she'd been sleeping. So he'd headed out to the bookshop. He'd tried calling her twice this morning, but had received only terse texts in response. We're fine. Can't talk.

He wanted to raise his daughter right. He'd just upended his entire life to do that. But he needed a little help, being a total novice and having rarely seen it done in real life.

He needed Deena's help and support, raising Willow

at the very least. He'd hoped for more, but it looked like he had screwed everything up.

Back in DC, for a brief moment, it had seemed like his coworkers liked him for more than his ability to make money. They'd seemed to genuinely care about him, to admire him, to be sad that he was leaving.

Here, though, with the people he was trying to make a go of it with, the most important people—Deena and Willow—he was failing miserably.

Deena had seemed taken aback, actually unhappy, that he'd sold the business. She'd looked at him like he was out of his mind. And that had made him question himself.

No question, he had plenty of money to take good care of Willow. But it was possible he'd be less wealthy in the future, having given up his major source of revenue. Deena was a smart woman and must have realized that immediately.

She hadn't liked it.

Without his wealth and potential for more, she would have no use for him. She'd actually called him "useless" last night.

He needed to go back to his usual modus operandi: work hard, make the store a success and forget any romantic feelings toward Deena as well as any hope that he could succeed at having a normal family life.

He swung the sledgehammer hard, and the last remaining wall crashed to the ground.

He cleaned up the demo site in record time, stacking broken boards to be hauled away to Jimmy's Junk Joint. Nothing was ever wasted on an isolated island. Someone could use the wood. He would have liked to go home and take a shower, but he didn't feel welcome.

So he cleaned up in the shop's little restroom and went out onto the sales floor.

A young guy, apparently a new hire, was ringing up something for a customer, making a hash of it, trying to figure out the cash register. Which wasn't at all complicated. "I'll do it," he said brusquely, stepping in front of the young guy. "Sorry, ma'am," he said to the customer.

The new kid was bagging her book, using a too-small bag, and Luis forced himself not to grab the project away from him.

"It's only my second day," the kid mumbled.

Excuses. Who had hired the kid? "Find the manual for the cash register and study it," he ordered, and strode out onto the sales floor.

Carol was there, putting together a new shelf, and she glared at him. "What's wrong with *you*?" she asked.

Obviously, respect didn't mean the same thing here that it did on the mainland. "Who hired the kid?" he asked, nodding toward the cash register.

"*The kid* is my nephew," she said, "and Deena hired him. At my suggestion. He's sixteen years old, and he agreed to come in today even though he's not fully trained, so I could work on a special project."

Her words, and more than that, her tone, brought him up short. He was being the kind of jerk boss he'd never wanted to be. "Sorry, sorry," he said. "Carry on. I'll help him out."

"If he doesn't quit," Carol said, her voice snarky.

Linda from the library came in then, with two older gentlemen he vaguely remembered, teachers who'd been old when Luis was here for high school. He greeted them and they were friendly enough, but clearly, they were looking for Carol, not him. Soon they were en-

LEE TOBIN McCLAIN 267

gaged in a lively discussion that seemed to have to do
with classic books, and which ones could be considered
beach reads. He listened a little more and discerned that
this was a project Deena had okayed.

So there'd been a lot going on here while he was busy
in town. Fine; he'd given Deena control as a manager
and couldn't second-guess her decisions.

The elders were laughing and arguing, having a fun
time. One of the guys seemed to be a bit handsy with
Carol, but she gave as good as she got, so apparently
the feeling was mutual.

He envied their friendship, the possible budding romance.

He forced himself to chat with the new employee,
apologized for his sharp words earlier, admitted he
hadn't gotten much sleep. The kid was pretty nice and
seemed to know a lot about science fiction and fantasy,
which would be an asset. So maybe Deena knew what
she was doing.

As he spoke with the kid and overheard the discussion of the elders, he realized they needed to have a
book club here, or book talks. Events to bring people
into the store, get them into beach reads.

He was going to learn to be good at this. This would
be his focus, at least for now. The fact that it wasn't the
warm and fuzzy experience he'd hoped to have on the
island, as a romantic partner to Deena—well, he wasn't
going to let that slow him down. He'd still do his best to
be a good father, even though his best wasn't any better than his new employee's efforts to use a cash register and bag a book.

He hated incompetence, especially in himself.

He'd seen a rolling ladder in a bookshop back in the

city, and he was pretty sure they could make something like that work here. He found a stepladder and brought it in during a lull in business so he could examine the top rim of the shelves and see if a clip could be attached there.

He was at the top of the stepladder when he saw what looked like a black fly. Then a bunch of them. Then he realized it was in his eyes, not in the room. He was seeing spots.

His head spinning, he started to climb down. He kept losing his grip with his right hand, though.

"Mr. Dominguez?" The kid was at the bottom of the ladder. "Are you okay?"

He opened his mouth to speak but couldn't get any words out. And then he was toppling backward.

THE CRASH STARTLED CAROL, and she rushed to Luis, her friends right behind her. He lay on his side, pale faced, eyes closed.

"I tried to catch him!" Her nephew was kneeling beside him, his expression worried. "I broke his fall a little, tried to protect his head, but he still came down pretty hard."

Carol snapped into action. "Call the clinic," she ordered her nephew. "I just hope they're open today. Explain what happened and ask if we should bring him there or call for a helicopter to the mainland. Linda, you call Betty. She should know his medical history and can meet us there or wherever we end up taking him."

"I'll put down the seats of the SUV," Israel said. He pointed at his brother. "Find something we can use as a stretcher."

Everyone went about their assigned tasks while Carol

knelt beside Luis. She rubbed his arm, gently. "Hey. Luis. Wake up."

He stirred but didn't open his eyes.

"We're going to help you," she said. What if he'd gotten a head injury? "Can you remember where you are?"

He moved his head back and forth as if shaking it "no."

"Where does it hurt?"

His eyes fluttered open, his handsome face twisting. He shifted and groaned.

"They say to bring him to the clinic if we can do it without hurting him," her nephew said. "If we can't keep his head and neck immobilized, we should call for a helicopter. I have the number."

"No helicopter," Luis said in a faint voice.

Israel rushed back in just as Gideon appeared with a large flat board.

"You do your best to keep his head still," she ordered her nephew. "You two, lift him onto the board real easy."

They lifted Luis onto the board in a smooth move that only made him groan once. Her nephew was agile and gentle, and Carol was proud of him.

She helped to guide Luis, her hand on his arm. When she touched his wrist, he winced.

The groan and the grimace of pain twisted Carol's heart. When she'd met Luis she hadn't liked him, had thought him arrogant. He could still come across that way. But now, having spent time with him and having worked with him in the shop, she felt only compassion for his pain.

Linda ended her phone call. "Betty will meet us at the clinic. She's bringing some medical paperwork and calling his brothers. She wants you to come over and sit with Deena."

Deena. Of course, she'd be upset, but she couldn't come to the clinic. She had to stay with Willow, who was sick.

They got Luis out to the SUV and her nephew volunteered to ride in the back, crouched down, to keep Luis steady.

"Call me the minute you know anything," she said to the men.

"If you give me the key, I'll shut down the store," Linda said. "You take my bike and go see Deena."

Carol only hesitated a minute. Linda wasn't a fan of the store, but she had way too much integrity to do anything destructive or dishonest. "Thanks."

Minutes later, Carol reached the front of the farmhouse and propped the bike against a tree. Deena waited at the top of the steps. "How is he? What happened?"

Quickly, Carol explained the chain of events.

Deena rubbed her hands down the sides of her jeans. "Betty said she'll call as soon as she knows anything. Willow's upstairs sleeping. I… I don't know what to do, how to help." Her voice cracked on the last word.

"You need to stay here for Willow," Carol said, "and I'm staying with you. Come on, let's go inside."

"Uh, sure, okay." Deena led the way to the kitchen, and Carol peeked into cupboards until she found tea bags and sugar. She turned on the heat under an old-fashioned teakettle.

Deena's phone buzzed and a few seconds later, so did Carol's. They both grabbed for them.

Carol's call was from Gideon. "They think he's fine for

now," he said without preamble. "He sprained his wrist, but no head injury, probably thanks to your nephew."

"Why did he fall?"

"They don't know, so it's more testing for him, but it can wait until tomorrow. They checked for signs of stroke and administered some medication in case that's what it was—"

"Stroke?" Carol interrupted. "But he's so young!"

"Apparently, it happens, and that could have been what caused his fall. They did some tests and linked up with a hospital on the mainland, and then they gave him an injection."

Deena was asking questions, nodding, and they both ended their calls at almost the same time. "How could they even suspect someone like Luis could have a stroke?" Deena said, and sank down into a chair at the kitchen table.

"I can't believe it, either," Carol said. "I didn't even ask—he's coming back here tonight, right?"

"Yes, and Betty's going to fix up a downstairs bedroom for him. In fact, we could do that together, if you don't mind staying."

To her own surprise, Carol didn't mind, and they walked back to a small bedroom off the living room, with a single, four-poster bed. Deena found sheets and they made the bed together.

They walked back out into the living room and sat down. Deena leaned her head against the high-backed couch and looked up at the ceiling, still clearly distraught.

"Do you want to talk about it?" Carol asked.

"No. No thanks. And you can go. I'm sure you want to get home."

"It's fine." The truth was, Carol didn't feel Deena should be left alone. The younger woman might not know it herself, but she had strong feelings about Luis, and his fall had upset her. "I'm staying," Carol said firmly, and cast about in her mind for a way to distract Deena. Quickly, the answer came to her. "Look, as long as I have your attention, can I show you some things about the project we discussed?"

Deena blinked.

"Just to keep busy." This was probably a bad idea. "If you don't want to…"

"No, I need a distraction. Let me check on Willow and then you can show me. Whatever will keep our minds off Luis."

So when Deena came back, Carol pulled out her phone and showed her photos of the shelf she'd put together. Then she read her a list of potential beach reads classics. They talked back and forth about them, with Deena suggesting changes. "I didn't know you liked the classics," Carol said. "Shut me down for jumping to conclusions. I thought, since you wanted only beach reads in the store…"

"That I didn't read anything else? No. I read everything. The beach reads choice was a business decision. Whatever else you want to say about Luis, he's a good businessman."

"He does seem to be. So you're okay with me putting in orders for these books?" They'd narrowed the list down to fifteen, and planned to get two to three copies of each so that couples or groups of friends could buy them for vacation discussions.

Deena scanned through. "Oh, wow, *Robinson Crusoe*. I never thought of that as a beach book, but it is," she said. "And *Persuasion*...oh, right! It has that great beach scene when Louisa Musgrove falls!" She continued skimming, exclaiming over several more of the titles Carol and her friends had chosen.

Carol felt pleased. Not only because Deena liked her ideas, but because she'd managed to distract the younger woman from her worries.

When they were finished, Carol propped her arms on the table and leaned forward, looking at Deena. "This request is going to surprise you, but I want you to recommend beach reads for me and my friends."

Deena's eyebrows shot up. "I thought you hated them."

"I did, too, but I've read a couple and they weren't bad. I need to learn more about them, open my mind."

"Impressive." Deena looked thoughtful. "I can think of suggestions for you. That's easy since I know you. For the others, you'll have to tell me more about their reading interests."

They discussed what Carol knew of the others, and within half an hour, Carol had a couple of choices for each one. "All right," she said, "I'm going to buy them with my employee discount and give them to my friends. It'll help me do a better job at our store."

There was the sound of a car outside, and they both rushed to the door. Betty's car pulled into the driveway. Two more cars pulled up behind it, tires spewing gravel. Ryan jumped out of one and Cody out of the other. Israel's SUV arrived and parked at a more sedate pace.

"No emergency," Betty called, "but he's not staying here. We hired a boat to take him to the mainland. The doc at the clinic thought he should have more tests." She turned to speak to Ryan and Cody.

"Looks like there are plenty of people to help," Carol

said. "I'll see if I can get a ride home with Israel. You can find out what's going on from Betty."

Deena hugged her. "Thank you for staying with me. You're more than an employee, you're becoming a friend."

As Carol walked out to Israel's car, she felt a spring in her step. She was coming to really like Deena. What had happened to Luis was worrisome, and he'd be in her prayers, but he had plenty of people watching out for him.

The good thing was that Carol felt useful, a part of things. She'd do what she could to help everyone out, both personally and at the shop.

More and more, she felt like she belonged here on the island.

CHAPTER TWENTY-ONE

ON SATURDAY MORNING, Deena woke up to bewilderingly bright sunshine. A few seconds later, Willow climbed on top of her and settled on her stomach.

"Ouch, honey!" She moved the child to the side and curled around her, blinking. Willow had just learned to climb out of her crib, so she guessed she needed to expect visits like this from now on.

It was warm in here, and she could hear sounds outside: a lawn mower running, a car driving by, a kid shouting.

"Mama," Willow said, patting her face. "Sleep."

Deena sat up and grabbed her phone to check the time: 9:30 a.m.? She *never* slept this late and neither did Willow. The house was quiet, with no sound of Betty bustling around. How much more neglectful could Deena be?

She ran a hand through Willow's hair and checked her for fever. Fortunately, she didn't have one, nor did she seem to be congested. Kids healed so quickly when they got good sleep, which Willow must have done. "What have you been doing, sweetie? Did you just wake up?"

"Wake up," Willow agreed. "Mama." She pointed.

At the foot of Deena's bed, every Tammalee memento they possessed was piled haphazardly. From the glamour shot in the crystal frame to a pillow Deena had made her with a photo of her and Willow on it. A sparkly halter top Tammalee had loved, an old pair of jeans, her phone in an inappropriate case, a book of poems entitled *Celebrate Every Day*. A pair of red Converse.

Willow must have dug into the box in Deena's closet. And Deena must have been deeply and inexcusably asleep not to hear her doing it.

Seeing all of Tammalee's things piled there made Deena's throat tighten. Quickly she pulled Willow close. "What were you doing with Mama's things?"

"Mama." Willow nodded. She extricated herself from Deena's arms, crawled down to the pile and started touching things, holding them up. "Pretty. Mama pretty."

Deena blinked but couldn't stop a tear from escaping to trail down her cheek. "Mama was so pretty. And she liked pretty things."

Willow used the jeans to wipe her nose. Then she held them to her face and stuck her thumb in her mouth. "Mama."

Deena's heart ached and her head spun. What should she do to help Willow process her feelings? That was the immediate concern, but two more major concerns came back into her mind to worry her: Willow's illness, and Luis's stroke. "How are you feeling, sweetheart?"

Willow dropped the jeans and gave a brilliant smile. "Hungry," she said.

"Then let's get you breakfast."

As she washed up and dressed in record time, Deena thought about Luis. How was he doing, stuck in a hospital in Pleasant Shores? What had his medical tests discovered?

On the kitchen table was a note from Betty: "Caught

an early ride on a fishing boat to take me to the hospital. Will keep you posted."

Did that mean he was doing worse?

Hurriedly, she got Willow into her booster seat with a cut-up banana and some toast. Then she texted Betty. How is he?

An answer came back quickly: Awake and feisty. Wants to come home, but docs are doing more tests.

Which didn't really tell her whether he was okay or not, what was the status of his stroke.

She wanted to talk to him. Wanted to *see* him, to ascertain for herself how he was doing, to learn from his doctors whether there were more lifestyle steps he could take to improve his health. Steps he might actually pay attention to, this time.

She also wanted to tell him about Willow's actions this morning, her focus on Tammalee. It seemed like an important milestone for the kiddo, talking about Tammalee without breaking down.

But Luis was sick, and he wasn't always reliable in the best of times. "What to do, what to do," she murmured aloud, and then realized she was asking the question on a bigger scale. What should she do about caring for Willow long term, about the feelings she'd developed for Luis, about the baggage they both carried?

A text pinged into her phone and she grabbed it. Luis.

Her fingers shook so much that she had trouble opening the message. Was he angry? Contrite? Had his health scare made him realize that she was important to him, more important than his work and moneymaking priorities? Was he reaching out to her in friendship, or something more?

Finally she managed to open the message, her heart in her throat.

Sorry you're stuck with Willow for weekend. Will pay you overtime and you can take time off next week.

And that was it. Nothing personal. Nothing about how he was doing or what had happened.

He cared about Willow—which was wonderful and the most important thing, of course—but he didn't care about her.

Her stomach felt like someone had put a shovel in it and dug a hole, and that was what told her for sure that, in her heart, she'd hoped for so much more. Somewhere, deep inside, she'd wanted a family, a home, a child…and a husband who was trustworthy and loved her.

She'd wanted to make sure that Willow was properly raised. That was her promise to Tammalee and to herself; that was why she'd agreed to come to Teaberry Island.

And true, she'd intended to raise Willow herself, to be Willow's surrogate mother. That was what her heart longed for, still.

But it wasn't going to happen.

Even so, she could put a check mark beside the goal of raising Willow properly; it was happening. Luis was reliable for Willow.

For Deena? Not so much. She'd been a fool to let him into her heart, to let herself hope even subconsciously that she could have it all.

She wasn't going to get it and so the question became: What was she going to do now?

She swallowed hard, looking at Willow. But before

LEE TOBIN MCCLAIN

she could formulate any kind of plan, there was a knock on the door.

When she opened it, there were Mellie and her eleven-year-old son, Alfie. "If you're not busy, let's go meet Taylor at the park," Mellie said. "We're all on our own today."

"Why's that?" Ryan and Cody usually stuck close to their wives on the weekends.

"Ryan and Cody went to be with Luis," Mellie said. "They plan to stay until he's better, which I'm glad about."

His brothers had both gone? "Betty is there, too," Deena said uneasily. She hoped that didn't mean that things were worse with Luis than anyone had let on.

"I'm glad he has family with him," Mellie said. "How's he doing this morning?"

Deena shook her head. "I don't know."

"Really?" Mellie's eyebrows drew together. "I thought you two were close."

"We…well, we had a falling-out." What did it matter if people knew? She needed to wrap her mind around it herself, this new certainty that she and Luis had no future together.

Alfie slipped past her into the house. "Can I play with the baby?"

"No, Alfie, come on," Mellie said. "We're all going to the park. You can play with her along the way and once we're there. Deena, get your things."

So it had been decided. Well, fine. It wasn't as if Deena had anything better to do, and getting out would be good for Willow. "She's recovering from a cold," Deena warned. "I don't know if you want Alfie near her."

"We'll be outside." Mellie waved a hand. "There's no keeping kids away from each other. Alfie will be fine."

Ambling along behind Alfie, who was holding Willow's hand, Deena and Mellie chatted about light topics. Or rather, Mellie chatted and Deena tried to listen. Half an hour later, they approached the park at the center of town.

Preparations for some kind of celebration were going on. People were putting up stands and kiosks, and there was a bouncy house for kids. Though it was early, the smell of meat cooking already filled the air. A woman was on a stepladder, attaching a big banner to the pavilion: Happy Father's Day!

Oh. Father's Day.

"There's a big Father's Day celebration tomorrow," Mellie explained, "but they do a kind of soft opening today." She saw someone and waved a hand back and forth, and Savannah came over with Nadine, the teenager who'd babysat the kids before.

"Hey, Nadine," Mellie said, tugging her aside. "Deena and I will chip in and pay you a good rate if you'll watch over Alfie and Willow."

"I was hoping you'd say that." Nadine smiled. "I have my eye on this amazing new speaker. Dad says my old one is perfectly good and he won't buy me a new one."

"It *is* perfectly good," Savannah said, then squeezed Nadine's shoulders. "For old fogies like us, but not for you."

"Right, what do the old fogies know?" Mellie grinned. "If you give us a couple of hours, you'll be a lot closer to getting your new speaker."

"Done," Nadine said. She brushed aside Deena's explanation that Willow could still be contagious, took

Willow's diaper bag from Deena and ushered the kids toward the playground. Willow didn't cling or put up a fuss, but followed eagerly.

"I think Willow has a crush on Alfie," Mellie said. "Look how she's looking up at him. It's so cute."

"He's a great kid," Deena said, meaning it. "And Nadine is terrific, too."

Savannah smiled. "She is. I love her to pieces. But it wasn't always an easy road for us. Still isn't. Teenagers are tough."

"*Kids* are tough," Mellie said. "But come on, we're free of them! Let's go visit Taylor in the bakery tent and see if we can score some free pastries."

Deena was swept along on the goodwill of these women, and it all made her feel a little better. She appreciated the way they'd welcomed her into their group, how they unquestioningly offered practical help with Willow.

She looked around the park and remembered being here with Luis. How he'd carried Willow, tossing her up into the air and making her shriek with joy. How they'd played with Willow on the blanket. How they'd cuddled together like a family as she'd drifted off to sleep.

She thought of how her hand had felt in his larger one for the briefest of unforgettable moments.

It's all wrong. Don't go there.

She should be glad that they'd disentangled themselves from each other. Doing that now would lessen later heartbreak. It was for the best, really.

They grabbed pastries and sat down in the bakery tent, and Taylor rushed over. "How is Luis doing?"

"Haven't heard this morning," Mellie said. "I'm as-

suming no news is good news. They got him medical
help right away, which is key."

"Hoping so, anyway." But Savannah looked worried.
"I'll text Ryan and ask him."

"And I'll ask Cody."

Responses came back quickly. He was feeling good.
They were running more tests. They were pretty sure it
had been a stroke, but a relatively mild one.

Conflicted feelings tossed and swirled inside Deena,
like two separate streams coming together to form a
river. Her intense relief to hear that he was feeling good
made her realize how terrified she'd been from the moment she'd heard the news about him. If he was feeling
good, he probably wasn't in imminent danger.

At the same time, if they were running more tests,
that meant that something serious could potentially be
wrong. A young man having a stroke was serious. It
could mean major medical issues, now or in the future.

Luis was so strong and vital and energetic. The possibility of him being somehow cut down made her almost physically ill.

Taylor shook her head. "I'm just stunned that he quit
his job to come back here and be with Willow," she said.
"Never saw that coming."

"Didn't just quit his job," Mellie said. "Sold his business. That's huge. He must have really wanted to come
back here to live."

"Maybe there are several reasons he came back."
Savannah nudged Deena. "When the two of you are in
a room together, it lights up."

"Not really." Deena didn't know what to say, but
they were all looking at her expectantly, so she blun-
dered ahead. "It's too little, too late. He let me down.

We fought, and now…well, it's not going to happen between us."

Mellie tilted her head to one side. "Let you down how?"

"Both Betty and I asked him to come back when Willow started having a bad time. She's been going through a kind of grief cycle, melting down all the time, talking about her mother, and we both felt like she needed her dad. He swore he'd be there for her, but when it got down to it, he was too busy to come."

Taylor frowned. "Did he let you know why?"

"Not really. Just said he was held up."

Mellie broke off a piece of a pink-tinted teaberry scone. "Um, Deena, do you know how important Luis is?"

"I mean," Taylor said, nodding, "everyone should keep their promises, of course. But Cody told me that his office surprised him with a big going-away party that held him up. He employs—employed—more than a hundred people."

Deena hadn't heard about the office party, but was that really an excuse? She looked at the table, picked at a sliver of wood. "He should live up to his promises."

"I'd be mad, too," Savannah said. "Being rich and important doesn't mean you can let people down."

"Exactly." Deena looked at her in relief. Someone was on her side.

"But how do you feel about him?" Savannah asked.

Deena spread her hands. "I don't know. And it doesn't matter."

A kid, about five years old, came sprinting into the tented area where they were sitting, ran up to a silver-haired man and flung his arms around him. "Pap Pap, come on, we're decorating signs and you gotta tell me things about Dad."

The man ruffled the boy's hair. "He was a rascal, just like you." The two of them walked out together.

Deena looked after them.

"What was *your* father like?" Taylor asked Deena abruptly.

She shrugged. "I never knew him."

"Oh. Wow. That's rough."

She looked around at the women who'd become her friends. "Maybe that's why Father's Day is getting me down a little bit."

"Understandable," Taylor said.

"It is," Savannah said, "but don't get too stuck in the past. You can learn lessons from it, and you should, but it's not a good place to live."

Deena pondered that, tucked it away to think about later.

"Anyway," Mellie said, "what are you guys doing for Father's Day?" She looked at Deena. "None of us have fathers, not living, so we'll help our kids celebrate their dads."

"Danny and Ava are cooking a meal for Cody," Taylor said.

"Which means *you're* cooking a meal," Savannah said.

Taylor shrugged. "I don't mind. What's Nadine doing?"

"She made Hank this *gorgeous* painting. If he doesn't at least get tears in his eyes, I'll be shocked."

"Alfie wants to go fishing with Ryan," Mellie said.

"You guys are lucky," Deena said. She watched an older couple come in with adult children and grandchildren, all talking and laughing.

She felt like the kid who hadn't got any toys at Christmas, watching the other kids rip into theirs.

Which was utterly stupid. She had so much. She was here in a beautiful place, with plenty of food and shelter and, from the looks of it, some wonderful new friends. She had a job she loved.

A better person would buck up and lift her chin and smile. You couldn't have everything in this world; no one did. Getting sad about what you didn't have was the road to depression.

But like Tammalee had always said, just because you don't have it as bad as someone else doesn't mean your feelings are invalid. Of course Deena felt sad. She'd lost her mother and then her best friend. She'd moved away from the neighborhood that had felt like home. These women were nice, great really, but they weren't old, comfortable friends.

She looked at the talking, laughing people of Teaberry Island and wondered if she'd ever feel like one of them.

Maybe she shouldn't have come out today, because all of this was getting her down.

Mellie was looking around. "All these multigenerational families. Enough to make you jealous."

"Really?" Deena was surprised. Mellie didn't seem like the jealous type. Plus, she seemed to have it all.

"Uh-huh. I didn't lose my parents early like these two," Mellie said, indicating Taylor and Savannah, "but I also didn't have a great relationship with my dad. Nor my mom, for that matter. She left when I was small."

"I'm sorry." Deena looked from face to face and thought, *You never know what people are dealing with.*

"I'm fine, now. But I do still get a little jealous sometimes. I'm only human."

"Are you taking Willow over to see Luis tomorrow, if he's still at the hospital?" Savannah asked.

"No," Deena said. "No plans to." Truthfully, she hadn't even thought about doing that.

"You're *not*?" Three reproachful pairs of eyes turned to her.

"No, I…" She searched for the right words to explain. "Look, I'm just the nanny. It's not my place to make a decision like that, to do something like that."

"Just the nanny, huh?" Mellie sounded skeptical.

"Yes," Deena said firmly. "I'm just the nanny."

Maybe if she said it enough times, she'd start to believe it.

LUIS WAS ACCUSTOMED to doing things on his own. He was *not* accustomed to people clustering around him and fussing over him. He'd told everyone to go home, and Betty finally had. But Ryan and Cody had insisted on staying in a dive of a motel near the hospital.

Staying here would mean they'd miss spending Father's Day with their families, and there was only one way to get them back home. Early Sunday morning, he left them a note at the nurses' station, checked himself out of the hospital and caught the ferry to Teaberry Island.

His brothers would find the note and catch the next ferry, which would allow them to spend the day with their families.

He didn't go directly back to Betty's house. Deena was there with the baby, and he wasn't sure of his reception. Wasn't quite ready to take on the emotional weight of all that. Instead, he walked the short distance to church—at an old man's pace—and slipped into the dark back corner of the sanctuary just before the service started.

He needed to find peace. To regroup after his stroke and figure out where his life was going.

The whole experience had been a wake-up call, one he was still processing. His earlier episodes of getting dizzy and passing out had been easy enough to brush aside. But a stroke…that could actually kill you.

If it happened again with a more serious outcome, if he died or became badly disabled—a possibility, according to the doctors—what would happen to Willow? What would his life have meant?

Not enough. He wasn't ready to go.

And he'd been spared, this time, which made him breathtakingly grateful.

His mind wandered a little bit during the sermon, but the singing and the prayers uplifted him. Despite all his uncertainty, he felt the glimmering of hope that things might turn out okay.

Not perfect—he might not capture the golden ring of love and a family—but okay. To the point where he could build a life here on the island, stay connected with his brothers and Betty, and be a good father to Willow. Running the bookshop, or overseeing it, anyway, seemed like it would be more satisfying than he'd expected.

After church, he tried to slip out the back before the crowd stopped socializing inside. But he felt a hand on his shoulder, and when he turned around, it was the pastor.

"Are you supposed to be up and about?" David

asked. He walked beside Luis toward the church's exit as if he had all the time in the world. That was one of the man's gifts, Luis had noticed in the time he'd spent on the island. He made every parishioner feel like the only person in the world.

"Had to make it back to see my daughter," he said to David. "First Father's Day with her." To his own mortification, his throat closed up, so that he had to choke out the last words.

David didn't call him on it; instead, he put an arm around Luis and clapped a hand against his arm. "Come see me when you get settled," he said. "I have some ideas about what you might want to get involved with, in the church and on the island." He stepped away and lifted a hand in a quick wave. "Now, I need to greet my flock and then get home to my own Father's Day fun."

"Thanks, Pastor. I will." And Luis meant it. Building a spiritual life and connections was one way he intended to create a more meaningful life.

Behind him, there was a shout, and then his brothers appeared, one on either side.

"Where have you been, man?" Cody asked, a bit of military steel in his voice. "You can't just walk out of a hospital when you're waiting for test results. Can't just leave us a note." He drew back a hand formed into a loose fist. "Man, if you weren't sick…"

Ryan grabbed Cody's hand and pushed it down, then pulled out his cell phone, scrolled and tapped. "We have him, he's fine," he said into the phone, and Luis could hear Betty's exclamation of "Thank the Lord" even without speakerphone.

"We were worried," Ryan said. He didn't elaborate, but Luis heard the feeling in his normally stoic voice.

It choked him up. Man, whatever other effects this stroke might have on him, it had turned him into a dishrag, emotionally.

As if by instinct, they started walking toward the water. It was what they'd done on so many days in their adolescence, when the world got complicated. The bay had provided all of them with an escape and a new perspective. It had set their various scars to healing. Today, the clouds that had rolled in made the bay gray as slate.

"Hey, do you still have a boat down here?" Cody asked Ryan as they approached an isolated dock with a crabber and several smaller boats tied up. On the shore, a couple of rowboats were upside down, both of them looking the worse for wear.

"I can borrow one." Ryan nodded at the older looking of the two rowboats. "Jed lets me and Alfie use it. What are you thinking?" He was already turning the boat over and hauling it toward the water. Ryan might be a science geek, but he was a strong one.

"Thinking we should row this one home and make him go to bed," Cody said, nodding toward Luis. "At least find him shelter before the rain comes."

"Hey, I can walk." The truth was, his legs felt sore after his fall and the walking he'd done today. But he wasn't going to give in to that kind of weakness; he couldn't.

"Wouldn't you rather boat, on a day like this?" Ryan's voice was kind.

Maybe his brothers were giving him an assist he should be grateful for. "I haven't been in a boat since I left the island," he admitted.

At that, his two brothers lifted him bodily and put him in the front of the rowboat, none too gently. Moments later, they were bobbing along the calm waters of the bay, with Ryan at the oars, Cody in the back and Luis in the front.

For the first few minutes, they were quiet, just taking it all in, and that was fine with Luis. He felt the gentle rocking of the boat and inhaled the soft salt fragrance of the bay water. A few drops of water hit Luis, but he couldn't tell whether it was rain or spray from Ryan's rowing.

"Eagle," Ryan said, pointing upward, and they all watched the majestic creature soar, then land on the top of a dead tree.

Why had Luis stayed away from here for so long? Why had he avoided the peace he knew the bay could bring?

He knew the answer: he was too busy driving himself hard. He didn't think he was allowed to relax and enjoy things; he thought he always had to be striving and succeeding, making money.

He'd learned differently in the past few weeks, and especially the past few days. Money wasn't everything. It couldn't buy health nor family nor friends. It couldn't give meaning to your life. Instead, it set you on a treadmill that you had to keep running on, faster and faster, never really able to keep up.

"So what's happening between you and Deena?" Cody asked unexpectedly.

"What do you mean?" He'd been trying not to think about her, but at his brother's words, an image of her appeared in his mind's eye, causing his mouth to go dry and his heart to ache.

"Taylor says you had a falling-out."

"Bad one, Mellie says," Ryan agreed without a pause in his rowing.

"Plus this stroke. You're a mess." Cody leaned forward, elbows on knees. "You need to get all this straightened out, man."

Luis was the younger brother, but not that much younger. He didn't need to be told what to do. But he knew Cody's words came from a place of concern. "The stroke, they're just going to monitor me. They don't think I had much damage. It's just, now that I had one, it's more likely to happen again."

"Bad." Ryan cut the boat to ease it through one of the waterways that bisected the island. Rain was starting to come down. "Heard you're staying here on the island."

Of course they'd heard it. No doubt everyone on the island who had an interest had heard it. News traveled fast here. "Yeah. Sold the business."

"Good decision," Cody said. "You gonna run the bookshop full-time?"

Luis shrugged. "That's part of it. I'll consult part-time, virtually. And I have a couple of other ideas."

"Running the bookshop, you'll work with Deena," Cody said. "Can be tough if you're at odds." He and Taylor had started off working together at the bakery she owned and ended up marrying, but there had been plenty of rocky and awkward moments along the way.

Ryan scooped the oar to dodge a sandbar. "Don't screw it up."

"We like Deena," Cody agreed, nodding toward Ryan. "More important, the women like her. Mellie and Taylor and Savannah and Betty. They've all given votes of approval."

"To what, exactly?" Luis asked, although he suspected he knew.

Cody and Ryan exchanged glances as the rain got heavier.

"Marry her, man." Ryan pulled the boat back into the bay, now close to Betty's farmhouse. "Don't let something stupid, like pride, get in the way."

"True words," Cody said. "Now, get out and go see your daughter. It's Father's Day. In fact," he added to Ryan, "I'll get out here, too. I'm guessing there's a cake or a pie waiting for me at home."

"For me, too." Ryan grounded the boat and got out, sloshing through the water to pull it higher onto the sandy shore. "Probably from the Bluebird Bakery."

"Dad!" It was Alfie, Ryan's son, running toward them at top speed. He hurtled into Ryan and wrapped his arms around him, unselfconscious despite his middle school age. "Come on, Mom made Sunday dinner, and if it gets cold, she'll be mad!"

"See you later," Ryan said, waving. He pointed at Luis. "I'd invite you over, but I think you have business at the farmhouse. Not to mention a daughter."

"Happy Father's Day, bro," Cody said, punching Luis's arm, lightly.

So Luis took a deep breath and strode toward the farmhouse.

CHAPTER TWENTY-TWO

DEENA WAS COOKING a Father's Day meal—and crying intermittently, her mood matching the rain that tapped against the windows—when the kitchen door banged open. Luis stood there, rain dripping from his dark hair.

She looked first at Willow, who sometimes freaked out when she was startled. Sure enough, her face screwed up as if she was going to cry. Then it suddenly brightened. "Dah!" she said, and held out her arms.

Luis strode to her and picked her up, swinging her high before settling her on his hip. That gave Deena time to grab a paper towel, wipe her eyes and dab cold water on her face.

When she turned, Luis was looking at her in that intent way he had. "Are you okay?"

She swallowed hard and nodded. She stirred the stroganoff sauce and then turned on the burner to start water boiling for noodles.

"We need to talk," he said.

"Tak, tak!" Willow batted a hand at his mouth.

He zoomed her down to the floor where she'd been playing and turned on her musical toy. He looked up at Deena, and then stood quickly and came over toward her. "Did you hear me? We need to straighten things out and make this work. I'm ready to do that now."

Through sheer force of will she kept the tears from overflowing, but her throat ached with the effort.

He was looking at her, expecting a reply.

"I don't believe you," she choked out. "It's not going to work."

She'd gone over and over it in her head. She'd taken account of what Mellie and Taylor and Savannah had said last night, how Luis was important and shouldn't be blamed for his unreliability. They'd even, as the night went on, produced examples of when their own husbands had been late or let them down.

Deena believed them. But she also saw a difference between herself and them.

They were the kind of women men stuck with and cared for.

She was not. "It's not going to work," she repeated.

His determined expression drooped for a moment and then returned to his face. She'd seen the change, though. It told her this separation was going to hurt him, too.

It would hurt Willow the most. She looked at the dark-haired child now pushing buttons on her bright plastic toy, making little noises of excitement and happiness, and her heart seemed to physically reach out for her. She loved Willow so much.

She'd promised Tammalee that she'd take care of her, which she had. But sometimes, taking care meant letting go. While Deena had no faith in Luis's ability to work things out between the two of them, she knew for sure, now, that he'd take care of Willow. Any gaps in his ability could be filled by Betty, Miss Arletta and others in this wonderful, warm island community.

Deena had to look at the long term. And long term,

being here with Luis, hoping for something she could never have, would break her. That would be the worst thing for Willow, having a mother figure by her side for months and maybe even a year or two, and then losing her.

Deena turned off the heat on the stove. She had to get out before she broke.

The best thing for Willow, long term, was for Deena to leave. That was the best thing for Luis, too, although looking at his face, the concern and pain replacing his determination, made it seem otherwise.

"Look," she said, "I appreciate all you've done for me, bringing me out here and giving me work. And I'm really, really happy—" Her throat closed and she had to pause and clear it. "I'm really happy you've stepped up as Willow's dad."

"I am, too. But I want it all, Deena. You're a part of me and Willow. Together, we make a family."

"This can never work." She gestured from her own chest to Luis's and back again. "And that means this—" she gestured in a circle then, herself to Luis to Willow "—this can never work."

"How can you say that without talking it through with me?"

Because talking about it will break my heart. "I've made a decision," she said. "It's best for me to go now."

"To *go*? *What?*"

She had to do it now or she never would; she'd give in to the strength of his personality, and it would destroy her. She walked over to the doorway, where her bag was sitting. "I'll send for the rest of my things," she said, her voice remarkably steady until it creaked on the last word. She sucked in a breath. "There's not much."

Rain was beating down outside now. She grabbed a slicker from the peg by the door.

She wanted to pick Willow up and clutch her to her chest and sob. Wanted to throw herself into Luis's arms and kiss the frown from his face.

But she couldn't. Couldn't do that to Willow, and couldn't handle it herself. She knew her own limits.

She threw on her slicker and started out into the rain.

"Ma-ma!" Willow cried.

It was as if invisible ropes connected her chest to Willow's, pulling her back to the child.

This is better for her. "Bye-bye!" she called in a funny voice, waving big.

Willow laughed and waved back. "Bye-bye, Ma-ma."

She caught a glimpse of Luis's fraught face, closed her eyes and turned, unseeing, into the storm.

AT THE CHARTER, she pawed through her purse for cash—the man, a mainlander, was charging an exorbitant fee for this holiday run—and came up short. Praying, she handed him her credit card, and he disappeared into the enclosed cabin of his boat to run it.

She stood hunched in the rain, trying not to think. Trying not to remember Willow's cute, smiling face that didn't understand the woman she now called Mama wasn't coming back.

Which made a second mama who'd let her down. How would Willow cope with that? Was Deena making a terrible, destructive mistake?

But each day she stayed drew Willow closer to her. Each day gave Luis the chance to dodge his duties. She had to extract herself from the situation if she ever wanted the two of them to live free and happy together.

To build a new family, one that didn't include her.

The thought of that dug a fresh, raw hole in her heart.

Headlights flashed through the dark and rain and a car pulled up. A figure got out and walked toward her.

Luis.

Luis, in a designer raincoat, bareheaded, his face shiny with rain.

"Where's Willow?" Deena asked.

"She's with Ryan and Mellie." He came closer and stopped two feet away from her, his gaze burning into her face. "Don't do this, Deena."

"I have to."

"Don't you think it could be your past talking? Can we at least try to make it work, maybe for a few more weeks while we hash things out between us?"

"No."

"A week? A few days?"

She could see the successful negotiator gearing up, and she couldn't take it. "Stop. I'm leaving."

The boatman came back and she turned to him gratefully.

He was shaking his head. "Your card didn't go through. I can't take you."

He gestured to the other couple who was headed out. They emerged from their car, and he directed them to a sheltered spot on the boat.

Why, oh why had she made that last big payment on the bill from her mom's illness? She'd been so eager to get out from under the debt that it had made her stupid.

Desperation made Deena feel like she was going to explode. If she didn't leave now, she never would. Her life, Luis's life and Willow's life would be the worse for it. She rushed after the man. "I'll get the money for you tomorrow! I'm good for it. I'll pay you double."

He glanced back and waved her away, then followed the couple onto the boat.

"Please, sir." She hated begging, but there was a fate worse than that. Staying on Teaberry Island felt like utter destruction.

A hand on her slicker-covered arm. Luis. "You're sure you won't change your mind?"

She nodded. "I can't." She tugged her arm away. "I can talk him into it. Sir!"

"Don't do it, Deena." Rain dripped down Luis's face. He ignored it. His eyes were fixed on her, those warm brown eyes she'd come to love.

Warm brown eyes that spelled destruction for her because he'd leave, like all men.

"I have to," she repeated, and called to the boatman again. "Excuse me, sir!"

The boatman started the engine, and she waved desperately.

Luis whistled, a loud sound that cut the noise of the motor and the rain and the wind. He jumped nimbly from the dock to the boat.

Inside the cabin, Deena could see him reaching into his pocket, pulling out a wad of bills, counting several off.

She closed her eyes.

A moment later he was in front of her. She still had her eyes closed but she could feel him.

"Go ahead, get on," he said, his voice gruff.

She should thank him, but now that he'd done this kind thing, she couldn't. "Why—"

"I want what you want," he said, still gruff. "Go on, go."

She turned and walked on the boat, glancing back. He stood in the rain, his expression inscrutable. She was about to go inside when she heard him say her name. "Deena."

She turned. Looked at him and gripped the railing so she wouldn't dive right across the gap into his arms.

"You're breaking my heart," he said. Then he turned and walked, broad shoulders slumped, toward the car.

And Deena clung to the railing of the boat leading her away from everything she loved.

LATER THAT NIGHT, in Betty's kitchen, Luis sat at the table, picking at the meal Deena had cooked for him before she'd left and enduring his brother's scorn.

"You *paid* for her to leave?" Cody shook his head. "I always thought you were smarter than me, but that's the dumbest thing I ever heard of."

"She wanted to go. I think she would have jumped in the bay and swam to get away from us." Luis pushed the plate away.

In her high chair beside him, up way too late, Willow rubbed her eyes with the backs of her hands. "Mama," she said.

Luis stroked her hair. He knew determination when he saw it, and Deena had been determined to go. He could argue her case to the boatman, or to Ryan and Cody and Betty.

But to Willow?

How did you explain that kind of loss to a child who'd already faced too many losses?

"Mama," Willow said again, louder. She struggled to get out of the high chair.

Luis lifted her out and sat her on his lap.

"Want Mama," she said, her face screwing up in a major pre-cry.

Luis felt like a kid being bullied, the comic movie kid who kept getting up, only to be knocked down again by a circle of bigger, laughing kids. Which was a pathetic way for a grown man to feel.

A better man would write off Deena as a lost cause. Would get angry at the way she'd abandoned Willow, the way she'd seemed to both promise and withhold love. He'd sever that connection, those emotions, and move on.

But Luis had grown up longing for that hole inside himself to be filled. Had tried to fill it himself with the approval that came from making money. The hard work he'd put in had seemed a small price to pay for what it got him: that momentary sense of being whole.

He'd felt whole, for short stretches, when he was with Deena. But Deena was gone.

When he looked at Willow, he saw the likelihood that she'd develop a similar emptiness inside herself, and he wanted to save her from it. Willow didn't deserve what had happened to her.

He couldn't beg Deena to come back for him. He wasn't worth that. But for Willow, he'd do anything.

He had to fix this. "I'll get her back. Daddy will get Mama."

Willow nodded and rested the side of her head against his chest and stuck her thumb in her mouth. The weight of her was the most precious thing Luis had ever felt. Gently, he stroked her hair.

When he looked up, two pairs of eyes stared accusingly at him. "You can't say that," Betty said quietly.

"Don't make promises you can't keep," Cody said. "You know better."

Luis waited until Willow's breathing indicated that she'd fallen asleep. "I'll get Deena back," he said. "I'll get her back for Willow. She'll come for Willow."

Betty shook her head. "You can't have a child be the only thing that's holding you two together. That's a bad reason to form a relationship, and too much pressure on the child. It won't work."

"Then...what *will* work?" Luis said bleakly.

Neither one answered.

He didn't look at their faces because he didn't want to see the pity there. Instead, with Willow in his arms, he stood and headed toward Willow's bedroom—Deena's bedroom, really, since you had to walk through that to get to where Willow slept.

After he'd tucked Willow in, he didn't want to leave. It took superhuman effort not to lie down and sleep in Deena's bed, just to catch a bit of the sweet honeysuckle fragrance of her.

But he couldn't give in to grief and melancholy. He had to get to work, had to find a way to get Deena back.

CHAPTER TWENTY-THREE

CAROL WAS SURPRISED when Luis came in to help her open the bookshop, rather than Deena. First of all, she didn't need help; she had her nephew with her, and it was a Tuesday, not a busy day.

Second of all, he looked terrible, as if he hadn't slept a wink. And third of all, he had Willow with him, letting her toddle across the porch and into the bookshop.

Once they were set up with the register on, the door open to the breeze and the sign outside, Luis touched Carol's shoulder. "I need to talk with you," he said.

Uh-oh. Those words, coming from a boss, made her stomach knot up. Too much like what Evie Marie had said when firing Carol from her university job. "Am I in trouble?" she asked, trying to joke. But her voice didn't sound joking, just shaky.

"No," he said, but he didn't elaborate. "We can talk out here." He gestured toward the chairs they'd put on the bookshop's front porch. He reached into a bag he'd brought, pulled out a set of colorful wooden blocks and dumped them on the porch beside them.

"Block!" Willow sank down onto the floor and started stacking blocks with more enthusiasm than skill.

Carol turned to her nephew, who was standing just inside the shop's door. "Can you work on your own for a little while? We have a new shipment of mysteries that needs to be shelved."

His face lit up. "Sure!" He went back inside at a quick pace.

As soon as Pete was inside, Luis gestured toward one of the red-painted chairs and waited until she was seated before sitting down himself. "I need for you to take charge of the bookshop, manage it, at least for a little while. Are you up for that?"

She stared at him. That was the last thing she'd expected him to say. "Really? Why?"

He hesitated. "Deena...she had to take a break."

She had the feeling that Deena's break was behind why Luis had Willow with him, and why he looked so bad. "And you're going to let her go?" she asked.

He met her eyes and then looked down at the porch's wide planks, not answering.

"Sorry, sorry," she said quickly. "Motherly tendencies. I'll do it interim, but I may have other plans long term." It was the first time she'd said that, the first time she'd thought it. But she did know she wanted to be more than a clerk at a store specializing in beach reads.

Although, being a manager here might be a different story. She'd have to see.

"That's great. Thank you." He looked over at Willow, reached to stroke a hand across her hair.

She studied the man, compassion filling her heart. He might be wealthy and a successful businessman, but inside he was just a man, and a young one at that. "I'm sorry you and Deena are having a hard time," she said, not even pretending she didn't know how much they cared for each other, or had.

He kept stroking Willow's hair. "It'll be okay. I'll

be okay." He looked over at her and gave her a crooked smile. "Sometime."

"Breakups hurt," she said. "A lot. But you *will* get through it, and most likely, come out stronger."

"Is that the voice of experience?"

She'd never told Luis about her past, her husband's betrayal, but she supposed it was obvious she'd moved here after some kind of life upheaval. "It is," she said. "I'm in the process of getting a divorce I wasn't expecting, and it's been an adjustment. But the truth is…" She paused, thinking it through as she went. "The truth is, I'm happier now than I've ever been."

"I'm glad for you." He smiled a weary half smile. "Really, I am. You do seem happier now than when I first met you."

"That day I hollered at you about the shop?" She rolled her eyes at her own foolishness. "That wasn't even two months ago, but it seems like a lifetime."

"A lot can happen in two months." His expression darkened.

"Look, Luis," she said, "my breakup made things better for me, but that may not be the case for you. Don't give up too soon."

He gave her a weary smile. "Thanks for the advice. I'll take it into consideration."

She was perfectly willing to continue bonding with him, enjoying the morning sun and thinking about how much life had improved for her, here on the island. Maybe even offer him more advice, or at least a listening ear. But Willow started to fuss and Luis stood. "I'm taking her to Miss Arletta's and then I'll be back," he said. "I can take over today. I know Deena—" His voice caught a little bit on the name. "I know she was supposed to work this afternoon."

"She was. I'd be fine staying, except I promised to spend the afternoon with my sister."

He started gathering up the blocks, and Carol scooted down to the floor and distracted Willow from her threatened tantrum by hiding her face and then revealing it, a baby game that made Willow chortle.

"I really do appreciate your being willing to take over," he said. "I'll be here for any questions or issues and I'll check in a lot and work some. But I also need to get my consulting business started."

They both stood and then Carol realized they hadn't nailed down the terms of their agreement. She sucked in a deep breath. "Since the new job will be full-time," she said, "I'd like pay and benefits equivalent to what I had at my old job."

"What did you make?" Luis asked.

She told him.

He nodded and looked thoughtful. Carol clenched and unclenched her hands. *Let him think. Don't cave.*

Finally, he looked back at her with the shadow of a smile. "You'll be in charge of the place. Why not ask for a raise?"

Relief washed over her. "I wouldn't object to a bigger salary," she said, "but what I'd really like is for you to give my nephew a raise and a promotion."

"Done," Luis said promptly. "After all, he caught me when I fell. Saved me from a head injury."

Did she dare to push her luck? "I'd also like for part of my job to be going through the boxes back in the storeroom, those books and maps and papers. There might be something valuable there, or something we could use in the shop."

"As long as you can keep the day-to-day operations of the shop running smoothly, sure."

"Thank you!" She shook his hand. Inside, she was doing cartwheels.

She could tell that he was trying to smile, to match her enthusiasm, but it wasn't working. He was still bummed out about Deena, and there was nothing Carol could do except say a quiet prayer for their relationship to be healed.

AN HOUR LATER, Carol pulled her car over at the grave-yard at the end of the island, her sister beside her. They'd thrown together sandwiches, and along with a bag of chips and some sodas, they were set for a cemetery picnic—something they'd used to do at least once every summer.

They found the bench near their grandfather's grave. Mary Beth sat down, but Carol turned a slow 360, look-ing at the place.

The graves, about thirty of them, were flat concrete slabs, most with weathered headstones in various states of mossy disrepair. Some were right at the edge of the water, and as Carol made her way over to look at them, her sandals squished in the marshy ground.

"Whoa," she said as she tiptoed back to her sister. "This place is sinking into the bay, isn't it?"

Mary Beth nodded, unwrapping her sandwich. "Has been for a while. Pretty sure we've actually lost some graves."

Their grandfather's plot was closer to the middle of the cemetery, not in danger of sinking into the bay any-time soon, but it was a fair warning. Everything changed.

Losing your ancestors to beach erosion, though, that was something to fight. Not only that, but if the cemetery was eroding, could all the beautiful places of the island, the shops and parks and homes where families lived their lives, be far behind?

That was a reason to preserve the past. Not to stay stuck in it, but to keep what was priceless and meaningful.

Then and there, Carol resolved that she would fight the erosion of the island. Maybe with the help of Linda and Israel and Gideon. They were all at the stage of life where they had the knowledge and time to work on issues, work for change. Whether they succeeded in such a big quest was another matter, but they could try.

"Remember when Pops would read to us from the old history books?" Mary Beth asked.

Carol nodded, laughing. "Nothing was ever so boring. But you couldn't say that to your elders, back in those times. You just had to shut up and listen."

Mary Beth looked wistful. "I remember how Nana would put down her work when he got to reading about the history of the bay," she said. "She'd just sit and listen with this rapt look on her face."

"Like she adored him."

"Yes." Mary Beth handed her a sandwich. "I always hoped for a partnership like that."

"Did you?" Mary Beth never talked about her divorce, and she wasn't likely to start now. But that had happened several years ago. "Do you think about dating, now that Pete's older?"

"No way." Mary Beth snorted. "No man has shown an interest."

"Have *you* ever felt an interest in anyone?"

"Nope. Too busy trying to keep Pete from spiraling down or flunking out, and food on the table."

Carol squeezed her sister's arm. "You've had a hard time. I wish I could have been more help."

"It's great to have you here now," Mary Beth said. "I hope you plan to stay on the island."

Carol thought. "You know, I'm pretty sure I will. I've made friends, and I love getting closer with you and Pete."

"Living well is the best revenge, as they say. You've come so far after what Roger did to you."

Carol chuckled softly. "I thought his affair was the end of the world, but to tell you the truth, I don't miss him much." She told Mary Beth about running the bookshop and how she'd gotten a promotion for Pete in the bargain.

Mary Beth studied her. "You really have changed. I'm in awe of it."

"I didn't have a choice. Kicking and screaming."

"Yeah, but however it started, it's worked out. I wouldn't mind following in your footsteps, although it's already taken me a few years longer." She stood. "Thanks for helping Pete. He's going to better this summer, I can tell, and I give you a lot of the credit for it."

"Thanks."

The two of them said a prayer by Pops's grave and then walked back to the car. "Dockside Diner for a cup of coffee?" Mary Beth suggested.

"Sure."

As they parked in the small lot between the ferry and the diner, the ferry chugged in. They stopped to watch the people disembarking.

"That looks like our old car," Carol said as one of the three cars that fit on the ferry came off. Then her eyes zoomed in on a woman walking off the ferry. Skinny, red curly hair, looking around in a timid way. "Either my eyes are playing tricks, or that's my old boss, Evie Marie."

Mary Beth had her hand up, shading her eyes. The car that looked so familiar pulled into the parking lot they'd just parked in, and a man got out.

She and Mary Beth stared and then looked at each other.

"That's Roger," they said together.

TRAFFIC NOISE, BUILDINGS THAT blocked the trees and sky, the smell of street food and car exhaust. Deena hadn't even noticed it when she'd lived in DC full-time, but now, after almost two months on Teaberry Island, she felt overwhelmed by it all. She missed the peace and quiet beauty of the island, the sight and smell of the bay.

But not nearly as much as she missed Willow and Luis.

She walked up the familiar steps to Mrs. Martin's apartment and knocked. Instantly the door burst open and kids started pouring out: Mrs. Martin's grandkids, and then the woman herself.

"Deena?" Mrs. Martin squinted into the window-less hallway. "It *is* you!" She wrapped her arms around Deena and hugged her close. "I've missed you so much! Where's Willow?"

"It's a long story." Reluctantly, she backed out of her friend's comforting embrace. "It looks like you're getting ready to go somewhere?"

"Midsummer Street Festival. Can you join us?"

"Come on, Miss Deena!" Mrs. Martin's oldest grand-daughter took her hand. "Where's Willow?"

"She couldn't come today," Deena said, her heart aching.

She might as well go along with them. She'd come to see her old friend in the hopes of feeling better, shaking off the gloom and sadness that had wracked her since leaving Willow and Luis and the island behind. She'd figured on a chat with Mrs. Martin, whose wisdom and life experience had proved more than helpful in the past. But words wouldn't do much for her now. Maybe attending the street festival with the family would help.

It couldn't make her feel any worse than she already did.

They went downstairs, the children rushing ahead and around them. Mrs. Martin shook her head as they exited the building. "Thomas, stay out of the street," she called. "Blanca! Hold Sara's hand!"

The summer heat and humidity felt like a damp, hot cloud.

The others didn't seem to notice the heat. Then again, they hadn't spent the summer enjoying the Chesapeake breezes, as Deena had.

"We're meeting my sisters at the Grove Street entrance," Mrs. Martin said. "They can keep an eye on the kiddos. Then you can tell me all about everything."

"Sure," she said, and when her friend looked at her sharply, she forced a weak smile.

The festival was an explosion of color and sound: jazzy electronic music, frying meat, shrieking kids running through a spray fountain. After they'd walked half a block, Deena was so overwhelmed that she stopped, holding on to the back of a park bench.

"There're my sisters. Kids, run and see your aunties."
She watched them go and then studied Deena. "How
long since you had anything to eat?"

Deena had tried to eat breakfast at her hotel, but
come to think of it, she hadn't eaten but a half piece of
toast before losing interest. "I haven't had a real meal
in a while," she admitted.

"Come on." Mrs. Martin tugged her along and got
them both street tacos and fruit seasoned with lime juice
and dusted with chili powder. Then she guided Deena
to a shaded picnic area. "Tell me everything," she ordered. "But eat, too. You need your strength."

For what?

Deena forced herself to sit up straighter. She couldn't
give in to negative thinking. Or rather, she couldn't
let it overwhelm her entirely. She took a bite of fruit,
sweet and sour and spicy, and the taste seemed to explode in her mouth.

"See, it's good," Mrs. Martin said. "Eat more. And
then tell me."

So, between bites of food, Deena did.

"I know leaving them behind was the right thing to
do, but it's so hard," she said, relieved to be able to share
her feelings with someone who knew and understood
her. "I can't sleep, I can't eat. I miss Willow so much."

"Of course you do. You love that child as if she were
your own."

"I do."

"And Luis?" Mrs. Martin prompted.

"Yes. I miss him, too," Deena admitted.

That was such an understatement that it felt like a lie.
Missing didn't begin to describe the ache in her chest
when she pictured him laughing, or bouncing Willow

in the air, or coming home in a rumpled suit, distracted by his busy life.

Somehow, in the short period she'd known him, Luis had found his way deep into her heart.

The older woman leaned forward. "Was there something between you?"

Deena looked away, then met her friend's observant eyes and nodded. "Yes, okay, there was. But ultimately, I was just the babysitter. It was never going to work between us."

"Tammalee wanted you to *raise* Willow," Mrs. Martin said. "Not just to be the babysitter. You were always more than a babysitter."

Was that true, if Willow could be so easily gone from her life? "Tammalee didn't know her father would take an interest and want to raise her. I have no rights compared to him."

"You're talking about the legal system." Mrs. Martin dismissed that with a brisk wave of the hand. "I'm talking about the heart. I'm talking about what Tammalee wanted and what you want and what's good for Willow. Tell me, do you want to be Willow's mother?"

"More than anything," Deena burst out. As soon as she said it, she realized it was true. Realized she'd always known it, in her heart.

And it couldn't happen, so she backpedaled quickly. "In an ideal world, yes, but it won't work. Not for me."

"Why not?"

"Grandma!" One of Mrs. Martin's grandkids came up. "We need money for the clown walk, please?"

She handed him ten dollars without a glance. "Go on," she said to Deena.

"Men don't love women like me," she explained,

and then, at the older woman's blank expression, she added, "I don't know why, exactly, but men aren't nice, and they don't stay."

Mrs. Martin frowned. "Women like you. What kind of woman is that?"

What kind of woman *was* she? She'd considered herself an independent person for years, had envisioned her future as a single. After caring for Willow full-time, and living on family-oriented Teaberry—and meeting Luis—she realized her view was starting to change. But it wasn't clear enough in her mind to articulate it.

Instead, she fell back on her old explanation. "Some women get good treatment and some don't. You're one of the lucky ones. I never have been. My mom wasn't, either."

In the midst of the oppressive heat and the carnival-food smells and the talk and laughter around them, Deena felt a sharp pang of sadness for her mother, for the life she'd wanted and couldn't have.

"You *are* lovable." Mrs. Martin reached across the picnic table and gripped Deena's hands. "You're a child of God and you can try again."

Hot tears formed in Deena's eyes as she shook her head. "I don't believe it."

"One man hurt you after knowing you. One. And that was a lot of years ago."

In a moment of loneliness, Deena had told Mrs. Martin what had happened to her during her high school years. She didn't say it, but there was her father. Her stepfather.

Mrs. Martin seemed to read her mind. "Your mother never got lucky with men, but you have the chance to," she said. "What does Luis say? How did you leave it with him?"

Just the thought of Luis made Deena's throat tighten. It was as if she could see his soulful brown eyes, feel his strong arms around her. She cleared her throat forcefully so she could speak. "He said he wanted to talk about it. About making it work. But talk is cheap. I saw how he acted."

The older woman's gaze sharpened. "Did he mistreat you? Like that other guy?"

"No! No, Luis would never do that." Because he was a good man. Not a perfect one, but a good one.

"Why are you so resistant to the idea of falling in love?" Mrs. Martin frowned. "You're such a smart woman in most ways, but I gotta say, in this regard…" She shook her head. "Not too bright."

Deena laughed a little through the tears that wanted to flow. "You're not wrong," she said. "It's like I can't get over it. I see what you're saying, but here…" She tapped her heart. "Here, I can't believe it."

Mrs. Martin stood suddenly. "Come on." She took Deena's hand, pulled her to her feet and led her through the crowds to a huge stone cathedral, one that was popular with tourists. Deena had heard of it but had never been inside.

She wasn't sure what Mrs. Martin was doing, but did it matter? She'd already messed up her life to the nth degree. Maybe seeing this beautiful place would at least distract her.

The quiet and darkness of the cathedral was a refuge in the midst of the noisy streets. Candles and incense spread a mild, spicy fragrance, and the sunshine through stained glass windows made mottled rainbows on the red carpet and dark wood.

"Now we're going to light a candle for Tammalee," Mrs. Martin whispered, guiding Deena to an alcove lined with candles, some lit, some unlit. She stuffed a ten-dollar bill into the locked box and handed Deena a candle.

"I've never—"

"You don't have to be Catholic to light a candle. Just do it."

So Deena lit the candle from the large central flame, and they knelt together and prayed. Deena pictured her friend, so wild and free, and tears flowed down her face. Thinking about Willow made the tears flow harder. How was the sweet child doing without Deena?

Several minutes went by. Finally, Mrs. Martin dug a tissue out of her purse and handed it to Deena. After Deena had pulled herself together, Mrs. Martin took another candle and lit it. "And one for you," she said quietly. "Ask to be healed."

Deena met the woman's eyes, nodded and bowed her head, quietly breathing in the cool, fragrant air. Mrs. Martin had pulled a pocket rosary from her purse and was passing the beads through her fingers, her lips moving soundlessly, so Deena stayed still.

Slowly, the peace of the place gave her the energy to pray more: for Willow, and for herself. And then for Luis.

She wanted him and Willow to be happy. If that meant happy with someone other than her, so be it.

A few more minutes, and they stood by mutual agreement and walked through the cathedral together.

As they collected the grandkids, Deena seemed to feel a little lightening of her heart. Not a lot, but a little.

She'd wanted to feel better and she did, but what that meant action-wise…that, she would have to ponder.

CHAPTER TWENTY-FOUR

IT HAD INDEED been Roger arriving on the ferry. Roger and Evie Marie. Now Carol was sitting with Evie Marie at a picnic table beside the dock. She felt almost dizzy with shock.

Mary Beth had offered to take Roger to the house, which made sense because he looked terrible, bloated and limping. "It'll give you a chance to catch your breath," Mary Beth had whispered. "I'll take care of him. Take your time."

Carol's heart ached for Roger, underneath her anger. But now wasn't the time to let those feelings free, so she turned back to Evie Marie. "I was half expecting to see him here one of these days," she said, "but you? What's going on? Did someone die?" Although she couldn't fathom that Evie Marie would care enough to come see her in person. Besides, Carol would've already heard through the grapevine if a close friend from work had passed away.

"It's not that," Evie Marie said solemnly. "Carol, we made a big mistake letting you go."

A thorny knot of emotion formed in Carol's chest. *I could have told you that. I did tell you that.* "What's going on?" she asked aloud.

Evie Marie leaned forward and propped her elbows

on the table, her hands fisted under her chin. "First off, Bambi quit."

"Really? Why?" When she thought about it, Carol wasn't shocked. Bambi hadn't seemed to have a strong connection to the university, the students or her colleagues.

"She got a better offer. Those tech skills."

"Ahhh."

"She didn't give any notice, so the tutoring center is...well, it's in disarray. I've been trying to manage things, but it's not going well." Her voice trembled a little bit at the end.

Carol felt for her, a young woman who just didn't have much experience. At the same time, what had Evie Marie expected would happen, promoting Bambi and leaving an important center in her hands?

Carol really, really wanted to say *I told you so*, but that would be both ungracious and unhelpful. "How are the student tutors doing? Are they able to pick up the slack?"

Evie Marie shook her head. "Three of them quit, so there are only two left." She blew out a sigh. "You were right about Bambi's social skills. She was hard to work for, from what I could gather."

"I believe that." Carol's mind was racing. All of this was leading to an offer for her old job back, unless she missed her guess. That was something she'd longed for, a triumphant return. She could probably even ask for a raise.

"On the plus side," Evie Marie said, her voice still tremulous, "our client numbers are way down. Students haven't been coming to the summer program in anywhere near the numbers they came for the past three years."

Carol winced. "That can get you in trouble with the grant. As well as the administration."

"That's what pushed me to come out here." Evie Marie turned to face her full-on. "Carol, will you come back and work for us?"

There it was, the offer she'd longed for.

She should take it. Get out of Mary Beth's hair. Go back to Baltimore, where everything was familiar. Even, maybe, to the old house, because there must be some reason Roger was here. Maybe he wanted to sell her the house.

Maybe he wanted to get back together.

Maybe she could have her old life back. Did she want it?

She looked out across the bay, sparkling in the early-afternoon sunshine. A couple of fishing boats headed to shore. Overhead, puffy clouds made their way across a mostly blue sky.

The air smelled soft and fresh, different from anywhere else she'd ever lived. She supposed it was some kind of island effect, being surrounded by water, that caused it.

"Didn't Bambi set up some online tutoring options before she left?" Carol asked. "You could try to hire someone remotely."

"She did, but it's not being used much." Evie Marie shook her head. "The latest research says that in-person tutoring is best."

Carol pressed her lips together to restrain a sarcastic response. But to her credit, Evie Marie understood what she wasn't saying. "Carol, I know you told us that, in your performance reviews and even on that last day we talked. I didn't listen."

"No, you really didn't."

"But now," Evie Marie said, "the faculty has gotten involved. Apparently the kids are coming to them because the tutoring center isn't helping. Online or what's left of the in-person side of it."

Those words cut into Carol's heart. *What's left of it.* She'd poured her soul into the tutoring center for twenty years, and it could all go down the drain.

"The students want you back, too," Evie Marie went on. "And we'd love to get you on board before the summer precollege program starts."

"Oh, man." Carol had gotten enough distance to forget what a scramble it was at this time of year, preparing for that program. A lot of students were admitted on condition of completing the summer program, including some of the athletes who were key to the sports teams' success. "You really do have a lot on your hands, don't you?"

"I do. I just… I feel so alone, with you and Bambi gone. The directors of the math center and the writing center are kind of letting me swing in the wind because they're mad about how you were let go. I screwed up badly, Carol. I think the only reason they're keeping me on is there's no one else to try to clean up the mess I made. But I can't do it alone."

This was tugging so hard at Carol's heartstrings. It wouldn't just be a triumphant return; it would be a rescue mission. And Carol had always liked rescuing people.

She breathed in more of that soft air and thought, *No.*

Evie Marie was being nice now because she needed

Carol, but what was to say she wouldn't get on another hobbyhorse in the future and decide Carol was too old or unskilled to compete?

And besides, Carol *liked* her new work at the bookshop. It was a special place, and she could help make it even more special. She liked tutoring high school students. And she liked the people here on the island, both family and friends.

Not only that, but she might just have a new cause to work on, saving the island from erosion.

Her decision made, she turned to the younger woman. "I don't want to come back, Evie Marie, although I appreciate the offer," she said. "I'm settled into a new job here, making more money. Living with my sister and nephew, and I love that." Reconnecting with Mary Beth had been a huge benefit of moving out to the island.

Evie Marie's lips trembled. "What am I going to do?"

Carol patted her shoulder. "I'll call a few of my contacts in developmental education. There are people who might like to move out of the community college environment, or who would rather live in the city. But you're going to have to pay them decently."

"I'll advocate for that," Evie Marie said.

Doubtful, when you didn't advocate for raises for me or the tutors for the past five years. Carol pushed aside the slight taste of bitterness. "You can get on the NOSS website and put the word out that you're looking."

"What's NOSS?"

Carol winced. What had the university administration been thinking, hiring and promoting Evie Marie? But she knew the answer to that. Evie Marie was young and cheap. And those things weren't her fault. "The National Organization for Student Success? Look, I'll text you the link. That and a couple others." The ferry-boat's horn sounded, and she gestured toward it. "I think they're headed back. Do you want to go, or wait for the next ferry in a couple of hours?"

Evie Marie stood. "You're sure you won't come?"

"I'm sure."

She watched Evie Marie climb aboard, shoulders slumped. Carol *would* beat the bushes to try and find some good people to apply for the job. The students deserved it.

Now, on to Roger.

CAROL TOOK THE long route back to the house, enjoying the sunshine and putting off the confrontation with Roger. But she couldn't avoid it forever.

Mary Beth met her at the door. "Good heavens. How did you stay married to him for so long?"

Carol looked past Mary Beth and saw that Roger was seated at the kitchen table. She drew Mary Beth out onto the porch. "Why, what's up?"

"He just complains and talks about himself and makes demands," Mary Beth said.

That was certainly true.

"And okay, he's disabled, but does that mean he gets a pass on being a decent human being?"

"It shouldn't." Carol thought of Gideon, who had a disabled hand, but never made a big deal of it.

"You girls talking about me?" Roger called.

Carol and Mary Beth rolled their eyes in unison, just like they used to do as teenagers.

"I'm going to leave you to it," Mary Beth said. "Just... be strong, okay?"

Carol looked at her sister, divorced and raising a teenager and struggling economically, but still fighting. "I will," she said, and straightened her spine.

Mary Beth headed upstairs, and Carol walked slowly into the kitchen toward her husband of thirty years. A sick combination of anger and hurt and defiance churned in her stomach.

The walls of the kitchen felt like they were closing in on her. "Let's talk on the deck," she said, and walked past him and out the sliding glass door.

She sat on one of the chairs that faced the bay. June sunshine beat down on her shoulders. She studied her legs. She was starting to get a tan.

Roger limped over and sank heavily into the adjoining chair. He didn't start a conversation.

Finally, she did. "So what do you want?"

He looked at her and then at the floorboards, sighing heavily. "I made a mistake," he said.

"There's been a lot of that going around." Carol couldn't keep the snide tone out of her voice, but at least she'd kept the language clean despite the cussing out he deserved.

He didn't seem to notice her tone. "Will you come back?" he asked.

The direct question made her stare over at him. "What happened to your nurse?"

He shook his head, blowing out a disgusted breath. "She wasn't what I thought." He didn't look at Carol.

Ashamed or... "She left you, didn't she?"

He sighed again. "Yes."

"So you came here. Why, Roger?" She held her breath waiting for an answer.

He was still a big man, with the same beautiful, dreamy eyes. She'd loved him so, and had thought he returned her love. Assumed it. But once he'd dropped her so readily, she'd started to wonder how long things had been going downhill. When he'd fallen out of love with her. Whether he'd *ever* loved her.

"The truth is…" He paused, looked at her, looked away. "I'm having trouble managing alone."

Anger roared through her, hot as fire. "You want a caregiver," she gritted out. She couldn't decide whether to punch him or cry.

He didn't want her for her. He wanted her for what she could do for him.

Maybe it had always been that way. Or maybe it had gotten that way since he'd become disabled and lost some of his sense of himself as a strong provider.

"We can go back to the way it was," he coaxed. "I talked to that Evie Marie on the way over, and she said she was offering you your job back. We could pretend none of this ever happened."

It was what she'd longed for: keeping things the way they'd always been. She was a traditionalist, always had been. She'd defined herself as a wife, Roger's wife, for as long as she could remember. It would be comfortable to take up her old life.

Or would it?

She'd never be sure if Roger was going to cheat again, never know if Evie Marie was going to fire her. She'd be in the same rut she'd been in for years.

She'd be bored, like she had been for years.

That thought startled her. Bored. Had she been?

She hadn't been conscious of it, but maybe that was because she didn't know anything different. She'd always lived life by the book. She'd made a choice—the university job, Roger—and stuck with it, no matter what.

She wasn't ashamed of that, because she knew she'd done good work at the university and been a good wife to Roger. If she could have, she'd have lived out her life without changing either aspect of it.

But change had been thrust upon her, and miracle of miracles, she'd loved it. She thought of sneaking around the bookshop planting classics after hours, of running away with Gideon and Israel and Linda and laughing about it afterward. She hadn't had so much fun since she was a teenager.

She'd come to Teaberry Island with her tail between her legs, and the place had changed her. The sun and breeze—and especially the good-hearted, interesting people, characters one and all—had restored her. Made her grow.

And now she couldn't smash herself back into the narrow confines she'd lived in before. "I'm not coming back," she said.

He must have heard the decision in her voice, because he nodded. "I guessed as much, when I saw you. You look good, Carol."

She couldn't help being pleased by that remark. She was human, after all.

"I'll come here, then," he said, looking out toward the bay and then back at the house. "It's nice."

"No!" She clutched the chair with one arm to keep from flying up out of it. She held up her other hand like a stop sign. "No, you can't. You're not invited. That wouldn't work."

"I'm not *invited*?" He looked affronted. "You're my wife!"

"Not anymore. I sent those divorce papers back."

"That can be stopped. I just have to say the word."

Once again, heat flashed through her body and she sat up straighter. "Listen to me. You're not the boss. You're not my husband. You don't get to decide you want to live with me and waltz right back into the life I've built here."

"You're seeing someone else?" He sounded incredulous.

"No, but if I want to, that's my decision. Just like you made a decision to have an affair with the little lady in the nurse uniform. That decision on your part took you off my guest list and out of the driver's seat in our relationship. Permanently."

He dabbed at sweat gathering on his forehead. "Then what am I going to do?"

She had to unclench her teeth before she could respond. Could the man be any more pathetic? "Look," she said, "if you manage your money carefully, you can afford a caregiver or even a personal care home."

"No way!" His knee jiggled up and down. His face had gone pale. It was as if he'd counted on her as a fallback, been confident that she'd return to him.

She took a slight satisfaction in letting him know he was wrong.

"I'm not old enough for a personal care home."

"Well, but if you can't manage on your own..."

"No!" He crossed his arms over his chest and looked away, his lower lip sticking out.

Pouting had worked for him in the past, many times, but Carol wasn't giving in to it. Not anymore. She shrugged. "Up to you. It was just a thought."

"No way would I go to one of those places," he repeated, his voice a little shaky now.

"Well." She stood and brushed her hands together. "I

have plans tonight, but there's another ferry in an hour.
You can catch it."

He stared at her, his brow furrowed. Then he got to
his feet with some difficulty.

You may not think you're old enough, but you are.
She sighed. She'd contact Roger's brother and explain
the situation, get him to help Roger find a new place to
live where he could manage and get help.

She couldn't leave the man entirely in the lurch. It
wasn't in her nature. But she didn't have to be the one
who fixed his life. Not this time.

"Just like that," he said with a slow headshake. "Just
like that, you're leaving me out in the cold."

"I'm leaving you where you decided to go." There
was a flutter in her chest, a floating sensation, like she'd
put down a heavy backpack and could move again. Run
again. Dance again. "Come on, let's get you down to
the ferry and out of here."

CHAPTER TWENTY-FIVE

LUIS STOOD ON the ferryboat, waving to Betty as it pulled out of the Teaberry Island harbor.

"Good luck," she called to him before turning back and heading toward her house.

He'd need it.

He'd learned from Betty that Deena was in DC. Meanwhile, he'd been busy packing up his own and Willow's things. If all went well, he'd arrange for a very interesting—and very local—move.

The boat was barely out on the open water when another ferry came their way, going toward the island. He watched it idly, then did a double take. There was a long-haired blonde woman leaning on the railing. Was that who he thought it was?

Sure enough.

Deena was on the boat.

"Hey, Deena!" he yelled, not caring that the other passengers were staring at him. "Deena, wait a minute!"

She must have heard her name, because she looked from one side to the other before scanning across the water. He could clearly see the surprise on her face, they were that close.

"Get them to stop the boat! I have to talk to you!"

She shook her head slowly, staring at him.

"Please! It's important."

She lifted her hands and shrugged, then went over to the cabin and spoke to the captain.

Hurry, hurry.

She came out shaking her head. "He can't stop."

Luis kicked off his shoes and shucked his jacket. What he was about to do was stupid for a man still recovering from a stroke and a sprained wrist.

He dived into the water anyway.

It hit him with a shock—the Chesapeake was cold, even during the summer—but his years of swimming experience came right back to him and he freestyled toward the other boat. Not easy when he was fully dressed and the water was choppy, but he was motivated.

He had to get to Deena.

Within minutes someone from her boat had thrown in a life preserver, and he grabbed it and let them haul him in. He climbed the ladder and was immediately surrounded by concerned customers, a couple of crew members and Deena.

"What were you doing, man? You could have drowned!"

"I'm fine," he said, shivering a little.

One of the crew members waved to the other boat, which continued on its way, its passengers lining the railing to watch the drama.

He was breathing hard as he stepped toward Deena. "I had to talk to you," he said.

DEENA STARED AT Luis as their boat started up again, headed toward Teaberry Island.

She had been thinking hard since her visit with Mrs. Martin. During that visit, and afterward, a lamp had been turned on—or maybe a candle had been lit—illuminating the darkness of her mind.

She was doing all this to herself. She was punishing herself, and she could decide to stop.

Luis had paid her boat fare away from Teaberry even though he didn't want her to leave. He hadn't used Willow as leverage. He'd done it because it was what she wanted.

In all their time together, he hadn't taken advantage.

He wasn't perfect, not in the least. But he *was* trustworthy.

He was a man, and he was trustworthy.

Even with her, who'd never evoked loyalty in a man before. Who'd never felt worthy of it.

What had Savannah said, that night in the park? The past had lessons to teach but was a bad place to live.

She was right.

And with that realization, she'd decided to go back.

She'd figured she'd probably ruined things with Luis by leaving. But maybe she could restore it enough to see Willow and to continue working at the bookshop. Especially if she apologized well, which she intended to do.

But now here the man stood, dripping before her. Was it possible she *hadn't* destroyed her own chances?

And could she let go of stifling her needs and punishing herself long enough to find out?

Several of the female passengers looked at him with admiration. And why not? If there were wet shirt contests for men, Luis would win by a mile.

But he was only looking at her, not at the other women.

Of course. Because he wasn't a womanizer.

"Where were you headed on the boat?" she asked as one of the crew members handed Luis a gray wool blanket. She helped him wrap it around himself and guided him toward a seat, grateful that the other passengers were giving them space.

"I was coming to find you."

She stared at him as the boat pulled into the harbor. "Why?"

"I think I can show better than tell," he said. He pulled out his cell phone—in one of those expensive waterproof cases, because of course Luis would have the latest technology—and sent a couple of messages. He wouldn't say any more until he'd apologized to the captain and they'd exited the boat.

He claimed one of the golf carts Hector Lozano had for rent at the docks and they buzzed toward the downtown area. Just before they reached it, he pulled up before a cute little house. "Willow and I are moving here," he said. "My brothers are helping. Don't even need to hire movers."

Deena's heart sank to her toes. From his attitude, she'd thought he wanted to show her something positive, something about the two of them. But instead, he was moving out of Betty's farmhouse. He didn't want to live with her. Their idyllic time playing at being a family was truly over; she couldn't rebuild it.

He glanced at her and could surely read some of what she was thinking, but he didn't address it. "Now, come on, let's walk down to the bookshop," he said. "I want to show you something there, too."

BY THE TIME they reached the bookshop, the sun and wind had mostly dried Luis's clothes and hair. He knew he still looked disheveled, and he knew he was confusing Deena, but he was still high on the adrenaline of swimming to her. He wanted to get the whole plan in front of her, visibly, before saying anything more.

There were a lot of people in the bookshop, as he'd expected after the messages he'd sent, but he focused on Deena. "I'm hoping you and Carol can run the place together," he said. "I want to become more of a silent partner."

She nodded, her lips pressing together. She didn't look happy.

"I'm not being lazy," he said. "I'm busy with my consulting work. And I'm starting a nonprofit."

"Oh?" She was clearly pretending interest, thinking about something else.

He pushed through his planned talking points. "Yes. I'm starting a nonprofit. Focused on funding FAS research."

Her eyes widened. That had gotten her attention. "You are?"

"Yes. And I've already committed most of my money to building up a starting base of capital." His stomach had butterflies. "That's why I bought a modest house. And why I need to continue consulting."

He watched her face, holding his breath. Would she approve of his plan, or would she turn away because now that he'd remade himself into an ordinary working joe, he was no longer worthy in her eyes?

Did she value him for his money, or for who he was? Deena had never seemed materialistic, but then again, she'd never been around Luis the nonexecutive, nonwealthy man before.

He closed his eyes briefly and remembered his talk with Pastor David. His value wasn't built on how much money he had.

When he opened his eyes, her face was stricken. Just as he'd feared.

But he'd lived by the business model of "finish what you start," and so he took her hand and led the way to the bookshop's porch. He'd been told by some older locals that this was the place people did what he was about to do.

He patted his pocket to make sure, then sank down onto his knees. "I've told you all the external ways I want to live my life now, and what I'm offering you," he said. "But there's an even more important part. Deena, I've fallen in love with you. I love the way you think and laugh and care for Willow. I love how pretty you are and how you don't even seem to know it. I love that you came to this island and made yourself a part of it."

She was staring at him, her expression hard to read.

"I know I haven't been the best so far," he pushed on. "As a father or a friend or a—a potential partner. But I have hope because you've put up with me. You help me to be better. And I know if you would commit to me, you'd keep on making me better. Just being around you makes everyone better. You're like the sun, Deena. To me, you're the sun and moon and stars. And so…" He reached into his pocket and pulled out the small, velvet box, damp from the swim in the bay. "Will you marry me?"

HE JUST PROPOSED. Deena looked down at his dear, up-turned face. Was she dreaming?

But no, because the box he was pushing into her out-stretched hand felt solid and velvety.

"Open it," he said.

His voice was strange. His eyes, very, very vulnerable.

She didn't take the box. "I left you alone here on the island, in charge of everything, with no warning," she said. "I'm so sorry. Why would you—why would someone like you—want to marry me, after I did that?" As she spoke, she was sinking down to her knees, too, until they were both kneeling, facing each other.

His smile was crooked as he reached out to touch her face. "You have baggage," he said. "Something about the whole situation pushed you back into the past. I get it. I'm willing to work through it with you. If you can put up with *my* baggage."

He was being understanding and trustworthy. Not anything like the men in her past.

Her chest felt like it might explode. Her throat was too tight to speak.

"Deena, I'm so imperfect it's ridiculous. I know it's a lot to ask, for you to make a commitment. If you can't—"

She put a gentle finger to his mouth, stopping his words. Then she swallowed hard and cleared her throat and found her voice. "Luis. I trust you."

He tilted his head, just a little, looking at her. Looking *into* her.

"I trust you. Do you know what that means? I don't think I've ever trusted a man in my life, but I trust you."

His smile grew, but insecurity still lingered around its edges.

"I've loved you for a while," she continued, talking fast now, "maybe ever since I saw you holding Willow. And I've loved watching you become a real father. I love working with you and arguing with you and sitting down to dinner with you." She paused for breath. "And now I trust you, too."

"Does that mean—"

"It means I'll marry you." She held his eyes. "Without even looking at the ring. Because that's not the important thing."

Understanding dawned in his eyes, and he swept her into his arms. He held her tight, his shoulders shaking a little, and she understood that he was crying. She was, too.

"Well," came a voice from the doorway, "what's the verdict?" It was Carol.

They let go of each other, mostly, and Luis looked up at the older woman, his face wet. "She said yes!"

Cheering erupted from inside the store. Deena turned to watch, confused, as most of the people they loved streamed out: Ryan and Cody and Mellie and Taylor, Betty, even Miss Arletta. Willow toddled out and threw herself into Deena's arms. "Ma-ma!"

Deena's breath was taken away. Taken entirely away.

She pulled Willow close and reached out for Luis, and he enfolded them both in his arms, and she realized: *I can have what I want. I can have it all.*

And despite all the congratulations of everyone around her, she found herself looking skyward, where Tammalee seemed to be watching. Seemed to be saying, *I told you, you could have it all.*

"Let's see the ring," Nadine said, and only then did Deena realize she was holding the unopened box in her hand. She sat back and opened it and gasped.

It was the biggest diamond she'd ever seen in real life, just this side of overdone. All the women raved over it, and the men made comments about how much it must have cost.

Luis hugged her from behind. "She's worth that and more," he said.

Deena leaned back into his arms. "So are you," she said. "You're worth everything."

"But you like it?" he asked.

"I value you for way more than this," she said, and turned to face him. "But yes, I absolutely love it!" She slid it onto her finger, and moved into the circle of his arms, and knew she was blessed.

EPILOGUE

Three months later

DEENA FELT THAT she was the happiest bride in the world. Some people wouldn't have wanted a wedding reception at their place of employment, but Deena was thrilled to celebrate her marriage at The Beach Reads Bookshop.

Mellie, Taylor and Betty were all helping with food, shooing her away when she tried to lend a hand. So she mingled with the guests, who clustered in small groups inside the bookshop, on the porch and in the new annex they'd built, filled with local history and books from the island's past. That was where Carol stood, of course, showing people around, in her glory. Deena stuck her head in the door, saw the woman talking intently with Gideon Bradshaw and went back out to spend a few minutes with Peg and her daughter, Ruthie.

Savannah sat down in one of the rockers on the porch, looking a little pale.

"Do you think she's okay?" Deena asked Peg, nodding toward Savannah.

"She's fine, better than fine. She's expecting a baby." Peg clapped a hand over her mouth. "Which I'm not supposed to know, so don't tell anyone. You either, Ruthie. This is a happy secret."

As Hank leaned solicitously over Savannah, hand-

ing her a bottle of sparkling water, Deena had to agree:
it sure looked like a happy secret.

Several of the older fishermen were talking with Weed,
who'd helped her move into the farmhouse, and who was
working on a veterans' aid program with Cody. Right
now, they were all sampling the food, giving Taylor a
thumbs-up, laughing together. They looked happy, too.

So did Luis, currently chatting with some of his old
colleagues who'd come over for the wedding. She went
to join the conversation, loving the comfort of Luis, the
way he reached to put an arm around her and include
her. It was all so, so good.

After a few minutes, she spotted Betty standing off
to the side, watching Luis with a fond expression on
her face. She walked over to join the older woman. "He
looks good, doesn't he?"

"So much healthier than when the two of you first
came back to the island," Betty agreed.

"I'm forcing him to eat lots of vegetables," Deena
said. "And of course, he already loves seafood. And
Willow keeps us both active. His doctor doesn't even
want to see him for a year, he's doing so well."

"I'm glad. You're a wonderful influence." Betty
smiled and put an arm around Deena. "And love is a
wonderful medicine."

"What's this about love?" A good-looking, silver-
haired man, who'd apparently been pursuing Betty off
and on for a while, came up behind her. "Why don't you
come explain it to me while we dance?"

Betty rolled her eyes, but she followed him readily
enough to the area where people had started dancing.

"Mama!" Willow's tone was demanding as she lifted
her arms to be picked up. It made Deena smile. Willow

sounded just like any other toddler, with no hint of the troubles she'd faced in her short life.

Deena picked her up, heavy as she was, and cuddled her close. Being Willow's mother, being able to form a family with Willow and Luis, was a dream come true. And Teaberry Island was such a perfect place to raise a child. She and Luis were talking about adding to their family, giving Willow a younger sibling to love, but there was plenty of time for that.

For now, she was savoring being Willow's mother. They talked about Tammalee often, and Deena would never let Willow forget her, but a child's world was here and now. In the here and now, Willow needed a mother. And Deena was so, so happy to be that for her.

Cody's little ones came over. "Can we play with Willow?" Ava asked. The sweet blonde child treated Willow like a doll, but Willow didn't mind and she seemed to be learning social skills from the older girl.

Willow struggled to get down. "Play!" she said, and Deena let her go, watching her run after Ava.

Her heart was full.

LUIS PULLED DEENA to his side. "Go get seafood," he urged his friends as he gestured toward the food tables. "I want to talk to my bride."

The truth was, he wanted to be alone with her. "Any chance we can cut out early?" he asked quietly, right next to her ear, catching a whiff of her honeysuckle perfume, so much her trademark that she'd worn it on her wedding day, eschewing anything fancier and more expensive.

"Nope. Behave." She softened the comment with a smile. "We need to thank Pastor David for doing the wedding."

"You're right." The island pastor had done a terrific job today, but he'd also been a rock of steadiness as Luis and Deena had worked through some issues from their pasts prior to tying the knot. They'd done counseling with him, both individually and as a couple, and it had reassured them both that they had what it took to make the marriage last.

So they hugged the pastor and his wife, Tiffany, including their baby in the hug. Their son, Justin, was running around with Willow. She chortled with laughter, happy and cheerful as any other child. She'd come so far in such a short time. They'd made sure she had counseling, too, and continued to have Early Intervention services. There would be challenges, but together, they'd help Willow overcome them.

As the night wore on, Luis danced with his new wife under the stars on a makeshift dance floor. When it got too crowded, some of their guests moved to the porch to continue there. Weed danced with Linda, and Israel cut in. Finally, Peg pulled Weed over to dance with her, and everyone was happy. Even Jimmy the Junkman was dancing with Goody, the cranky ice cream lady.

They took one more stroll through the bookshop and add-on museum. He'd been doubtful when Carol had proposed it, but he had to admit she'd done a stellar job. The boxes they'd originally found in the shop had held some rare books that turned out to be worth enough to fund some of the museum's construction. Deena and Carol had written a grant for the rest, waving away Luis's offer to finance the addition. Which was a good thing, since more and more of his money was tied up in the FAS nonprofit.

Now the walls held pictures of gatherings of townspeople from the bookshop's early days, along with old maritime maps. The locals loved it even more than the tourists.

Someone called Deena away, and Luis found himself in the annex with his brothers while the music and laughter sounded outside. Ryan studied the old photographs, looking a little pensive. "Kind of wish we had this background, ancestors on the island, like so many of the people we know," he said. "We're not part of this place the way they are."

Just then, Alfie came through carrying Willow, trailed by Cody's kids. He glanced briefly at the pictures, and then they all ran back outside.

"That's what we have," Cody said softly. "Our kids. They were born here, or close to it. They'll be raised here."

"Raised well," Luis said firmly because he believed, now, that with the help of Deena and their community, he could do it. "This place fixed us where we were broken."

"It did." But there wasn't time to elaborate, because their wives came in and pulled them outside.

Their wives. Luis still savored the fact that he had a wife, a family.

Teaberry Island *had* renewed and repaired them. And The Beach Reads Bookshop had played its role.

But it was really the community. It was the bay. It was Teaberry Island.

He pulled Deena close and she lifted her face to his. "I love you," she said almost shyly.

"Forever," he said. And he kissed her.

* * * * *

CAROL'S LIST OF
CLASSIC BEACH READS

(with input from Israel, Gideon and Linda)

Daniel Defoe, *Robinson Crusoe*
Jane Austen, *Persuasion*
Mary Shelley, *Frankenstein*
Louisa May Alcott, *Little Women*
Ernest Hemingway, *The Old Man and the Sea*
F. Scott Fitzgerald, *The Great Gatsby*
Daphne du Maurier, *Rebecca*
Truman Capote, *Breakfast at Tiffany's*
J. D. Salinger, *The Catcher in the Rye*
Kazuo Ishiguro, *The Remains of the Day*
Laura Esquivel, *Like Water for Chocolate*
Alice Walker, *The Color Purple*
Walter Mosley, *Devil in a Blue Dress*
Amy Tan, *The Joy Luck Club*
Terry McMillan, *How Stella Got Her Groove Back*

ACKNOWLEDGMENTS

As I END the Hometown Brothers trilogy, I owe thanks to so very many people:

Anna J. Stewart, who helped me pin down the main characters and their conflicts.

Karen Solem, my agent, who seized on my mention of a bookshop and basically insisted that I write about it. You were right.

Editorial Director Susan Swinwood, who steered the trilogy in the right direction, and Editor Shana Asaro, who pushed me to make the story all it could be.

Colleen, Jackie, Jonathan, Karen, Kathy and Sally—my beloved Wednesday morning writers' group—who helped me make Luis more lovable and encouraged me to carry through with Carol's story line.

My Seton Hill colleagues, who enabled me to write realistically (though with slight exaggeration) about the joys and tribulations of Carol's academic life.

The HQN art and sales teams: thank you for designing such perfect covers and for getting the books out into so many stores despite pandemic and supply chain challenges. I am fortunate to work with you.

My local booksellers, Completely Booked in Murrysville, Pennsylvania, and Barnes & Noble in Greensburg, Pennsylvania. Thank you for carrying and hand selling my books.

Karen Glass of Glass House Portraits: thank you for designing such a wonderful map for Teaberry Island. I asked for a map and you gave me a work of art.

Timons and the morning Zoom write-in pals: thank you for the inspiration and tough love.

Writer friends Dana, Rachel, Jo, Michelle, Susan, Valerie and Beth—you're my people and you help me more than you know.

Closest to home and to my heart, thanks are due to Grace, who may have provided a bit of the inspiration for Hank's teenage daughter; Sue, my sister and life-long reading companion; and Bill, who drives me to beaches and bookshops with tireless good cheer.

Do you love romance books?

Join the Read Love Repeat Facebook group dedicated to book recommendations, author exclusives, SWOONING and all things romance!

A community made for romance readers by romance readers.

Facebook.com/groups/readloverepeat

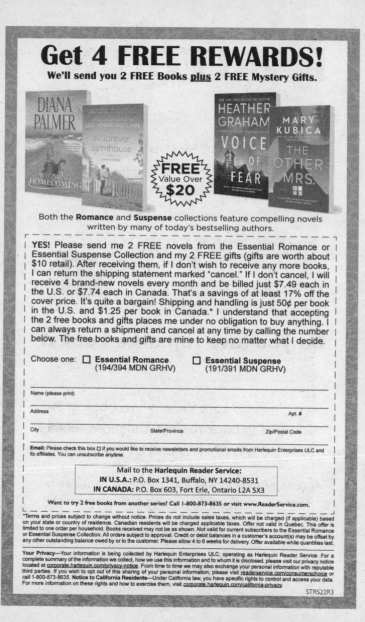

Get 4 FREE REWARDS!

We'll send you 2 FREE Books plus 2 FREE Mystery Gifts.

FREE Value Over **$20**

Both the **Romance** and **Suspense** collections feature compelling novels written by many of today's bestselling authors.

YES! Please send me 2 FREE novels from the Essential Romance or Essential Suspense Collection and my 2 FREE gifts (gifts are worth about $10 retail). After receiving them, if I don't wish to receive any more books, I can return the shipping statement marked "cancel." If I don't cancel, I will receive 4 brand-new novels every month and be billed just $7.49 each in the U.S. or $7.74 each in Canada. That's a savings of at least 17% off the cover price. It's quite a bargain! Shipping and handling is just 50¢ per book in the U.S. and $1.25 per book in Canada.* I understand that accepting the 2 free books and gifts places me under no obligation to buy anything. I can always return a shipment and cancel at any time by calling the number below. The free books and gifts are mine to keep no matter what I decide.

Choose one: ☐ **Essential Romance**
(194/394 MDN GRHV)

☐ **Essential Suspense**
(191/391 MDN GRHV)

Name (please print)

Address   Apt. #

City   State/Province   Zip/Postal Code

Email: Please check this box ☐ if you would like to receive newsletters and promotional emails from Harlequin Enterprises ULC and its affiliates. You can unsubscribe anytime.

Mail to the Harlequin Reader Service:
IN U.S.A.: P.O. Box 1341, Buffalo, NY 14240-8531
IN CANADA: P.O. Box 603, Fort Erie, Ontario L2A 5X3

Want to try 2 free books from another series! Call 1-800-873-8635 or visit www.ReaderService.com.

STRS22R3

HARLEQUIN
PLUS

Try the best multimedia subscription service for romance readers like you!

Read, Watch and Play.

Experience the easiest way to get the romance content you crave.

Start your **FREE TRIAL** at
<u>www.harlequinplus.com/freetrial</u>.